Alan Gibbons

bons is a full-time writer and a visiting speaker
urer at schools, colleges and literary events
de, including the major book festivals. He lives
ool with his wife and four children.

Gibbons has twice been shortlisted for the
Medal, with *The Edge* and *Shadow of the*
r, which also won the Blue Peter Book Award
ook I Couldn't Put Down' category. *Scared to*
he first of the Hell's Underground sequence,
2008 Salford Teenage Book Award.

Acclaim for Hell's Underground ...

' definitely scary ... builds tension slowly and
c y and is ultimately a more rewarding read for it.'
Jill Murphy, thebookbag

'e ainingly gruesome stuff' *The Daily Telegraph*

'A inely scary time-shift novel' *The Bookseller*

'A er gripping, action packed story full of mystery
a itement' *Primary Times*

Also by Alan Gibbons

Blood Pressure
Caught in the Crossfire
Chicken
The Dark Beneath
The Defender
The Edge
Ganging Up
Hold On
Julie and Me . . . and Michael Owen Makes Three
The Lost Boys' Appreciation Society
Not Yeti
Playing With Fire
Whose Side Are You On?

The Legendeer Trilogy

The Darkwing Omnibus

Hell's Underground

1. Scared to Death
2. The Demon Assassin
3. Renegade

Hell's underground 4

WITCH BREED

ALAN GIBBONS

Orion
Children's Books

First published in Great Britain in 2010
by Orion Children's Books
This paperback edition first published in
Great Britain in 2012
by Orion Children's Books
a division of the Orion Publishing Group Ltd
Orion House
5 Upper St Martin's Lane
London WC2H 9EA
An Hachette UK Company

1 3 5 7 9 10 8 6 4 2

The Orion Publishing Group's policy is to use papers that
are natural, renewable and recyclable products and
made from wood grown in sustainable forests. The logging
and manufacturing processes are expected to conform to
the environmental regulations of the country of origin.

A catalogue record for this book
is available from the British Library

ISBN 978 1 4440 0683 4

Typeset by Input Data Services Ltd, Bridgwater, Somerset

Printed in Great Britain by Clays Ltd, St Ives plc

www.orionbooks.co.uk

Prologue

'Tell me you will never forget me.' The quill pen falters on the page. The author swallows hard and drags the back of his hand across his eyes. He doesn't know whether anyone will ever read what he's writing. 'The dark heart of London is my home. Please think of me. In so many ways I'm closer to you than you think, but not in the only way that matters. I wish I could reach out and touch you ...' His attention drifts for a second, imagining faces printed in the darkness. '... but I travel alone. By an accident of birth, it's my destiny to use evil in order to fight evil. That's my burden.'

The writer of these lines twists in his seat and gazes across the candlelit room. There is a lead-lined box on the windowsill. He crosses the room to get it and places it on the table next to him.

His name is Paul Rector. He prays the specially made box will be his letterbox to the future, to the twenty-first century London he once called home. He imagines the people that will read the journal: Mum, Netty.

'I am continuing my journey, both back in time and

deeper into myself. Every day I struggle to cope with the things I discover about my true nature.

'Do you want to know what it's like here, in Hell's Underground? Ask Netty. She's seen it. It's lonely and it's frightening. There's hardly a single moment I feel at ease. Every day I want to go home and hold you both, but I know what I have to do. Is that all it is, seven months? I wonder, do those two simple words have meaning any more? In that period, I've journeyed through almost four centuries. I've seen cruelty, horror and war. I've begun to realise that time doesn't move in a straight line. It's not just a sequence of events that are fixed, ordered and unchangeable. It's a vast and complex structure, with many dimensions, many ever-changing faces and planes. Unpick a single thread of time here and countless events may unravel elsewhere.

'I'm travelling towards a meeting with the monster who poisoned our lives. Sometime soon I am going to meet Lud, desolate king of a demon world. He's here somewhere, imprisoned in his crypt. He orchestrates his disciples and plots to emerge from exile. Eventually he's going to break free of his living death. Then it's between him and me. One of us must perish.'

Paul opens the box and taps his teeth thoughtfully with his pen.

'Do you remember those first days when I discovered my true identity? You were worried about me, Netty. You too, Mum. You probably thought I was going crazy. We just wanted those horrible events to go away. That was never going to happen, was it? It was always going to come down to this. The demon seed contaminates me as it has so many of the Rector men. It puts down roots and grows, choking any goodness out of us. My ancestors Samuel and Harry lost their souls to Lud. Then there was John, my brother, the son you've

2

mourned all this time, Mum. He served Lud and he paid the price. Lud used them all, then cast them aside without a moment's thought. They did terrible things, but none of it was really their fault. It's him. It's Lud.'

He clenches his fist and presses his knuckles to his forehead.

'When's it going to end? I'm on the trail of the latest of the Rector men to serve Lud. I've only got a name. The man I must find is called Nathanael Rector.

'I hate what's happened to me. I left you, Mum. Then, Netty, you left me. I don't blame you. Who would choose to stay in Hell's Underground? I can say it now. You're the only girl I ever really cared about. I don't want to be here. I want to be with you. I'm no hero. I'm so scared.

'What am I doing telling you all this? Am I trying to hurt you? No matter how bad I feel, there is hope. I will find a way to complete my mission. Each step of the way, I'm getting stronger. Every day my powers seem more natural, more a part of me, like touching, like breathing. You know the first; I can instil mortal terror with a single stare. One day I will master my dual nature, part human, part demon.'

Paul snaps his fingers and watches the flames dancing from his fingertips.

'You know I can control fire too. But I have a third talent, if that's what it is. It's given me the ability to move small objects with my mind, even to feign death, but there's always a price to pay. If I want to take a demon's power, I have to kill him for it. To make myself strong, I must turn into a killer. That's what really scares me, you see, not the loneliness, not the danger, not even the thought that I may never make it home. It's this thing inside, the demon seed. Each time I kill, each time I draw on the dark arts, my human side weakens and my demon self strengthens.'

He sees his face reflected in the mirror. Menace seems to seep through the shadows. This is the face his victims see.

Paul takes up his pen once more. 'My mind opens to Lud. The nightmares flood in. He unleashes terrible visions of the white chapel in which he lies, preparing to return. Who knows? The next time I'm forced to use my abilities, it may cost me my sanity.'

He closes his eyes for a moment before completing the entry.

'I'm not going to feel sorry for myself. I won't give in. I will find a way back. Goodbye, both of you. I'm about to take the next step into Hell's Underground. I will find my ancestor, Nathanael Rector, and destroy him. '

He closes the book and places it in the box. Then he says the words he couldn't write to Mum and Netty. 'Or he will destroy me …'

One

6 June 1645

Grace Fletcher smoothed down her grey dress, tucked a curl of raven-black hair into her bonnet, and went to serve the troopers with cheese, bread and a pitcher of ale. The men were rowdy, but they weren't too much trouble.

'What,' the Cornet in charge of the men asked, 'do we not get a smile, fair lady Grace?'

Grace forced a thin smile and tolerated his banter.

'That's better,' the Cornet said. 'Why, when a smile lights your face, you make yourself quite presentable, a rare beauty, in fact. You should do it more often.'

'Thank you, sir,' Grace answered, resisting the temptation to pour the ale over the officer's fat head. What made men like him think that every woman he met should simper for him? What made him think that her only ambition in life was to make herself 'presentable'? She'd met King's men and Parliament's men and neither of them pleased her much.

There were a dozen men in the squadron. Rumour had it they'd been skirmishing with the King's men up country. Their faces were smeared with the dust and grime of a morning's hard riding and they had a raging thirst. The Swan was a regular watering hole for the men of the Eastern Association as they sallied forth to confront the Cavaliers. It was late May and there was hawthorn and elder blossom in the hedgerows. The fighting season had begun. Soon, there would be more broken bodies in the field. Wives would mourn husbands, and mothers their sons. As Grace made her way back to the kitchen, she shook her head and cursed man for his warlike nature. In this year of Our Lord, 1645, he still had nothing better to do than butcher his brother in a dispute over the divine rights of a single man.

As she deposited her circular, wooden tray on the table, she saw a familiar crimson stain the size of a small leaf spreading on the dark material of her sleeve. She felt the old hollowness inside her. Must she forever be reminded of her loss? She frowned, then glanced at the door. Hurriedly rolling up her sleeve, she examined her forearm. It was as she had suspected. There was the three-inch scar, the wound that never healed. It had flared up and was leaking fresh blood. Around the open wound, Grace's skin was so unbearably itchy that she started scratching, though she knew, from experience, that she risked making it worse. Stealing another look at the door, she rinsed the inflamed area with cold water from a jug before binding it with a clean cloth. That's when she heard the door hinges creak behind her. Feverishly, she rolled her sleeve down to the wrist to disguise the tell-tale mark.

'What are you doing over there, Grace?' Beldam demanded. 'Your customers are getting restless for another pitcher of ale.'

'It's nothing, Jacob,' Grace replied.

'If it's nothing, you should be out there serving those troopers,' Jacob said irritably. 'They've coppers in their pocket and I aim to get my hands on as much of their pay as I can. Now, what's wrong with your arm?'

Grace felt her heart flutter.

'I have suffered a horsefly bite,' she answered. 'It's no more than that.'

Try as she did to control the anxiety in her voice, she wasn't sure she'd succeeded. Beldam wandered over. Grace flinched at his approach. The more she got to know the landlord of the Swan, the less she liked him.

'Do you want me to take a look at it?' he asked. 'My wife may have a salve that will aid it.'

Something in his tone of voice told her he was less interested in helping than in finding an excuse to get close to her.

'Thank you for your kindness, Jacob,' Grace said, forcing herself to sound civil, 'but it's nothing.'

'That's what Elizabeth Clarke and all those other crones must have said out at Manningtree,' Beldam mused.

At the mention of the Essex town and its notorious witch trial, Grace felt the skin on her neck prickle. England's eastern counties were buzzing with the tale of Elizabeth Clarke and twenty-seven other women rotting in Colchester's rat-infested gaol cells. The good people of East Anglia now fancied they saw witches crouching in every hedgerow. Grace was left in no doubt which way Beldam's thoughts were turning.

'You know how it is with these witch-hunters, Grace,' Beldam continued, his breath hot on her neck. 'They are too eager by half. Like hounds after a hare, they are. Once their blood is up, they will pursue any suspect

7

female to her death. The moment they throw a wench in gaol, they will go looking for the Devil's mark. We wouldn't want them finding anything on your fair skin now, would we? That would be a great shame on such a comely wench.'

Grace was standing very stiffly, with Beldam immediately behind her. He made her skin creep. She could smell the heavy fragrance of ale on his apron.

'You wouldn't want to attract any unnecessary attention. You know full well that I set little store by the likes of Master Hopkins and his ilk. They treat their suspects cruelly, Grace. They strip them. Do you know what they're after?'

Grace nodded, then gave him his answer. 'They're seeking the sign of the Devil.'

'That's right. They're intent on finding a red spot,' Beldam whispered, his whiskery chin brushing the top of her ear. He stuck his hand out in front of her face and made a gesture with his thumb and forefinger. 'That's all they're looking for, a tiny red spot.'

'Do you think it is seemly,' Grace asked in a trembling voice, 'that these witch-hunters should be allowed to strip a woman of her clothes and her dignity?'

'I'm not the one who makes the rules, Grace,' Beldam said, feigning a yawn. 'I'm only telling you the way it is.'

'Well, it's wrong,' Grace protested. 'You failed to give me a proper answer, Jacob. Do you think it is fair that a woman should be examined without any right of appeal?'

Beldam ignored her question and pressed on with his speech. 'The mark doesn't have to be much at all, they say. Sometimes, it is just this little, red spot, like the bite of a flea' – he let the word hang for a moment – 'or a horsefly.'

8

Grace closed her eyes. Dear God, this man will be the death of me.

'They say the spot is immune to pain,' Beldam reminded her. He laid his large hands on her shoulders. 'Do you know, when it is pricked, there isn't even a trace of blood?'

Revolted by his presence, Grace seized on his words. 'Then I have no need to worry, Jacob.'

On impulse, she thrust out her right arm. 'Do you see my sleeve? Do you see the stain? Is that blood enough for you?'

Instantly, she regretted her outburst. Sweet heavens, she thought, have I lost my reason? Her mark was so unusual, it would be bound to excite the witch-hunters far more than a mere flea bite. She had just made him more, not less suspicious.

'Let me see that,' Beldam commanded as he seized her wrist. He dabbed at her sleeve with his forefinger. 'Why, the material is soaked through! This is no horsefly bite. Roll up your sleeve.'

Grace snatched her hand away. 'I shall do no such thing!'

'I will examine this mark,' Beldam snarled, his mood changing. 'You must give your permission this moment or I shall put you out of the door!'

'Then I will leave your employment forthwith, Jacob Beldam,' Grace snapped, trying to wriggle out of his grasp. 'You have no right to command me in this. It is a private matter.'

But Beldam held her tight. 'God's blood, woman, you have a fiery temper. Have you not listened to me these last few weeks? If you did but learn to control it, you would be able to live a comfortable life in this town.'

'Is that right, Jacob?' Grace retorted, turning her head to get a look at him. 'So tell me this, what would I have to do in order to secure this comfortable life you offer me? Speak straight, for I will have no more of your teasing and taunting.'

Taking her words as a sign of encouragement, Beldam softened his attitude. 'All I seek, Gracie, is a smile now and then.' He squeezed her shoulders, his fingers kneading her flesh. 'I have no sympathy for those who would see the Devil's mark in the slightest blemish. I have your best interests at heart, my flower.' His fingers strayed over her cheek and throat. 'Maybe you could show me a little kindness in return.'

With that, he leaned forward and pressed his lips against the nape of her neck. Grace responded by spinning round and slapping his face so hard it made his teeth rattle.

'The only kindness I would show you,' Grace cried, a little too loudly, 'is the same kindness those troopers show to a horse with a broken leg, for you deserve no more, sir. Maybe I should tell your wife about the things you whisper in my ear. It is high time the old shrew saw you in a true light.'

She had her back to the door, but she felt a draught as somebody entered the kitchen. The quarrel had attracted the attention of the russet-coated Cornet.

'Is the wench giving you trouble, landlord?' the officer asked, an amused smile playing on his lips. He had spotted the telltale redness on Beldam's cheek.

'No more than usual, Cornet Leech,' Beldam answered. 'I am afraid Mistress Fletcher has the tongue of an adder sometimes.'

'What is the cause of so hot a dispute?' Cornet Leech demanded.

Beldam relished the information he now gave Leech. 'There is a strange mark on Grace's arm.'

Grace's throat tightened. Did I anger him so much

that he would put my reputation at risk? Does he now want revenge? She was beginning to regret the force she put into that slap.

Leech threw his head back and laughed out loud. 'You're talking to a soldier, landlord. I have had my fair share of cuts.'

'You misunderstand, sirrah,' Beldam weaseled. 'This is a strange thing, a wound that does not heal.'

Grace's eyes widened in horror. He had known about it all along. He had been biding his time, planning to use it as a bargaining counter against her.

'That's right, my girl,' Beldam gloated. 'Though you have tried to disguise it, I have seen you tending to it often.'

'What are you getting at?' Leech demanded, the smile vanishing from his face. He was beginning to wish he had never allowed his curiosity to draw him through the door.

'Are you blind to the ways of Satan?' Beldam asked. 'Mistress Fletcher has long harboured a most unusual sore on her forearm. It is always livid and raw and never does it heal.'

At last, the scales fell from Leech's eyes. He was the son of a gentleman farmer from just outside Ipswich. He had heard about the spate of witch trials that had broken out across eastern England.

'Landlord,' Leech said gravely, 'I would counsel caution here. They hang women for witchcraft. If this is no more than a quarrel between master and servant that has got out of hand ...'

Beldam remembered Grace's final insult and rubbed his cheek. A moment later, he smirked. His next words chilled Grace's blood. 'I understand the consequences of what I am saying. If there is nothing to it, then let Mistress Fletcher submit to a physical examination.'

'I will do no such thing!' Grace cried. She knew there could only be one outcome.

'Perhaps we can resolve the matter quickly,' Leech suggested. 'I am sure you have nothing to fear, mistress. If you would just roll up your sleeve ...'

'Let me be,' Grace pleaded. 'I have done nobody any harm.' She pointed at Beldam. 'He is the one who harbours wicked thoughts, not I. Sir, I am innocent.'

Beldam chuckled. 'So that's the lie of the land. Now you're trying to transfer the guilt to me, hussy. But I am not the one with an unexplained sore on her forearm, am I, Grace?'

Leech reached out to take Grace's wrist. She drew away. 'Stop this foolishness immediately,' he ordered, the look of indulgence vanishing from his face. 'If you would but permit me to take a look at your arm, then we can have done with this tomfoolery.'

But Grace's voice was now laced with panic. 'Please, sir, just let me leave.' She gave Beldam a sideways stare. 'That man is wicked to the core. He means me harm.'

'But do you not see?' Leech said. 'Now that an accusation has been made, I must ascertain whether there is any evidence of the Devil's mark.'

Grace shook her head fiercely. 'Why must you?'

Leech allowed his arms to flop by his side. 'You see, my father is a magistrate.'

At that, Grace swallowed hard. She detected that the officer was a fair-minded man with little time for the witch-hunters, but here he was, the son of a magistrate, being confronted with an allegation of witchcraft, an offence punishable by death. He had no choice but to see the matter through.

'Pray roll up your sleeve, mistress,' Leech said.

Grace shook her head.

'Then I regret I must use force,' Leech said. 'Ruddock, Cate, come in here this minute.'

Grace tried to bolt for the inn door, but the troopers had her pinned by both arms before she could lift the latch. The soldiers would remember later that she had raised her hand as if to throw something, then thought better of it. For a moment or two, she struggled in vain and then her body sagged in despair. Leech drew back her sleeve.

'What is this?' he asked, seeing the strip of bloodstained white cloth.

Grace maintained her silence. Leech peeled back the hastily applied dressing and gasped. The wound reminded him of a sword slash. It was deep and angry. 'How do you explain so grave a wound?' he demanded.

Grace's eyes burned with indignation and resistance. 'I don't.'

'Put away your pride, for pity's sake,' Leech said, uncomfortably aware of Beldam looking over his shoulder. 'Do you not understand that I am trying to help you?' He was willing her to provide a rational explanation. 'Did you perhaps cut yourself with a knife?'

'You'd like to believe that, wouldn't you?' Beldam said, catching the trooper's eye. 'She has had the wound ever since she turned up at my door, asking for work, and that is three months since. What, do you have a soft spot for a fair-faced doxy?'

'I am no doxy,' Grace retaliated, 'as you know only too well.'

'Then what are you?' Beldam spat back. 'Are you a witch, a servant of Satan? Do you consort with the Prince of Darkness? Is that why you refuse to explain this mark?'

'You must speak,' Leech implored Grace. 'You must

say something in your own defence or suffer the consequences.'

'But you can't, can you, Grace?' Beldam said, seizing on Leech's words with glee. 'Because you have no defence. You see, I got talking to one Master Sudley the other day. He is a shoemaker from out Framlingham way.'

Not for the first time that day, Grace's heart missed a beat.

'Did you see that, Cornet?' Beldam chortled. 'When I mentioned Framlingham, she looked like I had struck her in the stomach. Now why's that, Grace? Could it be because he told me the tale of Mistress Grace Fletcher who left the town in mysterious circumstances? Three months have elapsed since she vanished.'

Grace struggled against the troopers, who were still restraining her.

'Tell the officer why you fled Framlingham in such haste,' Beldam continued. 'No? Very well, I will.' He turned to Leech. 'The story is, you see, that Mistress Fletcher flew the coop in some haste so she didn't have to explain her daughter's disappearance.'

Leech, who had been sympathetic until now, stared at Grace.

'That's right, Cornet,' Beldam crowed, 'Mistress Fletcher has committed the most demonic act possible. She gave up her only daughter to Satan himself. Remind me of the child's name, mistress.'

Grace dropped her gaze. 'Susanna.'

She saw the trooper's gaze grow cold. In that moment, she knew she was lost.

Two

6 June 1645

inety miles away from the Swan, Paul Rector
climbed wearily to his lodgings. It had been
another fruitless day. He had gone from tavern to
tavern enquiring after his ancestor, Nathanael Rector.
He had been met everywhere with blank looks. Back
in his room, he dropped heavily on to the edge of the
bed and sighed. Outside, he could hear the sounds of
the street. There were tradesmen selling their wares.
There were cries of fish and eels, sugar apples and
fine moleskins. Paul wandered over to the window
and looked out at the winding lanes and alleys that
led down to the Thames. Here and there, a lantern
bobbed in the deepening darkness. A stray dog
scratched and whined amongst the refuse that littered
the unpaved street. Paul lit a candle and shook his
head. He must have scoured every inch of London in
the last three months, but Nathanael was nowhere to
be found. Lud had refused to show his hand. The

demon lord's designs remained as mysterious as ever.

Paul had not wasted his time in all those weeks. He had begun to learn the ways of seventeenth-century London. He had made the acquaintance of a footpad by the name of Tom Catchpole. Catchpole scratched a living thieving and selling the goods he had stolen. They had met in a murky tavern and become friends, though Paul had never divulged his origins. Catchpole had shown him where to find the richest merchants, how to fleece them of their purses and vanish into the maze of passageways where whores and bargemen rubbed shoulders with half-dead vagrants. Paul counted out his coins and nodded. Even after paying Tom his share, he had more than enough to pay for his room and board for the next few days. Then there had been the more mundane skills, such as swordsmanship, aiming a pistol and riding a horse. The horse Paul had taken from a captain of arms. Tom had helped him find a stable.

For a while, Paul was happy to watch the people of the night shuffling by, but soon he grew bored of keeping vigil at the window. He pulled out a manifesto he had bought, one of the many chapbooks doing the rounds of London. It detailed the various crimes of Charles Stuart, King of England. He tried to decipher it by the light of his candle, then sighed and put it away. Accustomed as he had become to the way people spoke, he was having much greater difficulty reading the books, pamphlets and newspapers of the time. The conventions of spelling and grammar were unfamiliar. Frustrated, he tried lying down on his bed, but he wasn't ready for sleep. After a few minutes spent staring up at the beamed ceiling and trying to picture Netty's face there, he decided to venture back out into the night. The dark, lawless neighbourhood held few terrors for him. His demon nature was enough protection. He was confident that his powers of fear and fire would help him survive, at least until Lud finally made his move.

Making his way down the creaking stairs, Paul let himself out and set off through the hot, humid night. His footsteps took him north-east intuitively. He crossed Tower Street and carried on up Mark Lane. Eventually he found his way to the church of St Katherine Coleman. Even after three months, he was dazzled and disturbed in equal measure by this other London, so different to his own. It was a city that would, in less than a quarter of a century, be largely razed to the ground in the Great Fire of 1666. It was a lost world.

After a few moments spent gazing up at its facade and the star-studded sky above, he crossed Magpie Alley and found his way to Camomile Street. He stood on the very spot where, in another time a hundred and ninety years in the future, he had fought Lud's forces and been out-thought and defeated. He gazed at his surroundings, trying to recognise the Victorian street in these seventeenth-century surroundings. The shifts backward in time seemed to cut him free of reality. Everything seemed dreamlike. 'Where are you, Lud?' he murmured. 'What are you up to? Why don't you make your move?'

When Paul first arrived, he expected to be thrown into a life-or-death struggle for the three gates that still contained Lud. But the battle didn't come. Instead, Paul roamed alone, learning how to survive in a city where all the talk was of the savage civil war that was raging beyond its ramparts. He explored the recently built earthworks and fort, built to reinforce the city's ancient defences. The threat of a Royalist invasion had receded, but the outcome of the war still hung in the balance. England was like a runaway locomotive that had left the tracks of normal life and was plunging into uncharted wastes. Paul arrived at Aldgate and examined the fortified archway. Somewhere beneath his feet, Lud lay waiting in his crypt, preparing to rise again. War, fear and want were his tools. They opened the way for his return. Yet he waited.

'But why don't you attack?' Paul wondered out loud. 'You have an army of disciples while there is only one of me. Why don't you send the demon brotherhood against me?'

'It could be a sign that you are more powerful than you think,' came a familiar voice.

Paul turned to see a translucent form, his sometime guide through Hell's Underground. 'Cormac.'

'You don't sound pleased to see me,' Cormac observed.

'What the Hell do you expect?' Paul asked. 'It's been three months. I came to the conclusion that you had abandoned me.'

'I will not abandon you,' Cormac said simply. 'You are indispensable if we are to defeat Lud. I will be with you until your final reckoning with the demon master.'

'When were you ever by my side?' Paul snapped, scowling at the ghostly presence. 'I don't see you giving me much help now either.'

'I have told you before,' Cormac said. 'I am not a free agent. I do what I can, but there are limits to the support I can give. I must answer to a higher authority.'

'That's always the excuse, isn't it?' Paul sneered. Three wasted, miserable months in an unfamiliar London had taken its toll on his spirits. 'You're going to start talking about the mysterious Courts of Destiny again.'

'Yes, I am bound by the decisions of the Courts of Destiny,' Cormac said. 'If I overstep the mark they will deny me passage into this world. Then you really would be alone.'

'Isn't that convenient?' Paul snorted. 'You love your little secrets, don't you? The famous Courts of Destiny again. What about them? Are you ready to tell me who they are and what they do?'

Cormac shook his head slowly. 'You must earn the right to stand in their presence. That time has not yet come.'

Paul turned his back. 'Will it ever come? What kind of game are you playing, Cormac? I need help and guidance but all I get from you is riddles.'

Cormac's cloaked form shimmered. 'If you are to win the war against the demon brotherhood, Paul Rector, you must learn patience. Lud has broken many an opponent because they raced too eagerly into battle. He uses cunning as well as strength. Everything I say is true. I am indeed constrained by a higher authority. You do not understand the risks I have taken to guide you this far.'

'I hope you don't expect me to be grateful!' Paul yelled, his voice crackling through the darkness.

'No,' Cormac said patiently, 'but I do expect you to rein in your eagerness to do battle. It is a game of strategy and tactics. You must have your wits about you.'

'Oh great,' Paul snapped. 'Do you really expect me to sit here waiting for Lud's disciples to come for me?'

'I expect you to prepare yourself,' Cormac said. 'Lud's methods are different this time. Three times he has thrown his henchmen against you in open battle. Though he succeeded in breaking one of the seals that bound him in his crypt, he has failed to destroy you. He understands that your strength is growing. That is making him change tack. This time he has a different strategy.'

'Do you know what it is?' Paul demanded.

'We will only understand Lud's motives when we find Nathanael, his latest accomplice,' Cormac replied. 'There must be no complacency. You will still be tested to the limit. Thus far you have done well. You have mastered horsemanship and you have some command of the weapons of this time.'

'I didn't have much else to do,' Paul grumbled. 'I've tried to find Nathanael. You don't know how much shoe leather I've used tramping the streets. Can you imagine how bored I am . . . how lonely? I miss my mother. I miss my friends. I miss television and mobile phones and traffic noise. I miss seeing planes cross the sky. Most of all I miss Netty.'

'Loneliness is your condition,' Cormac reminded him. 'You are the demon who can be all demons.'

'Yes,' Paul retorted, 'thanks for reminding me. Aren't I wonderful? What a gift I have. I can slay any demon I encounter and take his powers. So what does that make me? It sounds like the description of a murderer, or a parasite.'

'I see you have doubts about your mission.'

'Of course I've got doubts,' Paul cried.

'You must be strong,' Cormac said. 'You are approaching journey's end. You are here to delay Lud's escape as long as possible. You are here to create an even playing field for the final conflict when you must face him alone. One wrong move and you face defeat and death.'

'Tell me something I don't know,' Paul snapped.

'Then why must I keep saying it?' Cormac demanded, striking back. 'Why do I have to keep beating the same tale into your stubborn head?'

This rare show of temper from Cormac reduced Paul to silence for a few moments. 'Is there anything else?' he asked rather meekly.

'Only this,' Cormac said. 'You understand how Lud is held. My three brothers and I used four magic seals to bind him all those centuries ago. Let me describe them. We made them out of fire, storm, flood and blood. One has been broken. You must defend the others at all costs. Should the demon master rise now, he would be unstoppable.'

Paul wondered what the consequences would be? Would future generations cease to be? What would happen to Mum, Netty, Evelyn, Betsy, Chaim?

'What can I do to stop him?'

'You must understand the power that holds Lud,' Cormac continued. 'We used the ancient elements of Beltane. Fire broke the Bishopsgate seal.'

'You mean Samuel's explosion?'

'Yes, that's how he did it.'

Cormac's explanation started to make sense.

'So that's how Lud's disciples will open the seals,' Paul said, 'by storm, flood or blood? I have to stop them and delay his escape until my power equals his.'

Cormac nodded. 'There are three seals left. They will hold the monster. They are located at three of London's ancient entrances: Aldgate to the east, Ludgate to the west and Aldersgate to the north.'

'In what order is it meant to happen?'

'I don't know. The spells we used to contain Lud were both powerful and intricate, drawing on the skills of the four greatest sorcerers of our time. His solution will be no less cunning. I am not privy to the demon master's thoughts. Suffice it to say, his disciples will use storm, flood or blood.'

'So what do I do now?' Paul sighed. 'I've scoured every inn and tavern looking for Nathanael Rector. I've knocked on hundreds of doors. So where are you, Nathanael? Come out, come out, wherever you are!' He waited for the echo of his voice to die away, then stabbed a finger at Cormac. 'That's what I've been hearing for three months, silence. Nobody has even heard of Nathanael Rector.'

'Are you sure about that?'

'I think I can tell when somebody's lying to me,' Paul retorted.

'Can you really?' Cormac said. 'That would be a rare skill indeed for one so young. You don't believe that one man or woman, of all those you have interviewed, may not have hidden the truth?'

Paul frowned. He felt slightly ridiculous about his boast. 'If you put it like that . . .'

'May I try something?' the fire priest asked.

Paul stared at the ghostly form. 'Like what?'

'Sometimes there are things we barely register at first glance. On re-examination, we may understand their importance. Put your trust in me and I will help you relive your memories of the last three months.'

He had Paul's attention. 'You can do that?'

'I am a priest of Beltane,' Cormac said. 'It is one of my gifts. Or rather, it is one of yours. All I have to do is help you to realise your own abilities.'

The priest's ghostly, shimmering hands floated around Paul's face. At first, Paul shrank back from the phantom touch, then he steadied himself.

'Let me bring your memories to life,' Cormac said.

Suddenly, without warning, vivid images exploded into Paul's consciousness. He tore himself away, clutching his temples. 'What did you do to me?'

'I apologise,' Cormac said. 'I will take it more slowly this time. Are you ready?'

Paul nodded. The images blazed so intensely he was tempted to break away again, but this time he kept his nerve, gradually overcoming the sense of nausea and invasion. It was as if the film of his life was being rerun before his eyes. He didn't just see it. He smelt it, felt it, tasted it. He experienced every moment once more, in all its dazzling reality. What's more, he sensed things he had missed the first time round. As he learnt to trust Cormac, the fire priest varied the tempo of the recollections, speeding through some, creeping through others. Further and further back he delved, to the moment Paul first appeared in this time. After maybe ten minutes, Paul shouted for Cormac to stop.

'What is it?'

A busy thoroughfare hovered in Paul's mind, as real as when he had first come across it.

'Camomile Street,' Paul said. 'Of course, I've been there before. I was standing in Camomile Street when Lud breeched the first seal.'

'There's a pattern here,' Cormac said. 'Tell me. What did you see?'

'Can you rerun it?' Paul asked. He saw the fire priest's look of confusion. 'Can you make it live again?'

'It's your turn,' Cormac said, stepping back. 'I have done nothing that you can't do yourself. Trust your own abilities.'

Paul raised his own hands to his temples. Falteringly at first, then with growing confidence, he explored his memories. He peered into the fluttering mind-pictures.

'There! I'd only been here four or five days. I started my search in Whitechapel, where my quest began. I was asking about Nathanael in a tavern.'

'So you now think the landlord lied to you?'

'I don't know,' Paul answered. 'I can't say if he was in on it or not. I remember hearing a scraping sound and looking round. Now I know what it was. One of the doors was ajar. A little girl was watching me through the crack.' Cormac went to speak, but Paul raised his hand. 'Do you remember I told you my hearing and eyesight were becoming more acute?'

'Yes, you are beginning to explore your nature, to understand who you are.'

'Somebody came to fetch the girl,' Paul said. 'It was a woman. I could tell from the tap of her shoes on the stone floor.' He stared at the swirling images. 'I can see the hem of her dress. The material looks expensive.'

Cormac was puzzled. 'But what does this have to do with Nathanael?'

'The tiniest thing caught my attention,' Paul said. 'It was the woman's reaction when she heard me ask for Nathanael. I heard a gasp.' He threw his head back. 'I didn't give it much thought at the time. I was curious for a moment, then I put it to the back of my mind. Now that I hear it again, I know this woman, whoever she was, recognised the name Nathanael Rector.'

'Would you know her again?' Cormac asked.

'No,' Paul answered. 'There's nothing but that one glimpse of the hem of her skirt. She dragged the girl out the back way.' He ran his thoughts forward. 'I was leaving the tavern when a carriage went by.' He saw a four-wheeled hackney carriage pulled by two horses. 'There's a little girl watching me. She's got black hair and she's holding her arm for some reason. She seems to be hurt. Cormac, it's the same girl!'

'Are you sure?'

'I know what I saw,' Paul said. 'Even better, I remember the crest painted on one of the doors. I'd know it anywhere.'

Cormac watched Paul for a moment before speaking. 'You have been searching for your ancestor for three months. He may have even left the capital. At least we have the girl. She may lead us to him.'

'So we're on to something at last,' Paul cried

jubilantly. 'I'll set about tracing the carriage tomorrow.'

For the first time in three months, Paul went to bed happy and full of hope. He used his new ability to make his memories live and pictured his home, friends and family. The last thing he saw as he slipped into a deep sleep was Netty's smiling face.

Three

Present Day

Netty still calls on Paul's mum from time to time, though her visits are becoming less frequent. There doesn't seem much to say. They both know the fading police investigation is doomed to failure. Doctor Who might use an old police box but the Met don't have a time-travel department.

'It's good of you to call round,' Mum says.

'That's OK,' Netty says. 'I want to keep in touch. I suppose it's my way of saying Paul hasn't gone for good.'

'What if he has?' Mum wonders out loud.

'Don't talk like that,' Netty says. 'You've got to believe he'll come home.'

Mum sighs. 'I don't know if I do.' She catches Netty's eye. 'It's funny the way you've stayed so devoted. I mean, you didn't go out for long.'

'But we went through so much together,' Netty says. 'There were monsters . . .'

Her voice trails off as she remembers Mrs Rector's eldest son John was one of the monsters. 'Oh, I'm sorry.'

'Don't be,' Paul's mum says. 'I've learned to live with what John did ... was.'

There is a moment's silence while Netty plucks up the courage to ask her question. 'Do you ever feel like you're being followed?'

'No, why?'

'Oh, nothing.'

'Netty, I think you'd better explain.'

'There's this man,' Netty says. 'The first time I saw him, I was browsing the tops on the stalls outside the tube. The next day I noticed him leaning against the lamp-post across the street from my house.'

'Are you sure?'

'Of course I'm sure,' Netty replied. 'You don't think I'd make something like that up, do you?'

'Oh, Netty!'

'I even saw him standing outside the school gates. I went back into Reception to report a stranger hanging round. A couple of teachers came, but he'd gone. It's got so I feel like a stalked deer.'

There's a detail she doesn't confide in Mrs Rector. It would be too painful for the mother of John Rector, the boy who became a creature called Redman. It's the stalker's eyes that have got Netty spooked. She's familiar with that demon stare, so dark, so cold, so intense with menace. The stranger's eyes remind her of Redman. They're the eyes of a killer.

'You should contact DS Hussein,' Paul's mum says.

'What's she going to do?' Netty asks.

Mrs Rector is concerned. 'Netty. You can't just ignore it.'

'Don't worry,' Netty answers. 'I won't.' She glances

27

at her watch. 'Look, I'd better be going. I'm meeting Charlotte in half an hour.'

'Don't go,' Paul's mum says. 'We need to talk about this.'

'Look,' Netty replies. 'Forget it. I shouldn't have worried you. I really have got to go.'

Mrs Rector follows her to the door. 'At least promise you'll come again.'

'I will,' Netty says. 'I'll call tomorrow, about six. We'll talk then.'

'See you then, and Netty?'

'Yes?'

'Be careful.'

Netty takes the tube to Whitechapel. She's halfway across Whitechapel Road when she pauses to glance back. A shadow has just crept over her. The driver of a sapphire-blue Audi screeches to an abrupt halt and pounds his horn.

'Are you trying to commit suicide or what?' he snarls through the open window.

The car has stopped just centimetres from Netty's right leg. Flustered, she hurries to the opposite pavement. People are staring. The moment Netty steps off the road, the Audi roars off with a squeal of tyres.

'Stupid cow!' the driver yells.

Netty doesn't pay him the slightest attention. What's one bad-tempered driver compared to the fright she's just had? She's still searching for the face in the crowds that pack the pavement around the street-traders' stalls. Her heart is slamming. No, she thinks, my eyes must have been deceiving me. It can't all be starting again. Netty stands on the central reservation for several moments, darting panicky looks to her right and left. Where did he go? she wonders. She knows she isn't imagining it. That dreadful, empty stare, the mischief that dances for a moment, then dies, leaving nothing but an intense emptiness. She will never forget that look. She remembers how it burned into her soul that November night last year. She remembers the way Redman transported her to the killing room. By now, she is trembling. If not for Paul, she would have died there, amid the squalor of the Ripper's London. A thought that has occurred to her often. Now that Paul is gone, there is nobody to protect her. She becomes aware of somebody talking to her. It is an elderly Asian woman wearing a jilbab.

'Are you feeling all right?' she asks.

'Oh, yes, I'm fine,' Netty splutters. She forces a smile. 'I really am. Thanks for asking.'

Then she hurries to the other side of the road and starts jogging towards the Idea Store and her meeting with Charlotte. The moment she enters the cafe, Charlotte waves to her.

'Your call sounded urgent,' Charlotte says. 'Why did you want to meet here anyway? There are plenty of places nearer to home.'

'This is where you saw Paul's photograph,' Netty says, pulling up a seat.

A change comes over Charlotte.

'This is where I saw a photograph of somebody who *looked* like Paul,' she says, correcting Netty. 'Aren't you having anything?'

'I'll go to the counter in a minute,' Netty says. 'Listen to me, Charlie, you're my closest friend.'

Charlotte pulls a face. 'OK, where's this going? Usually, when people tell me I'm their best friend it means they want to borrow money or they're going to tell me something I don't want to hear.'

'I'm not bothered whether you want to listen or not,' Netty says. 'I just want you to hear me out. That *was* Paul

29

in the photo.' She holds up a hand to ward off the protest. 'No, don't interrupt.' She pulls out a photocopy of the picture. 'Just look at it, Charlie. Tell me it isn't him.'

Charlotte barely gives the picture a moment's glance.

'It isn't him,' she says patiently. 'Think about it, Netty. What you're saying just isn't possible. This photo was published in the *Daily Mirror* in 1941. Netty, that's nearly seventy years ago.'

'Look at his face, for God's sake,' Netty says stubbornly. 'Look at the hairstyle. Did they look like that during the war?'

Charlotte studies the picture, then meets Netty's stare. 'OK, it looks like Paul. I admit it, the resemblance is uncanny.' She folds her arms. 'What do you want me to say?'

'I never told you what happened, did I?' Netty says. 'You don't know what happened when Redman broke into our house, not the whole story.'

Charlotte looks uneasy. She doesn't want to know what happened that night. Every time she thinks about Netty's shattered look the morning she returned to school, she wonders about the events that left that haunted shadow in her friend's eyes.

Netty doesn't care how her story is going to sound. 'Redman wasn't human, Charlie. He was a monster. When I looked into his face, I saw into Hell. He transported me back in time. I saw ...' Her breath catches. ' ... I saw a half-dismembered body on a bed. I was the body, Charlie. I was the murdered girl.'

'Netty,' Charlotte whispers, 'keep your voice down. People are staring.'

'Let them stare,' Netty says. 'Don't you understand, Charlie? Redman was going to kill me, to make me into that poor murdered girl. Paul saved me from a monster. Now there's another one stalking me.'

'What?'

'Somebody's been following me,' Netty says. 'Remember that day I reported somebody outside school?'

'Ye-es,' Charlotte says, wondering where the conversation is going.

'That's him. It's Redman all over again.'

Charlotte leans forward and takes Netty's hands. 'This is crazy.'

Netty pulls her hands away. 'You mean *I'm* crazy.'

'I mean,' Charlotte says patiently, 'that you're upset. You went through a terrible ordeal. That Redman character was crazy, yes. Then there's the fact that Paul is still missing and I know how much he means to you. That's got to shake you up. Maybe you should see somebody.'

'See somebody? Who?'

Charlotte becomes a little defensive. 'They have these counsellors.'

'You think I'm nuts, don't you?'

'Of course I don't,' Charlotte says, uncomfortably aware of the other customers turning to look. 'I'm not talking about a shrink. They offered you counselling for post-traumatic stress. Maybe you should have taken them up on it.'

'Don't you believe somebody's following me?' Netty glares at her friend and sees the hesitation. 'Well, either you do or you don't.' When Charlotte drops her eyes something snaps inside Netty. 'I've got to go.'

Charlotte tries to call her back. 'Netty. Netty!'

But Netty is halfway down the stairs. She races into the street, tears streaming down her cheeks. A dark-clad figure drops his copy of the *Evening Standard* in the bin and follows.

Four

7 June 1645

Henry Lampkin, the town gaoler, admitted his guests and led the way down the stone steps to Grace Fletcher's cell. The individuals that followed him were Cornet Leech, Jacob Beldam and his wife Margaret. Only one of the trio was smiling and that was the innkeeper. Margaret was scowling at her husband. Like Leech, she suspected his motives. He had always had a wandering eye, especially when there was a pretty girl around. Lampkin turned the key and stepped aside to admit his visitors. Leech looked around the plain cell and sniffed.

'These quarters are damp, gaoler,' he said.

''S' good enough for them that winds up here,' Lampkin muttered. 'You don't end up in the gaolhouse unless you've done something wrong.'

Leech was unimpressed. There was no window to admit light and air. Nor was there any form of heating. The cornet approached Grace. 'Are you being treated kindly, Mistress Fletcher?'

Grace didn't answer.

'I am enquiring after your health,' Leech said.

Grace turned on the wooden stool that, besides the grubby mattress, was the only piece of furniture. There was a scattering of straw on the stone floor. It seemed more suited to keeping livestock than providing accommodation for people.

'My health would be better served if you would permit me to leave this noisome hovel,' she declared.

'I told you she was a lively minx,' Jacob chuckled.

Grace fixed him with a stony look, then rose to her feet. 'What is the cause of your visit?'

'These gentlemen wish to examine your wound, Grace,' Lampkin said.

Grace glanced at Margaret Beldam. 'What's that miserable creature doing here?'

'I insisted upon her presence,' Lampkin said. 'If a woman is to be examined in my gaol, then there has to be another female in attendance. It is only proper.'

Grace found this little speech odd. Did the gaoler have some measure of integrity after all?

'Will you permit Mistress Beldam to roll back your sleeve, Mistress Fletcher?' Leech asked.

Grace's eyes lit with indignation, but only for a moment. In the end, she nodded and consented to the examination. Margaret Beldam slowly rolled back Grace's right sleeve. When she saw the bloodstained dressing, she clapped a hand to her mouth. Evidently, she was more superstitious than her husband, and more prone to believe in witchcraft. 'By the gospels!'

'You must continue, wife,' Jacob said.

Margaret lifted the dressing and recoiled at what she saw. The wound was seeping and there was fresh blood trickling down Grace's skin. 'It is just as you said, husband. She has a wound that will not close. This is unnatural. It is true. She is a servant of Satan.'

'Mistress Beldam!' Leech exclaimed. 'You are jumping to conclusions. Please consider your words carefully. These are dark times. You must not let your head be turned by the fears that sweep the land. There is no proof of any crime. I beg of you, do not divulge what you have seen to a living soul. Until Mistress Fletcher is examined by someone qualified to pass judgement, we must keep secret what we have witnessed.' But he knew the cat was already out of the bag.

Margaret stumbled backwards, pointing a trembling finger at Grace. 'You are a witch. You do evil magic.'

'Keep pointing that bony finger at me, you old crow,' Grace spat back, 'and you will see what magic I can do.'

At that, Margaret Beldam set up such a screeching and caterwauling that half the town must have heard her. 'She threatened me. You heard her. She said she was going to put a curse on me!'

'Dear lady,' Leech pleaded. 'Please control yourself.'

But it was past the point when reason would have any effect on the innkeeper's wife. She stumbled to the door, her face utterly drained of colour. Darting a final look of triumph at Grace, Jacob helped his wife back up the steps.

'Are you done here?' Lampkin asked.

'Give me five more minutes, gaoler,' Leech said.

'I can't leave you alone with her,' Lampkin grumbled.

'I didn't ask you to,' Leech replied. 'You may wait over by the door.'

Lampkin's brow furrowed for a moment, then, remembering the authority the soldier's russet coat conferred on him, he gave way. Leech drew Grace to one side.

'You are not helping yourself, Mistress Fletcher,' he whispered. 'Must you be so wilfully defiant all the time?'

'That is easily answered,' Grace said stubbornly. 'I protest because I am wholly innocent of any crime.'

'That's as may be,' Leech replied. 'I dare say most, if not all of the poor wretches now rotting in Chelmsford Gaol are innocent too. That will not prevent them being hanged by the neck until they are dead. Believe me, if people want witches, they will have witches. There are men wandering the land whose very purpose in life is to condemn women to the gibbet.'

He had Grace's attention.

'You must listen to me,' he said. 'I am under orders to return to my regiment, but you will not be without representation while I am gone. My father is a magistrate. He is a fair-minded man. He has spoken out more than once against the fever of witch-hunting that has broken out across the Fenland.' He sighed. 'I have sent word to him that there may be a miscarriage of justice here.'

Grace softened her expression. 'Thank you, sir.'

'Don't thank me,' Leech said. 'I fear there is more I could have done to prevent you being placed here in the first place. I was weak.' He hesitated.

'What concerns you, sir?' Grace asked.

'Jacob Beldam alleges that you gave up your only child to Satan,' Leech said. 'He is accusing you of infanticide. You must prepare a defence.'

'My poor Susanna was taken from me three months since,' Grace answered, tears welling in her brown eyes. 'She was abducted.'

'By whom?'

It was Grace's turn to hesitate. 'That I can't tell you.' Her voice was so low Leech had to strain to hear.

'But you must,' Leech told her. 'If you will not provide an explanation you are doomed. Your enemies will seize on your silence. Grace, you will face charges of witchcraft and child murder. You will hang for sure.'

Grace hung her head. 'If you knew my story, you would understand my silence. I regret, sir, that I have nothing more to say.'

Leech stared at her. 'You are making a great mistake. I want to help you, but you refuse to tell me anything.'

Grace maintained her silence.

'Very well,' Leech said. 'Admit nothing until my father communicates with you. Do you hear me, mistress? No matter what they do, you must not say a word to them. I will be gone but a few days. You must say as little as possible until I or my father comes to see you.'

When Grace continued to stare at her hands, Leech shook his head in frustration and brushed past Lampkin. The gaoler locked the cell door and followed Leech upstairs. He watched the trooper climb into the saddle of his grey mare and ride off down the Cambridge Road. Soon, he was joined by Jacob Beldam.

'Did you eavesdrop as I asked?' the innkeeper inquired.

'I did,' Lampkin said, 'though I don't feel good about it.'

'It is rather late for an attack of conscience,' Beldam said. 'Give me an account of what passed between them.'

Lampkin told his tale.

'I knew Leech had an eye for her,' Beldam said. 'Well, he is going to be disappointed. I knew about the letter to his father. I have already intercepted it.'

Lampkin raised an eyebrow. 'And why would you do that?'

'Oh, let's say I have a bone to pick with Mistress Fletcher,' Beldam replied. 'I have no doubt that she is indeed a daughter of Hecate and a witch as accused.'

'Just yesterday you thought she was a comely maid you wanted to tumble,' Lampkin commented sourly.

Beldam's face changed. 'Repeat that to anyone,' he warned, 'and I will make things very difficult for you, Master Lampkin.'

Lampkin scowled. Beldam was an influential man in the town. 'How did you persuade the messenger to hand over the letter?'

'Why, the same way I persuaded you to send mine,' Jacob said, nudging Lampkin in the ribs. 'I hope you carried out my instructions, Henry. I would be disappointed if you didn't.'

Lampkin remembered the coins in his breast pocket and wished he had refused the errand. 'I did as you asked me. Matthew Hopkins will be opening the letter as we speak.'

'Imagine that, Henry,' Jacob said. 'The man is the talk of East Anglia and soon he will be riding into our quiet little town.'

'Jacob,' Lampkin said, 'are you not afraid that we are stirring up forces we will not be able to control?'

'There you go with that conscience of yours,' Beldam said. 'You have been paid for your services, so be sure to keep your lips sealed about this. I know what I'm doing, Jacob. Soon we will be as famous as Manningtree, and all thanks to the Witchfinder General.'

Five

Present Day

Netty runs across the road. She's too upset to notice which way she's going. Only when she hears her feet clanging on the tube-station walkway does she realise where she is. She finds herself facing the Sports Centre. Her stomach twists with growing unease. What has led her to run *here*, of all places? Instinctively, she turns left. There, by the old Board School, is the spot where, in the autumn of 1888, Jack the Ripper killed his first victim, Mary Nicholls. It is also the site of Redman's second murder. This is where he killed one of her teachers, Mrs Petersen. Netty is standing on a fault-line of evil.

I've got to get out of here.

She turns ... and her scalp freezes. Striding towards her is the man in black, the unmistakable figure who has been stalking her for months. His sleek, voluminous coat flutters about him like a giant pair of wings. A broad-brimmed hat shades his face, but fails to disguise eyes that are deep pits of menace. She takes a couple of steps backward and stumbles into somebody. It is a woman in early middle age wearing the garb of an office manager: pinstriped trouser suit, black shoes and crisp white blouse. The woman scowls at Netty.

'Don't you kids have any respect?' she snaps and continues on her way.

'No, don't go,' Netty says, 'I'm sorry I bumped into you. Come back!'

The man in black turns and watches the woman stride towards Whitechapel Road. Then he turns. His smile is so cold and artificial it could have been painted on his gaunt features.

'I think you've offended her,' he says.

'Who are you?' she asks.

'Oh, let's not talk in clichés,' the man in black says. 'You must know why I am here, and who sent me.' He cocks his head. 'Let's guess, you're going to scream. That is usually the next stage.'

Netty feels a rush of hot air. Dark clouds are gathering around her. She has been transported like this once before, by Redman.

'No,' she cries. 'No!'

Already, she can feel herself sinking through the concrete pavement, through the earth, through the tangle of cables and pipes. Soon, she is standing on the platform from which Paul departed on his journey, seven long months before.

'You've got to let me go,' Netty croaks. Her voice is dry with fright.

'Do I?' the man in black asks. He sounds genuinely curious. 'Do I really? Why is that?'

'If you think I can lead you to Paul, you're wrong,' Netty tells him. 'I haven't seen him since November.'

The man in black considers what she has just said.

'Don't you think I know that? My dear, you are a pawn in the game, no more. It is my intention to sacrifice you to take the knight.'

'I won't let you use me to trap Paul!' Netty cries.

'Oh, I think you will.'

'Never!'

Her captor finds the outburst funny.

'Don't you dare laugh at me!' Netty cries. She stares into the grinning face. 'I know how long you've been following me. Why's it taken you so long to make your move?'

'I was busy enjoying the fleshpots of London,' the man in black answers. 'Yes, I love it all: the money, the cars, the clubs, the drink, the fights, the drugs, the mad, selfish pursuit of pleasure.' He looks her up and down. 'Then there are the girls, of course. Is it me, or do they wear a little less with each century that passes? Yes, London in the Civil War is such a dull place compared to this ...' He searches for the right word. 'What's the word I'm looking for, Bernadette? Your London is a playground, an Elysium. There is so much self-indulgence, such a hunger for self-destruction. It is demon Heaven!' He sweeps off his hat. 'I am Nathanael Rector, by the way. I'm sure you already knew my family name.'

Netty tries to make her getaway. Nathanael seizes her by the wrist.

'My poor, addled child,' he says. 'Where do you think you are going to run? Look around you. Do you imagine that, up those stairs, you will find Whitechapel Station? That London has burned away like morning mist. Why, you have already entered Hell's Underground.'

Netty skids to a halt. The stairs have given way to a country lane bordered by fields where cattle graze. 'Where am I?'

40

'You are standing in Hog Lane,' Nathanael replies coolly.

'I don't ...'

'Turn around,' Nathanael says, enjoying his little game.

Netty sees a row of timbered houses teetering on the edge of a deep ditch. They represent the outer limits of a great city. Smoke rises from many chimneys.

'Is that ... London?'

'Well done, my dear,' Nathanael says. He places his hand casually on her shoulder. Though Netty flinches at his touch, he seems oblivious to her obvious revulsion. He starts pointing out the landmarks. 'That is Houndsditch.'

'The one in the City?'

'The very same. This is where, four centuries from now, Redman will hunt down the policeman Ditchburn and drown him in a storm drain.'

'I don't believe it.'

'Suit yourself,' Nathanael says, 'but it is true. Here, where a cart now trundles, you can see Wentworth Lane. Look over to your left. Do you see the church in the distance? That is St Botolph.'

'I know St Botolph,' Netty objects. 'It doesn't look like *that.*'

'Do you still not comprehend?' Nathanael asks. 'The church you know will not be built for another hundred years.' He moves his finger slightly to the right. 'Now that should interest you. Do you see the large gate within the wall?'

Netty nods.

'That is Aldgate.'

'So these fields ...?'

'The ground on which you are standing will one day be part of the East End of London,' Nathanael said. 'The city in which you grew up is yet to take shape.'

'What year is this?' Netty asks.

'The year is 1645. England is torn by conflict.' Nathanael shakes his head. 'Mankind is such a sad tribe. He is so intent on war. Sometimes I think the demon brotherhood would be better standing back and letting you get on with destroying yourself. But where's the fun in that?' He turns Netty and strokes her cheek. When Netty pulls away, he chortles merrily. 'Let's take a walk.'

'But where are you taking me?'

'Did you not listen to what I told you?' Nathanael asks. 'The game has begun. We are moving to the next square on the board.'

Six

7 June 1645

Grace heard the key turn in the lock and looked up. She recognised Henry Lampkin and Jacob Beldam immediately. As to the identity of the other men, she had no idea. That didn't stop her watching them with suspicion.

'This is the hag,' Jacob said. 'She serves Satan.'

Grace had been perched on the end of the bed. She rose to her feet and glared at Jacob. She was in her twenty-eighth summer. With her mane of glossy black hair and dark-brown eyes, she had always been thought something of a beauty. If she were such a hag, why did Jacob rarely seem more than a few feet away, his covetous eyes roving over her?

'Let me alone,' she warned.

'Oh, I intend to, Grace,' Beldam said. 'This business has passed out of my hands.'

At that, Grace's senses tingled. For the first time she

43

gave the two newcomers due attention. 'Who are these men? What is their business here?'

'Let me introduce our honoured guests,' Beldam said. 'This is John Stearne.'

Grace's skin crawled. She knew the name. Who hadn't heard of Stearne the witch-hunter? She also guessed what was coming next.

'And this, Mistress Fletcher, is Matthew Hopkins, a gentleman of some renown.'

Though the men were of a similar height, in build there could not have been more of a contrast. Stearne was a brute, thickset and muscular, his features blunt and bulbous and his wiry hair dark. Hopkins, on the other hand, was painfully thin. He seemed lost in his sombre Puritan clothes. While Stearne sported heavy stubble, Hopkins' beard was wispy and fair. As to the hair on his head, it was blond and thinning.

'I am pleased to make your acquaintance, mistress,' Stearne said. 'I will assist Master Hopkins in his investigations.'

'I am innocent,' Grace declared. 'I have done nothing wrong.'

'That,' Hopkins said, speaking for the first time, 'is precisely what a witch would say.' He dusted the stool with a kerchief and sat down. 'Woman is Satan's vessel, Mistress Fletcher. She sets little store by honesty. Is that not so, Stearne?'

'I've heard it said many a time,' Stearne answered. He was watching Grace keenly, clearly looking forward to his day's work. 'Many's the unsuspecting man who has been led astray by some foul temptress.'

'I swear that I am telling the truth!' Grace said hotly.

'Do not raise your voice to me, harridan!' Hopkins roared, surprising everyone but Stearne by the force of his voice. 'Do you not know the story of Eve and how she tempted Adam with the apple?'

'I know the gloss men such as you put on it,' Grace retorted.

'There,' Jacob cried, seizing on her words. 'She rejects the scriptures. Did you not hear the blasphemy pour from her lips?'

Hopkins raised his right hand and adopted a pained expression. 'Leave this to us, innkeeper. Stearne, ask Mistress Pettigrew to come down.' He looked directly at Grace for the first time. 'It seems you have already terrified this man's good wife so badly that she dares not leave her room.'

'That is true,' Beldam said. 'All that she does every moment of the day is cloister herself in her chambers, quoting scripture.'

'It's not terror that keeps her up in her chamber,' Grace scoffed, 'but the sweetmeats with which she stuffs her fat face.'

'I would advise you to speak with a civil tongue,' Hopkins said. 'Or have you forgotten the gravity of your situation?'

A tall, grey-haired woman entered the cell. She was dressed from throat to toe in Puritan black. Only her face was plainer than her dress.

'You must uncover yourself, Mistress Fletcher,' Hopkins said. 'Stearne will examine you. Mistress Pettigrew is here to ensure that the examination is conducted properly.'

'I will not consent to this!' Grace cried. She retreated across the cell, holding out her hands. 'Get away from me!'

'Stearne,' Hopkins ordered, 'restrain her.'

Stearne seized Grace roughly and pushed her face down on the bed. While he pinned her, Mistress

Pettigrew ripped open the back of her dress. Grace writhed and twisted, trying to break free.

'You are doing yourself no good,' Hopkins said in that flat, controlled way of his. 'Do stop struggling. It is most wearisome.'

'Do you have the bodkin?' Stearne asked, panting slightly as he fought to control Grace.

Mistress Pettigrew nodded and produced a long needle. Hopkins shifted his stool and leaned forward so that his face was close to Grace's.

'Do you understand the nature of the examination, Mistress Fletcher?' he asked.

Grace turned. Her dark eyes blazed out from an untidy forest of black hair. She fixed him with a stare full of contempt and barely suppressed rage. 'You enjoy inflicting torture, don't you, Witchfinder?'

Hopkins pressed on, using the same flat, purposeful delivery. 'This is England. There is no torture here. Mistress Pettigrew will prick any spots she discovers on your body. As you know, witch spots do not bleed.' He rose to his feet and sauntered across the cell. 'Now do stop struggling. If you are innocent as you say, surely this examination is going to help your case.' He gave a little cough. 'Some water please, gaoler. My throat is dry.' Lampkin set off to get the water. 'Oh, and bring a more comfortable chair please. The examination may be long and the stool is not fit for purpose.'

During the next hour Grace screamed many times. Each time she resisted the bodkin, Stearne forced her arm against its joint, causing her agony. It wasn't long before she realised that he was enjoying his work more than any man should. Eventually, Hopkins called a halt to the examination.

'There are no witch spots yet, Master Hopkins,' Mistress Pettigrew told him. 'Every time I've pricked the wench, she has bled most generously.'

Hopkins gazed down with distaste at Grace's prone form. She was sobbing with frustration and misery.

'Tell her to stop that wretched noise,' he ordered.

'Master Hopkins wishes you to desist,' Stearne said.

In an effort to obey, Grace swallowed hard, but it only made the sobs come again. Stearne wove his fingers through her hair and slammed her face against the frame of the bed. Grace screamed. Even the stern and normally expressionless Mistress Pettigrew looked startled.

'She stopped her whining, didn't she?' Stearne said.

'There will be no physical torture,' Hopkins instructed, realising that his lieutenant might have gone too far. 'This isn't France, John.'

Stearne nodded.

'You are fortunate to live in England, Mistress Fletcher,' Hopkins drawled. 'On the Continent witches are tortured and burned for the offence of sorcery.'

'I hope you're not laying claim to moral superiority,' Grace cried. 'What's this but torture, you cold-hearted monster? And try telling your victims that hanging is better than burning.' She was disturbed to see that Hopkins didn't react to her outburst.

'Instruct her to sit up,' he said.

Grace heard him. She sat up, gripping the dress to her to preserve her modesty.

'Let me see the mark on your forearm,' he said.

Holding her dress up with her left arm, Grace showed him the open wound.

'Do you see this mark, John?' Hopkins said eagerly. 'This could be the entry point of an imp. Then again, it may be a scar made when she was separated from one of her familiars.' He caught Mistress Pettigrew's eye. 'Do you understand the idea of a familiar, Ann?'

47

'I think so, Master Hopkins,' Mistress Pettigrew replied. 'It is the witch's animal companion, is it not?'

'Oh, it is so much more than that,' Hopkins told her. 'It is a supernatural being that accompanies a witch. It may take the form of an animal, it is true, but the familiar is no mere beast of the field. It is a bridge to the Devil himself. It is the way the witch communicates with her master.' He shuffled his stool nearer to Grace. He was so close; his knees were almost touching hers. 'Now, Grace, what is your familiar? What caused this wound that never closes?'

Grace bit her lip. 'The wound is a mystery. I do not know its origin.'

'Liar!' Hopkins snarled. 'You must confess, witch. You must name your victims.'

'What victims do you mean?' Grace said.

'There is the innkeeper's wife,' Hopkins said.

At this, Grace snorted.

'Then there is your greatest abomination,' Hopkins continued. 'I am talking of the child you gave up to be a bride of Satan.'

The blood drained from Grace's face.

Hopkins smiled. 'Yes, I am talking of your daughter.'

Seven

7 June 1645

'**P**ick up your feet,' Stearne commanded. 'Well, are you ready to reveal the methods by which you serve Lucifer?' He had been forcing Grace to walk back and forth for hours. He hissed in her ear. 'Maybe you will tell us what you did with your child's body.'

'She has a name,' Grace told him defiantly. 'She is called Susanna.'

'You talk as if she is still alive,' Stearne said brutally.

Grace gave him a ferocious stare, then sagged back, knowing she dare not let her anger show. She pressed her hand to her temple. 'Providence willing, she is. No matter what, she will always live in my memory.'

'Sweetly put,' Stearne scoffed. 'Now move your feet, baggage. There will be no rest for you until you tell me how you do the Devil's work.'

Stearne drove Grace back and forth, hour after hour. From time to time, he would tell her to stop and interrogate her about imps and familiars and visitations by the Devil. Exhausted as she was, Grace accepted it all stoically. When Hopkins arrived about nine o'clock the following morning with a breakfast of porridge and eggs inside him, Stearne looked almost as weary as the prisoner.

'Get yourself off to the Swan, Stearne,' he said. 'Master Beldam is preparing your breakfast and your bed has been made. Get some sleep, then come back refreshed and ready to continue the interrogation.'

Stearne shot Grace a frosty glare and stamped up the stairs.

'Sit down, mistress,' Hopkins said.

Grace dropped heavily onto the bed and waited. Hopkins drew his chair up, just as he had done the previous evening. Lampkin's eldest son, taking his father's place, watched from a distance.

'Do you understand your predicament, Grace?' Hopkins asked.

She noticed that his voice was softer and he had addressed her by her Christian name.

'I know full well that you intend to deny me sleep until I confess,' she said.

'I am no rustic brute,' Hopkins told her. 'I take no pleasure in these interrogations.'

Grace wanted to throw the comment back in his face, but she held her tongue.

Hopkins continued. 'You can end your ordeal this moment. You will eat a hearty breakfast and be permitted an uninterrupted sleep. Isn't that what you want?'

'You know that it is,' Grace answered. 'What must I do to earn it?'

'Make a full confession,' Hopkins said eagerly. 'Name your accomplices.'

'You know that I have none,' Grace said. 'I have

resided in this town only three months, Master Hopkins. I know but a handful of the local folk.'

Hopkins ignored her. 'Three months is time enough to do the Devil's work. Name them, Grace. List their familiars. Describe their acts.'

Grace drew on her remaining reserves of defiance and examined her interrogator's face. 'What are you afraid of, Witchfinder? What can have led you to this dismal trade?'

She saw Hopkins' eyelids flutter. He didn't like her replying with questions of her own.

'You were a lawyer, I hear.'

'I am administering the law at this very moment,' Hopkins answered indignantly.

'Then it is law without justice,' Grace said. 'What happened to you, Master Hopkins, to make you so cruel? Why do you hate womankind so?'

Hopkins was unsettled by her gaze. Her dark-brown eyes seemed to peer into his thoughts. 'Did your mother reject you, I wonder? Did young Matthew Hopkins sit on the bottom stair, alone and neglected? Perhaps you suffer from some unrequited love. Was she pretty? Did she leave you for another? What is the nature of the pain you suffer, Master Hopkins?'

She had touched something in Hopkins. His eyes flashed with rage. 'I am the interrogator here. You ask me why I hate women. The question is wide of the mark. Witches are not women.'

'What are they then, Master Hopkins?' Grace retaliated.

'They are nothing but savage beasts,' Hopkins ranted. 'They are related to the vermin: rats and serpents and scuttering roaches. They are the lowest things in nature.' He threw his arms up as if he were giving a sermon. 'They are the consorts of Satan. The Prince of Darkness

51

is everywhere, mistress, and his vessels are many. The Earth is his empire. Let us stop playing games. I know full well what you are.'

Grace tossed her head. 'You know nothing. You can't even imagine ...' Immediately, she regretted her outburst.

Hopkins half-turned, checking that the younger Lampkin had heard. The gaoler's son nodded.

'What can't I imagine?' Hopkins hissed, prowling nearer. 'Tell me, Grace. It is obvious that you wish to unburden yourself. Is it that you take part in sacrilegious and diabolical activities? Describe the rituals. Tell me every detail. ' His eyes lit with a cruel hunger. 'Confess, sorceress.'

'Do your worst, Witchfinder,' Grace spat. 'Deny me sleep. Prick me. Cut me. No confession will escape my lips. You will never make me talk. I have endured greater torments than you can imagine, you miserable beanpole. Do your worst!'

Hopkins leapt to his feet at such speed that his chair clattered to the floor. 'Oh, you can be assured of that. You will regret defying me, mistress!' He stormed to the door and addressed the younger Lampkin. 'Tell your father, she is to be kept awake every minute of the day. She is to be denied both food and drink.'

He pointed at what furniture there was in the cell. 'Remove the bed and stool. This is no ordinary witch. The air hangs heavy with her profanity. What we have here is a high priestess of her kind.'

At this, Grace burst out laughing.

'Do you hear that?' Hopkins screamed, his voice shrill with thwarted ambition. 'She laughs at the mention of her satanic breed. She mocks a man who does God's work. Perfidious woman, I will see you condemned.' He glanced at the stone floor. 'Have this floor swept regularly. The Devil will send imps to visit her. They can be so small, they hide amongst the straw.'

'Invisible imps!' Grace said. 'Master Hopkins, you are making yourself look ridiculous.'

'There is nothing ridiculous about the Lord's work,' Hopkins said. 'You won't be smiling when you're dancing from the gibbet.'

Unease crept back into Grace's face, something Hopkins noted with satisfaction. 'Have the floor cleared by the time I return.'

Having said his piece, he swept out of the gaolhouse and strode down the main street. Passers-by stopped. Some pointed. Others whispered behind their hands. News of the Witchfinder General's arrival had swept every household. Hopkins did not break his stride, sending chickens fluttering in panic as he approached the Swan. There, Stearne had just finished his breakfast.

'Get to you, did she?' Stearne said. 'She's a cunning besom, that's for sure.'

'We have to break her,' Hopkins panted.

Stearne could see that he was quite hysterical. 'You're right, Matthew, we must. The town elders have just been to see me. They have offered to pay twenty-three pounds to cleanse the town of sorcery.' He rubbed his palms together. 'Did you hear that, twenty-three pounds for a single witch.'

Jacob Beldam heard the proposed amount and let a pewter pot fall to the stone floor.

'Why,' he exclaimed, 'the daily wage in these parts is only tuppence halfpenny.'

'This is not about the money,' Hopkins objected.

Stearne met Jacob's eye. Not about the money, indeed!

'It is about serving the Lord with all your heart,' Hopkins said. 'I am fighting for the soul of the people of this town. Where there is one witch, you can be sure there will be others. Mark my words, there is a coven here. We must steel ourselves for a long campaign against this one, Stearne. We need evidence and we need witnesses.'

Stearne grinned. 'It is all in hand, Matthew. I have not been idle. The moment Mistress Beldam started telling her story, all manner of people came forward. You've met some of them.'

Stearne listed the witnesses. Susan Hackett had arrived with her husband, complaining that their hitherto healthy baby boy, Miles, had not stopped crying since the family first encountered Mistress Fletcher in the street one day. He had spoken his first word soon after and it had been Beelzebub. Ester Hoskyns reported that her cow had given birth to a litter of puppies. Finally, George Mabb swore on the Holy Bible that he had seen Grace Fletcher and 'divers other females' consorting on the heath.

'Circumstances are tending our way, Matthew,' Stearne crowed. 'We have three witnesses, four with Mistress Beldam. That should be enough to see the hag condemned. Yet you do not look content.'

'Susan Hackett is a new mother,' Hopkins said wearily. 'The child is teething and she seeks a reason for her sleepless nights. Mistress Hoskyns would see three-headed rabbits if it got her a hearing from her neighbours. As to Mabb, he is five years a widower. Is it any surprise that he dreams of seeing females consorting on the heath? Stearne, are we reduced to such slim pickings?'

'We have hanged women for less,' Stearne reminded him.

'We have,' Hopkins said. 'But Grace Fletcher is our greatest challenge. What we have here is the high priestess of a coven, I know it. Stearne, what if Cornet Leech discovers that we intercepted his letter? If a magistrate does arrive to examine what we are doing here, our case must be strong. I want nothing less than a complete confession supported by irrefutable testimonies.'

'What if you don't get them?' Stearne said. 'Are you really saying you will let the harridan walk free?'

Hopkins leaned back, gazing up at the ceiling.

'You won't read the answer on Master Beldam's crumbling plasterwork,' Stearne said. 'Tell me your intentions. Matthew, look me in the eye.'

Hopkins sighed and faced his companion.

'Don't go talking about conscience to me, Matthew,' Stearne said. 'The Devil is a cunning opponent. You don't defeat him without bending the rules. I ask again, Matthew, if Mistress Fletcher continues to offer such stubborn resistance, do we allow her to walk free?'

Hopkins finally gave his answer. 'No, that is out of the question. We must not let her escape the wrath of the Lord.'

'So we are willing to use trickery?'

'Yes.'

'We are willing to use the witnesses we have, even if they are as mad as half-starved hunting dogs?'

'Yes.'

'We are willing to starve her and deny her sleep, no matter how much she begs for mercy?'

Hopkins nodded.

'And if I overstep the mark and chastise her with fist or boot, you will support me in that?'

Hopkins lowered his head.

'Matthew,' Stearne said, 'I must have your answer.'

'Yes, damn you!'

'Then I have the very thing,' Stearne said. He noticed

Jacob listening and drew Hopkins to one side. 'I have designed this for just such an eventuality.' He produced a bodkin with a wooden handle. It looked convincing enough, but when Stearne pressed it against his skin, the point retracted. 'It pricks, but the mark does not bleed.'

Hopkins shook his head vigorously. 'I will have nothing to do with cheap tricks, Stearne.'

'Cheap?' Stearne declared. 'It was not cheap. It cost me five pence.' He gripped Hopkins' sleeve. 'Just answer me this; are you sure of Mistress Fletcher's guilt, Matthew?'

'I have never been more convinced of anything in my life,' Hopkins answered.

'Then will you not consent to a little trickery to snare so wicked a sorceress?' He saw the hesitation in Hopkins' eyes. 'Remember your scripture, Matthew. Did not Christ himself tell us to turn the other cheek?'

'You know that he did. What relevance does that have?'

'But did he not also turn over the moneylenders' tables?' Stearne asked. 'The scriptures are God's truth, Matthew, but they can be read in various ways. So it is in the affairs of men. We would simply be interpreting the truth in a slightly different way.'

Hopkins struggled with his conscience for a moment or two, then held out his hand. 'Let me see the bodkin.'

Stearne handed it over and Hopkins pressed it against his hand.

'It is no good,' he said. 'If a witness were to ask to examine it, he would spot the trick instantly.'

'Which is why,' Stearne announced triumphantly, 'I have its twin.' He started to demonstrate. 'You simply slip the false bodkin into the folds of your tunic and produce this one.' He gripped the bodkin in his fist and stabbed it into the table top next to them. It did not retract, embedding itself into the wood 'Simple, but effective, don't you think?' He examined Hopkin's features. 'Well?'

'The Lord's work will be done,' Hopkins said piously. 'I am content. This is good work, Stearne.'

Eight

Present Day

Lisa Hussein jogs triumphantly down the steps and opens the car door with her key fob. She walked into the interview as a detective sergeant. She is leaving it as an inspector. She is still purring over the quality of her performance when she switches on her mobile and sees the missed call. Still smiling at the good news over her appointment, she contacts the station.

'Hi,' she says, starting the engine. 'This is Lisa. Yes, I got the promotion. You'd better start calling me ma'am.' She enjoys the uniformed officer's congratulations, then remembers why she called. 'Why did you want to contact me?' She listens and the smile drains from her face. 'Say that again.' She cancels the call and sits staring out of the car window. Her lips begin to move, repeating the message. 'Netty Carney ... missing.' She closes her eyes. 'It's starting again.'

It is a few moments before she signals and pulls out into the busy East End traffic. She drives on autopilot, weaving her way through the choked streets, barely registering the familiar landmarks. She pulls into the estate where Bernadette Carney lives with her mother. DI Hussein mounts the kerb behind a patrol car and kills the engine. Sitting there, she remembers a night seven months earlier. She stared into the eyes of a killer and saw her own death. Soon after Paul Rector disappeared.

DI Hussein closes her eyes. 'Now the girlfriend,' she murmurs.

The Redman case remains the strangest in which she has been involved. It led the normally level-headed Hussein to believe in the supernatural. How else could she explain a killer capable of scaring his victims to death? It also cost the life of her superior, DI Matthew Ditchburn, in circumstances that still mystify her. Hussein alarms her vehicle and crosses the road. A female constable meets her at the door of the house. She introduces herself as PC Elton and shows Hussein into the living room, where Mrs Carney is sitting in an armchair. There is a shattered look on her face.

'When did you last see Netty, Mrs Carney?' Hussein asks.

'It's two days,' Mrs Carney said. 'I phoned the local station, but they didn't take me seriously. '

'I'm sorry,' Hussein says. 'Were you the last person to see her?'

Mrs Carney shakes her head. 'No, that was Charlotte. They met at the Idea Store in Whitechapel. Charlotte says Netty was really upset. That's not all. Mrs Rector phoned.'

'Paul's mum?'

'Yes,' Mrs Carney says. 'Netty was at her house before going to see Charlotte. Netty told Mrs Rector she was being followed.'

'Did she tell you that?' Hussein asks.

Mrs Carney shakes her head. 'I think that's why she still saw Mrs Rector. I couldn't talk to her about ... those things.' Her bottom lip trembled. 'I tried to blot it out, you see. Oh, I knew something was wrong. Netty didn't tell me what exactly. Why didn't I try to talk to her?'

'You mustn't blame yourself,' Hussein says.

'Believe me, I don't,' Mrs Carney says. 'I blame the police. Why did you never get to the bottom of those terrible murders? If you'd done your job, Netty wouldn't have disappeared.'

'Mrs Carney,' Hussein says. 'None of us know what we're dealing with here.'

She notices the way the PC Elton frowns.

'Oh yes, we do,' Mrs Carney snaps. 'I wouldn't listen to Netty to begin with, but I know she was right. There are demons in this city, creatures from Hell.'

Five minutes later, PC Elton follows Hussein outside. 'Do you think she's quite right in the head, ma'am?'

'She's as sane as you or I,' Hussein tells him. 'You think you know what's out there in those shadows, don't you? Constable, you have no idea.'

With that, she jumps in the car and drives off, leaving a bewildered PC Elton looking down the street after her.

Nine

8 June 1645

Paul was standing in the shadow of St Clement Danes Church. The building was a decrepit, crumbling shell. It was in urgent need of demolition and reconstruction. But he wasn't there to go sightseeing. He was waiting for his sometime accomplice, the footpad Tom Catchpole, a man who knew all there was to know about London's wealthy families. He had plans to fleece most of them. Paul gazed down Fleet Street and the Strand, hoping to spot the hackney carriage with the distinctive coat of arms. A sighting would make Catchpole redundant, which might not be a bad thing. Catchpole made a good companion, but he was, for all that, a thief and a cut-throat.

'Have you had any luck, young Paul?' Catchpole asked, his voice leaping unexpectedly out of the night.

Paul spun round. 'How did you manage to creep up on me like that?' He was annoyed. His senses had been growing more acute by the day, but they had failed to alert him to Catchpole's approach. What if it had been Nathanael or one of Lud's other disciples? Lapses such as this one merely reminded him how much he still had to learn. 'It's a while since anybody surprised me so easily.'

'It isn't easy,' Catchpole said with a grin. 'It's a skill that's been many years in the learning. I can creep up on a man, slit his purse and be away before he has noticed my presence.' He followed the direction of Paul's gaze. 'You left a message at my lodgings. How can I help you?'

'I'm looking for a carriage,' Paul said. 'I'll know it immediately. There's a coat of arms painted on the door.'

'What does it look like?' Catchpole asked.

'There are three silver bars . . .'

'Argent,' Catchpole said, correcting him. 'In the field of heraldry, silver is called argent. You need to know these things if you are to rob the rich. What else?'

'There's a lion's head.'

Recognition lit Catchpole's face. 'Follow me.'

They crossed the pitted road and walked past a row of reasonably well-to-do homes.

'The middling sort has been moving in lately,' Catchpole said. 'These houses belong to the merchants that have grown fat on the city's trade with Europe.' He winked. 'I've relieved a few of them of their purses.'

'Why are you showing me this?' Paul asked. 'None of these houses are grand enough to possess a carriage like the one I saw.'

'Maybe not,' Catchpole said. 'This is the property I brought you to see.'

He was pointing to a large mansion, set back from the road. Paul saw something on the ornate iron gates and hurried forward.

'Catchpole,' he said, 'you're a diamond!'

The gates bore a coat of arms: three argent bars and a lion's head.

'What do I owe you for the information?' Paul asked.

'Nothing as yet,' Catchpole said. 'The next time you go taking purses, I will expect half the proceeds.'

Paul nodded. 'Done!'

'You do talk strangely for a London-born Englishman,' Catchpole observed. 'Are you sure there's no foreign blood in your veins? Every day, the city swells with new arrivals.'

'Tom,' Paul answered, 'I'm as English as you are.'

'Well, I must be on my way,' Catchpole said. 'I trust you will find what you're looking for, Paul.'

Paul smiled goodbye, but the moment Catchpole had turned the corner any expression of pleasure drained from his features. He had used his demon powers just once since his arrival in this time. That was to rob a merchant and secure the funds to feed himself and put a roof over his head. Now he would have to call on them again, though he remembered the dark shadows that would come. He had been dawdling in the road for twenty minutes or so when a maidservant slipped through the gates and set off towards Charing Cross. She was carrying a basket. Paul hurried after her.

'Just a moment,' Paul said.

The maid looked startled.

'There's nothing to fear,' Paul told her. 'I just want some information.'

'Sir, I have nothing to tell you.'

'I think you do,' Paul said. 'I saw the coat of arms on those gates through which you've just passed. Whose house is that?'

He heard the maid breathe a sigh of relief. 'It is the home of Sir James Rokeby.'

63

'Of course,' Paul said, trying to sound knowledgeable. 'Thank you.'

The maid hurried away, pausing just once, when she had gone about fifty yards, to glance back.

'Sir James Rokeby,' Paul said out loud, ignoring her cautious stare. 'Let's see what we can find out about you.'

He came upon a nearby tavern and lunched on beer, coarse bread and bacon. He had soon gathered what little information he could glean from the innkeeper and his customers. Sir James had inherited his wealth from his Norman ancestors, but lately he had amassed a considerable fortune shipping coal from the northeast. Sir James had sided with Parliament in its dispute with the King, while his brother Sir Charles had raised a regiment on the Royalist side. So what's the link to Nathanael? Paul wondered. He toyed with what was left of his food, pushing a thick, fatty piece of bacon to one side. Having eaten his fill, he gazed at the ceiling. Soon, he was interrupted by a stranger's voice.

'You have been asking about the Rokeby family, I hear.'

Paul turned to look at the man who had sat down opposite him. 'That's right. But who told you?'

'It was Bridget,' the newcomer asked.

'Bridget?'

The man pointed at a figure standing in the doorway. 'You remember the maid you accosted in the street, do you not? She was under instruction to alert me should anything untoward occur at the house. What's your interest in Sir James?'

'I wish to help him,' Paul said.

The newcomer was in his thirties, lean and muscular. Paul noticed that he held his right leg stiffly.

'You look like a military man,' he ventured.

'You are most observant,' Bullen said. 'I fought my first engagement at Edge Hill. I was sorely wounded at Roundway Down. Permit me to introduce myself. I am Nehemiah Bullen.'

'How do you know Sir James?' Paul asked.

'It was under Sir James I served,' Bullen said. 'He was a fine man until . . .'

'Pray continue, sir,' Paul said, striving to mimic the patterns of speech he heard around him.

'A few weeks ago, I was sufficiently recovered from my wounds to call upon Sir James,' Bullen said. 'I wanted to thank him for supporting me financially during my convalescence. I was in for a great disappointment. Bridget ushered into the presence of a man who didn't even recognise me.'

'I don't understand,' Paul said.

'At first I believed that Sir James was suffering from some mental affliction,' Bullen said. 'That was before I met the true cause of his transformation.'

'What was that?' Paul asked.

Bullen interlaced his fingers on the table and stared at them. 'Sir James has fallen under the influence of a man so wicked, I fear for his very soul. He manipulates my old friend the way a puppeteer plays with his marionette.' Bullen looked up, meeting Paul's gaze. 'Why, Sir James does not say a word unless bidden by the rogue.'

'The name of this advisor,' Paul said uneasily. 'Would it be Rector?'

Bullen's eyes widened. 'Yes, that's the fellow.'

'Nathanael Rector?'

'How in God's name do you know this?'

'I am about to tell you something which may affect your opinion of me,' Paul said. 'You see, my name is also Rector.'

Bullen leaned forward. 'I am listening.'

'My family is divided,' Paul continued, wondering how to broach the matter. A thought occurred to him. He could use the Civil War that was raging far beyond London's walls. 'It is divided much as Sir James' family is.'

Bullen nodded gravely. 'This conflict sets father against son and brother against brother.'

'It does,' Paul said. 'Nathanael has shamed his family. I have been asked to find him, bring him to justice and salvage our battered reputation.'

Bullen thought for a moment. 'Has your relative always been able to hold sway over men's minds?'

'I don't know him personally,' Paul answered truthfully. 'What makes you ask?'

'Did you not hear what I said?' Bullen replied. 'Sir James was once a brave soldier, a successful merchant and a doting husband. Now he sits day after day in a darkened room alone. All he ever does is gaze into the shadows. This is your relative's doing.'

'But what has he done to Sir James?' Paul asked.

'Perhaps you need to see for yourself,' Bullen said.

Paul leaned forward. 'Can you get me into the house?'

'In the sorcerer's absence, I am able to gain access,' Bullen told him.

'So Nathanael is out of London?'

'It appears so,' Bullen said. 'There is no sign of the devil. Would you like me to arrange the visit?'

'Very much,' Paul said. 'If I am to make amends for my relative's evildoing, I must see what havoc he has wrought.'

'Where can I find you, Master Rector?' Bullen inquired.

Paul gave directions to his lodgings.

'You will hear from me soon. Good afternoon, sirrah.'

'There is one other thing,' Paul asked. 'Are there any children in the house?'

'Children?' Bullen repeated. 'Sadly, there are not. Lady Sarah lost her first child. She miscarried. The poor woman will have no more. Is that all?'

'Thank you, yes,' Paul said.

He sat for several moments, considering what he had heard, then left.

Ten

8 June 1645

Grace read the list of witnesses. 'What have I done to earn the hatred of these people? It is but three months since I arrived here from Framlingham. I hardly know a soul.'

Mistress Pettigrew entered the cell.

'Prick her, Stearne,' Hopkins said.

Stearne grinned and produced the fake bodkin.

'But I thought we were done with all that,' Grace protested.

Stearne made her stand spreadeagled against the wall. Holding her by the nape of the neck with his left hand, he used the right to press the retractable point against her back.

'There,' he exclaimed triumphantly. 'The bodkin pricks her, but there is no show of blood.'

Grace struggled. 'What tomfoolery is this? I felt no pinprick. There is no puncture.'

'Do it again,' Mistress Pettigrew urged. 'Let me see.'

Stearne repeated the procedure and walked away, holding the bodkin high in the air.

'May I examine the bodkin?' Mrs Pettigrew asked.

'Why, of course, good lady,' Stearne said, effecting the exchange and handing her the second, rigid needle.

Mistress Pettigrew pressed the bodkin against the wall and professed herself satisfied that there was nothing suspicious about Stearne's tools. 'Grace Fletcher is indeed a witch. I suspected it all along.' She caught Hopkins' sleeve. 'I never did like the way she paraded herself through the town with her hair loose about her shoulders, attracting the eye of every man she passed. I knew her for a wanton hussy. I did not know her for an evil sorceress too.'

'Now will you confess?' Hopkins demanded, his face close to Grace's. 'Will you at last name your accomplices and describe the satanic practices that you have introduced to this quiet, god-fearing town?'

Grace swayed wearily on her feet.

'Mistress Fletcher?' Hopkins hissed eagerly.

Grace watched him for several moments, then spat in his face. 'No matter what you do, Witchfinder, no matter how long you deny me sleep, no matter how many witnesses you find or how many lies you tell about me, I will never submit. Do you understand me, Master Hopkins? Though Hell may freeze and angels skate upon its surface, I will never indulge you in this cruel mischief. Condemn me if you must. There will be no confession.'

Hopkins stood open-mouthed for a moment, taken aback by Grace's defiance, then he guided Mistress Pettigrew out of the cell. 'You may go home. You have done your duty.'

Mistress Pettigrew smiled and went on her way. Once she was out of earshot, Hopkins took Stearne to one side. 'Do what you have to. Just do it in such a way that there are no broken bones, nor obvious bruises or swellings. When we have her confession, any fair-minded soul must be able to look at her and see that it was extracted without torture or mistreatment. Can you do that, Stearne?'

Stearne stroked his beard. For a moment or two he seemed to turn the matter over in his mind. Finally, he gave his answer.

'You can rely on me, Matthew. I will have her confession by the morrow.'

But there was no confession that night, or the next day, or the day after. Lampkin and his son heard Grace's screams and feigned ignorance of her suffering. Late one evening, in a break between Stearne's visits, Lampkin entered the cell.

'What's this?' Grace asked through parched, cracked lips. 'Have you come to gloat, gaoler? Have I not suffered enough at the hands of Stearne and Hopkins?'

Lampkin glanced anxiously behind him. 'I've come to give you this. ' He held out a cup of water.

'Is this a trick?' Grace asked. 'Have you laced it with salt?'

'It's no trick,' Lampkin said. 'I know not what you are, Mistress Fletcher, or what you have done. I come from plain, labouring stock and I am ignorant of witchcraft. When Jacob involved me in this matter, I took his money. Hearing you scream like that, I wish I had never pocketed those coins. I cannot stand to see one of God's creatures mistreated so. Drink. But do not let it slip that I was the one who gave you water.'

Grace snatched the cup from him. Wisely, when she raised it to her lips, she did not gulp it down. Instead, she sipped it, still wary. Finally convinced that Lampkin was honest in his intentions, she drank heartily.

'Thank you for this kindness,' she said. 'I am in your debt.'

'Just remember,' Lampkin said. 'Don't let Stearne know that I let you drink.'

Grace gave him a thin smile. 'I will keep your secret.'

Without another word, Lampkin hurried from the cell, locking it behind him.

Eleven

9 June 1645

Nathanael waited impatiently in the sitting room of the modest lodgings above a tavern. Finally the door opened and Netty appeared, accompanied by an older woman. The moment he saw her, Nathanael clapped his hands.

'Well, well,' he chuckled, 'what a transformation.'

'I can't wear this,' Netty protested. 'It's itchy and I'm burning up under here. I'm so hot!'

'Of course you are,' Nathanael said with a grin. 'But this is the seventeenth century and women dress with a sense of modesty unknown in your age.'

The woman Nathanael had entrusted with the task of dressing Netty was hovering nearby. 'What shall I do with these?' she asked, wrinkling her nose as she held out the clothes Netty had been wearing when she was taken.

Nathanael examined the jeans, sandals and bright orange top.

'Burn them immediately, Mistress Caulker,' he ordered.

Netty went to protest, then thought better of it.

Mistress Caulker held up the sleeveless top between forefinger and thumb. 'These are the vestments of a Jezebel.' She darted a scandalised stare at Netty. 'Is the wench from foreign parts?'

Nathanael's expression changed from wry amusement to anger. 'Mistress Caulker, have you learned nothing in your dealings with me? You are well paid for your services, but more importantly for your discretion. Do not presume to ask questions.' His eyes flashed, hinting at the demon within. 'You must know the penalty for curiosity.'

Mistress Caulker saw her own worst nightmares dance in Nathanael's pupils and the colour drained from her face. 'I am sorry, sir.'

'So you should be,' Nathanael snorted. 'Now bring us something to eat.' He listened as Mistress Caulker's footsteps died away, then turned to Netty. 'You don't say much, do you?'

'I don't talk to the likes of you,' she told him.

'No? Why's that?'

'You hurt and kill for the pure pleasure of it,' Netty answered. She tried not to imagine what he would do to Paul. 'All your kind are obsessed with violence.'

'Ah, of course,' Nathanael said. 'You have already met one of my demon brothers, haven't you? You're thinking about Redman.'

'He nearly killed me,' Netty snapped. 'He was a monster and so are you.'

'That really depends on your point of view,' Nathanael said. 'I am content to be a member of the demon brotherhood. You see, mankind always justifies everything in terms of a greater purpose. While we kill

73

for the pure pleasure of the act, they do it in order to serve God, or democracy, or their country or some other grand ideal. Oh, they do like a good cause. In the name of the greater good, they can excuse any atrocity.'

'What about you?' Netty demanded. 'You said it yourself. You kill for *fun*.'

'Do you think the accusation offends me?' Nathanael asked. 'If you do, then you greatly misunderstand the demon brotherhood. To us, experience is everything. Some say life is about wine, women and song. That is true, and what joys they are, but the observation leaves out so much. Life is also about power, strength and the sheer wonder of exploiting the weak. A demon is like a naughty boy in a nursery, and the likes of you, pretty Bernadette, are his playthings.'

All the while she was listening to him, Netty was wondering how she would ever escape from such a creature.

'That's the difference between man and demon,' Nathanael said. 'Your kind wants your experiences to be done with as quickly as possible. Take war, for example. You perfect ever-more destructive machines of terror. You are so squeamish you want your dirty work done at long distance so you don't have to witness the effects of your weapons.'

'Not all humans want war,' Netty protested. 'I went on a peace demonstration with some of my friends from school.'

'How laudable,' Nathanael sneered. 'Did you carry little placards? Did you blow whistles and beat drums? I saw all that starry-eyed nonsense during my sojourn in your time. Oh, the masters of war must have been trembling in their boots!' He rolled his eyes. 'You're right. Some milksops do want peace. They want to place flowers in the barrel of a gun.'

'It's better than firing the thing,' Netty said.

Nathanael scratched his chin. 'Do you really think so? So why do all your entertainments feature them?' He pressed his fingers against Netty's forehead and made a gesture with his thumb to imitate the trigger. 'Bang!' Netty pulled away.

'Can you really imagine a world without conflict?' Nathanael asked. 'What would people discuss? It would all be so *dull*. Did Paul go with you on your peace march?'

'No.'

'I thought not,' Nathanael said. 'Now what was I talking about?'

'You were talking about machines of destruction,' Netty said reluctantly.

'Ah yes,' Nathanael said, warming to his theme. 'We demons could not imagine anything worse. I don't want to kill with a machine. I would derive no pleasure from a gun. It is too distant. You pull the trigger and a tiny figure falls. I mean, it's just so *disappointing*. No, I want to watch my prey's eyes as I tear his flesh asunder. I want to feel his hot blood spray my face.'

'Dear God!'

'That's right,' Nathanael said, revelling in Netty's reaction. He breathed deeply as if enjoying the fragrance of blood. 'I don't want to rush on to the next victim either. I want to sense every second of my victim's death throes.' He stretched out both arms and mimicked the death quiver. 'Ah, the dying breath of the victim, the tears of his widow, is there any greater joy in life?'

Netty couldn't disguise the shudder that passed through her.

'You are shocked, aren't you, soft-hearted Bernadette?' Nathanael said. 'Why? You are not repulsed by a lion or a hawk. They kill their prey and feed on hot flesh.'

'They're wild beasts,' Netty protested. 'It's their nature.'

'Yes,' Nathanael said, 'and this is mine.'

Netty's eyes were wide with fright.

'Oh, there's no need to fret,' Nathanael said. 'You're safe for now. What interest would the renegade have in you if you were damaged?'

Netty found the choice of words disturbing. To Nathanael, she was a mere bargaining counter, an object. It was some moments before he spoke again.

'You are right in what you say,' he said suddenly. 'We will use you to destroy the renegade. His downfall will usher in our freedom. Then there will be blood, pleasure, *fun*. Already, my master's disciples are preparing to break his crypt's second seal.'

'And you're going to use me as bait,' Netty said, seizing on the information.

'There you go again,' Nathanael said, 'stating the screamingly obvious. I expected more insight from you, Bernadette.'

'Call me Netty! I hate the name Bernadette.'

'Your name,' Nathanael said. 'Oh, I should have said something about that.'

'What do you mean?'

'The Parliamentary side might be suspicious of a name that sounds French,' Nathanael said, seeming to enjoy himself. 'Your cousins across the Channel are supporting the King in this conflict. As for the name Carney ...' He sucked in his cheeks. 'Oh dear, oh dear.'

Netty waited patiently for him to explain.

'The name Carney is Irish, is it not?' Nathanael asked.

'What if it is?'

Nathanael laughed out loud. 'Do you know nothing of the present conflict, girl? There is nothing the good people of Roundhead England hate more than the Papist Irish.' He reached out to stroke her cheek, but she batted his hand away. 'You think I'm the worst monster you could encounter. Believe me, Netty Carney, man that is born of woman is a far more savage beast than any member of the demon brotherhood. We would never destroy all our enemies, and we have absolutely no interest in that dangerous cocktail, politics and religion. What would we have to play with? We enjoy our tortures, but only your despicable race is capable of extermination.'

The return of Mistress Caulker put an end to the conversation. She set the meal down in front of them.

'What is it?' Netty asked suspiciously.

'There is beef broth and a quart of ale each,' Mistress Caulker said. 'Why, what's wrong with it?'

Netty's rumbling stomach overcame her doubts. 'There's nothing wrong with it,' she said, reaching for her spoon.

As she ate, her thoughts drifted from this room. Where was Paul? Did he have any idea the demon had her? She had been angry with him for a long time, ever since she had discovered he had found another girl. Angry as she was, how she longed to see him walk through the door and wipe the sinister smirk from Nathanael's face.

Nathanael turned his attention to Mistress Caulker. 'How are your guests?'

Netty turned at the mention of guests. She was burning with curiosity.

'They give me no trouble,' Mistress Caulker answered.

'I'm pleased to hear it,' Nathanael said, sipping his ale. 'You will not need to shelter them much longer.' He noticed that she was watching him closely. 'Is there something else?'

'You have not paid me for the next week,' Mistress Caulker said.

Nathanael grunted and produced a drawstring purse. 'Here.' He ate greedily and wiped his lips with a napkin. 'Watch Netty while I look in on my other charges. Keep the door locked and only reopen it when I knock to be admitted.'

Netty finished her meal under the supervision of the dour Mistress Caulker. Neither of them said a word. Netty listened to Nathanael's tread on the floor above. Who were these 'charges' he had gone to see? Already, she was wondering how she could gain entrance to the room upstairs. Presently, Nathanael knocked at the door and Mistress Caulker admitted him.

'Show Netty to her room, Mistress Caulker,' he ordered, 'and make sure you keep her under lock and key. Believe me, I would be most displeased if she were to escape. Do you understand me?'

Mistress Caulker met his glance for a moment, then tore her eyes away. 'I do, sir.'

Twelve

9 June 1645

About an hour later Netty heard a key scrape in the lock. Nathanael walked in on her washing.

'Don't you ever knock?' Netty demanded angrily, as she wiped her hands and face and quickly buttoned her dress.

'Is it privacy you want?' Nathanael asked. 'Well, I am afraid that is a luxury I cannot allow.'

'Are you telling me you might walk in at any time?' Netty cried.

'Did you expect anything else?' Nathanael responded. 'You must understand our relationship. It is that of a proprietor and his property. You will have enough to eat and drink, but you will never have freedom ... and you will certainly not have privacy.'

He was about to say something else when he broke off. Something had caught his attention. Netty couldn't understand what it was.

'What's this?' he murmured, his voice low and

troubled. It was obvious he wasn't talking to her.

Netty looked around. What had distracted him? She watched as Nathanael staggered backwards, slumping into a seat by the barred window. Immediately, he slipped into a restless dream.

'Who's there?' he inquired under his breath. 'Is that you, Bridget?'

'What are you doing?' Netty asked. She took a couple of steps forward. 'Nathanael?'

There was no answer. His head was at an uncomfortable angle, saliva bubbling on his lips. She pushed him. It was like touching dead meat. He was in a deep trance.

'Nathanael, can you hear me?'

Seeing him so vulnerable, a thought formed. He was a monster. He would destroy Paul. If there was any way home for her, it could only be in Paul's company. Netty ran her gaze over Nathanael. He was quite unconscious. Soon, she came across the sword and dagger that hung from his belt. Surely she would never be able to draw the sword without disturbing him, but the dagger, that was a different matter. She edged closer.

'Nathanael?'

One final time she pressed her fingers into his upper arm. There wasn't even a grunt from him. Still he stared at some distant, invisible object. Reaching across him, she wrapped her fingers around the hilt of the dagger and started to draw it from its sheath. She held her breath and directed every iota of concentration on drawing it steadily and evenly from the leather scabbard. The blade was halfway out. Already she was trying to picture herself driving it into him. How would she do it? Should she cut his throat? Should she sink the blade into his stomach? She chanced a look at him. To her horror, his eyes were wide open. His unblinking stare seemed to search her mind. How long had he been watching her?

'Do continue,' he said. 'Stab, cut, slash. I find this strangely compelling.'

On impulse, Netty seized the dagger and pulled it free. She drew her arm back and lunged at him. Nathanael moved with unnerving speed, allowing the blade to thud into the chair's head rest. In the same fluid movement, he knocked Netty off her feet. He straddled her, pinning her arms to the floor. She threshed from side to side for a moment before facing the fact that he was too strong for her. She stared up at him and saw nothing but contempt in his eyes.

'How did that feel, Bernadette?' he taunted. 'Did hope taste sweet on your tongue? Did it turn to ashes of disappointment?' He tilted his head in a gesture of curiosity. 'Is your heart pounding?' He pressed his hand to her chest. 'I see that it is.'

'Get off me!' Netty yelled.

'Did you really believe that you might sink the blade deep into my heart?' He read her reaction. 'What's this, you didn't choose the heart? Where then? Oh Bernadette, what am I going to do with you? You struck at me without any idea of your target, didn't you? Did you really think you could possibly be successful, a weak mortal like you, flailing without thought at a member of the demon brotherhood?' He released her and got to his feet. 'Pick yourself up. You shouldn't feel bad. Proud warriors have tried to kill me and failed. Think yourself lucky. I bathed in their blood. You are a woman and you are useful to us. You will escape unscathed.'

Netty turned her head. Tears of frustration were stinging her eyes.

'What's wrong?' Nathanael asked, his voice laced with mock sympathy. 'Are you feeling helpless? Do you resent my power?'

'I hate *you*!'

'Of course you do,' Nathanael said. 'I would expect nothing else.'

After a few moments Netty was sufficiently recovered to venture a question.

'What were you doing?' she asked. 'You were in a kind of trance.'

'Not a trance,' Nathanael said matter-of-factly. 'I was in complete control. There was an unexpected call on my abilities, that's all.' He reached out and played with a lock of her hair. 'Did you feel neglected, sweet Netty?'

She drew back in revulsion, making him laugh.

'I have a few tricks up my sleeve, you see,' he said. 'Paul plays with fire. I play with ... people. They are my puppets. I was visiting one of them.'

'I don't believe you.'

Nathanael led her to the windows. 'Do you see that hawker?' He was pointing to a shabbily dressed trader who was calling on the crowds of passers-by to buy his sugared apples.

'Yes.'

'Watch what I can do.'

Once more, he closed his eyes. This time, Netty made no bid for the knife. She understood now, that no matter how deeply Nathanael appeared to have slipped into his trance, he continued to be aware of what she was doing. She was still watching Nathanael when she heard the labourer's boots on the hard-baked earth. He was dancing. Without opening his eyes, Nathanael chuckled. 'Do you like my little show?'

'Are you controlling his movements?'

'That's what I meant when I spoke of puppets. Of course I am controlling his movements, and his mind.'

'Can you influence his mind and continue to behave normally at the same time?' Netty asked.

Nathanael's eyes opened. 'Keep watching.'

He walked to the middle of the room and started to dance himself. His movements matched the street salesman's perfectly. When the dance was over, the hawker continued on his way. He never knew why the people around him were staring and pointing.

'I wager you are wondering how much effort my little trick requires,' Nathanael said, circling the man. 'How many puppets can I manipulate at the same time without being distracted?'

'I wasn't ...'

'Yes, you were,' Nathanael interrupted. 'Already, you are trying to conceive of a plan so that you can escape my clutches and fly to Paul. You are wondering how much my mastery of this man's mind hinders my own thoughts and movements.' He grinned. 'How many people can I control before it stops me functioning properly?' He wrinkled his nose. 'Sorry, Bernadette, I'm not telling.'

In the middle of this speech, he broke off as he had before. Putting a finger to his lips to stop Netty disturbing him, he closed his eyes just as he had several minutes earlier. His mind had drifted away to another place.

'Bridget?' he said. 'Wait, who's that with you?'

This time he dropped to the floor, where he sat with his back to the wooden panels. He tossed back and forth, mumbling under his breath. At one point, he reared up, pointing his finger at the middle distance. His body was in the same room as Netty, but his mind was elsewhere.

Who are you talking to? she wondered. What are you seeing? Her pulse quickened. He had mentioned somebody called Bridget. But what about Paul? Was he coming?

Thirteen

9 June 1645

$\mathfrak{I}$t was after dark when Bridget opened the gates to admit Paul and Bullen.

'Are you sure this is the right thing to do?' Bridget hissed. 'The mistress is away from the house. I should not make such a decision without consulting her.'

'You have done it before,' Bullen reminded her. 'You were quite happy to admit me then.'

'You were alone,' Bridget observed pointedly, glancing in Paul's direction. 'You were also a regular visitor. I already knew that you had the master and mistress's best interests at heart.' She gave Paul a sideways glance. 'This person I do not know. Can you vouch for him?'

'Do you want to see this house restored to its former happiness?' Bullen asked impatiently.

'Of course I do,' Bridget told him, offended that he had even posed the question.

'Then you must lead the way to your master without further delay,' Bullen said. 'This is a matter of the utmost urgency. Bridget, I believe that he is in mortal danger. If we do not act, he could lose control of his house, his wealth, his reputation, even his family. I am convinced this young man can help.'

Bridget stole a second wary glance at Paul, then led the way indoors. 'You trust him then?'

'That I do,' Bullen replied.

The Rokeby house was as quiet as a sepulchre. The only light came from the guttering candle that Bridget was carrying.

'Why are there no lights?' Paul asked.

'My master forbids them,' Bridget said. 'All light, whether from the sun, from a candle or from a lantern, hurts his eyes terribly. For weeks he has been so sensitive to light that he suffers terrible headaches should the sun not be completely hidden from his gaze.'

'It was not always so,' Bullen said. 'This is the intruder's doing. The moment Nathanael Rector set foot in the house, a shadow fell over it. I have come across such men before, scoundrels, leeches, good-for-nothings, but none have been so determined, nor so successful. I would never have believed that my old friend could be manipulated by so transparent a rogue.'

'You underestimate Nathanael,' Paul said. 'He is no ordinary trickster. Tell me, how did Sir James first meet him?'

'It was through my friend's coal business,' Bullen explained. 'Nathanael posed as a wealthy merchant. I am convinced that he is nothing of the sort.'

'I'm sure you're right,' Paul said.

The trio climbed the broad staircase.

Bullen peered into the shadows as if expecting some evil to seep forth. 'When I discovered the influence the scoundrel had gained over Sir James, I went to investigate Nathanael's premises. They were deserted.'

'Did you convey the information to Sir James?'

'I tried,' Bullen said. 'Sadly, by then the creature had so insinuated himself into Sir James' confidence that my old friend and mentor would believe no ill of him.'

At this point, Bridget stopped. 'You know the way, Master Bullen. I can go no further. Sir James must never know that I took it upon myself to admit you to his rooms.'

Paul had a question for her, the same one he had put to Bullen in the tavern. 'Before you go, tell me this; has there ever been a child in the house?'

Bridget took a moment to answer. 'Sir James and Lady Sarah have no children of their own.'

Paul was alive to the evasion. 'That isn't what I asked, is it? I repeat: has there been a child in the house recently?'

Bridget's gaze fluttered across to Bullen.

'If you know something, you had better reveal it now,' Bullen said.

'There was a child,' Bridget admitted in a faltering voice. 'She was a strange little creature, prematurely wise. The mistress brought the wench home in her carriage.'

'When was this?' Paul asked.

'It was just before Easter if my memory serves me right,' Bridget told him.

'So about three months ago?'

'Yes.'

'What reason did Her Ladyship give for the sudden appearance of a child in the house?' Paul asked.

'She said the girl was her niece,' Bridget answered.

'But you don't believe that, do you?'

Bridget shook her head. 'No, sir, I know it to be false.'

'Why?'

'I have been in Her Ladyship's service for five years,' Bridget explained. 'I know all Sir James' and Lady Sarah's family. There is no niece by the name of Susanna.'

'That is her name, Susanna?'

'Yes,' Bridget said. ''Susanna did not come from gentry, I am sure of that. Why, you only had to look at the poor waif. The child was wild and unused to the ways of society.'

'In what way?'

'You should have seen the way she behaved around the house,' Bridget explained. 'She protested most strongly at having to wear shoes.'

'Did she give you any idea where she came from?' Paul asked. The child was important. But where was the hunt for her leading? He felt a deep unease.

'I have no idea as to her origins,' Bridget replied. 'In truth, she was as quiet as a field mouse most of the time. There was the outburst over the shoes. Otherwise she spoke little, save to say the same few words.'

'What were they?'

'She asked for her mother, of course.'

'Is that all?'

'No,' Bridget said. 'There was something else. It was most odd. She said that she must find her mother or their wounds would never heal. What could that mean?'

Paul frowned. 'I don't know, but I intend to find out.'

'May I go now?' Bridget asked.

'In a moment,' Paul said. 'I do have one more thing to ask.'

Bridget waited, nervously biting her bottom lip.

'When did you last see Susanna?' Paul asked.

'About a week ago,' Bridget told him. 'Her Ladyship ordered a plain carriage with no insignia. She was tying the child's bonnet and telling her not to take off her shoes.'

'A carriage with no insignia, you say?'

Bridget nodded. 'Secrecy had become important to

Her Ladyship. It is not just Sir James who has changed these last few months.'

'But why would they move the child?' Paul wondered out loud.

Bridget glanced at Bullen. 'I think it was on your account, Master Bullen.'

'Mine?'

'Yes,' Bridget said, 'I overheard Master Rector talking to Sir James. He thought you were ... meddling too much.'

'Meddling!' Bullen cried. 'I was trying to save my friend's family from destruction. Can nobody see that?'

Paul continued to press Bridget for information. 'Do you know where Lady Sarah and the child are now?'

'No, sir, I do not.'

Paul examined her face for a moment. Convinced that she was telling the truth, he let her go.

'What is the significance of this child?' Bullen asked. 'Why is Nathanael Rector going to such lengths to keep her whereabouts a secret?'

Paul shrugged. 'As yet, I have nothing to go on.'

'But you believe it is important?'

'Yes,' Paul replied, 'I know it is.'

Important, and possibly deadly. Without the benefit of Bridget's candle, they had to negotiate the landing by the shafts of moonlight that lanced across the floor. Presently, Bullen stopped outside a heavy oaken door. He knocked and entered.

'Who's there?' asked a voice from the shadows.

'It is I, James, your friend Nehemiah Bullen.'

'Ah, Bullen, do come closer.'

Bullen approached Sir James, who was sitting upright in a high-backed chair.

'Wait,' Sir James said. 'I detect another presence. Who is this stranger?'

'I have brought a friend,' Bullen said. 'This is Paul . . .'

Paul interrupted quickly before Bullen could blurt out the name Rector. 'Catchpole's the name. I am Paul Catchpole.'

Bullen caught Paul's eye and briefly acknowledged the correction. Goodness knows how Sir James would have reacted if he discovered that there was another member of the Rector clan under his roof.

'Why have you brought him here, Nehemiah?' Sir James asked. 'You know I do not want strangers entering my home uninvited.'

Bullen interrupted him. 'Paul has intelligence of your tormentor, James.'

Sir James snorted. 'How many times must I repeat it, Bullen? Nathanael is not my tormentor. He is my protector.'

'That is arrant nonsense!' Bullen cried. 'Do you not understand what he is at, James? He is stripping you of your wealth. He is taking you for a fool.'

'I am no fool!'

'Then why do you allow this man Rector to dictate your every move?'

Sir James scowled.

'Master Bullen is right to suspect Nathanael Rector,' Paul said.

Sir James turned to look at him. For the first time, in a beam of moonlight, Paul was able to see his features. His face was drawn and furrowed with deep lines. His eyes were so dark and deep set, the sockets could have been completely empty.

'Nathanael serves but a single soul in this world,' Paul said, taking care to frame his words according to the customs of the time. Sir James was suspicious as it was. A single error of judgement on Paul's part and the interview would be over.

'And who, pray, is that?' Sir James asked.

'His name is Lud,' Paul said.

At the demon master's name, Sir James' mouth yawned open in terror. Bullen looked on bewildered, trying to make sense of the exchange.

'You know of the creature's existence?' Sir James groaned. His hands were trembling.

'Yes,' Paul said, 'I know him. So, it seems, do you.'

'How do you know the monster?' Sir James asked.

'He made his first appearance some months ago,' Paul said. 'He destroyed my life. I am sworn to defeat him. Would you like me to prove that I know Lud?'

Sir James said nothing, but there was encouragement in his eyes.

'Does he come in a swirling vortex of darkness?' Paul asked. 'Do you see the glow of a white chapel? Does the demon lord rise from the shrieking depths?'

Bullen tried to interrupt, but Paul waved away his protests.

'That is how it is,' Sir James said, astounded. 'Yes, that is precisely the way it is. Lud came to me some months back. The ground opened before me, and the beast rose from the hellish depths before my very eyes. He had come to take my soul.'

'He *and* Nathanael,' Paul said.

'You misunderstand,' Sir James croaked, barely recovered from his shock. 'You do Nathanael a terrible disservice. He does not serve the monster. He guards me. I told him of the monster that visited me. Nathanael professed knowledge of the dark arts and offered to conjure a spell to keep Lud away.'

'I bet he did,' Paul snorted.

'You speak strangely,' Sir James said.

'Answer my questions honestly,' Paul said, shrugging aside his lapse into twenty-first-century idiom. 'Did

Nathanael insist on you withdrawing from society? Was that at his behest?'

'Yes. He said that only within the precincts of my home could he protect me.'

'And retiring behind drawn curtains, was that on his advice?'

Sir James looked away. 'You know that it was.'

'Who is this Lud?' Bullen demanded, 'and what is this talk of magic? Why have you not mentioned any of this before, Sir James?'

Paul waved Bullen away. 'You must leave this to me,' he said. 'It is a matter of urgency. Please listen to me, Sir James. Ignore my warning and you will put your life in peril. Lud has many disciples. Nathanael is but one of them.'

'No,' Sir James said, 'I refuse to believe it!'

'You must,' Paul insisted. 'You have to come with us this instant. We have to get you out of this house.'

'Why?' Sir James asked, still resisting.

'Here,' Paul said, 'in this house, Nathanael holds sway. The walls are infected with the demon presence ...'

'Demon, did you say?' Bullen's face was taut with anger. 'What madness is this? I brought you here to help Sir James break free of Nathanael Rector's malign influence. Suddenly you are talking about demons!'

'I was unable to tell you everything, Bullen,' Paul said. 'You would never have believed me.'

'You betrayed my trust!' Bullen roared.

Before either of them could say another word, they became aware of a terrible change in Sir James. His eyes suddenly lit with a strange, dark fire.

'Who attends me?' he growled, his voice a whole register deeper. The voice still belonged to Sir James, but they weren't his words and gestures. An alien presence had entered the room.

Paul pushed Bullen forward. 'You speak,' he hissed. 'My identity should remain a secret.'

Still angry, Bullen frowned, but finally allowed himself to be guided into his friend's presence.

'It is I, Nehemiah Bullen,' he said. 'But you know that already, James. I don't understand. We have been talking together these last five minutes.'

'Who is that?' the creature inside Sir James demanded, pointing past Bullen at the figure in the shadows. 'Command him to show himself.'

Bullen glanced behind. Paul gave him a warning shake of the head.

'You are mistaken, old friend,' Bullen said, still not understanding why he had to lie. 'Nobody is there.'

'I am not mistaken,' the voice rasped. 'What are you concealing?'

'I am hiding nothing.'

'Step forth, intruder,' Sir James commanded, speaking for the intelligence that was manipulating him.

'Listen to his voice,' Paul whispered. 'It's changing all the time. This isn't Sir James. He is possessed.'

But by whom? Was this Lud's doing or one of his disciples?

'What did he say?' Sir James hissed, almost hysterical by now. 'Make him come forth. Show him to me!'

He rose from the chair. There was something mechanical about his movements. 'Reveal the intruder!'

'James,' Bullen pleaded, 'you must not exert yourself so. Your strength has drained away while you have been confined in this room.'

'Get out of my way, you interfering oaf,' Sir James yelled.

Finally, he glimpsed Paul's face, pale in the moonlight. 'You!' Sir James stumbled to the grate and seized a cast-iron poker.

Paul grasped the tip and the whole poker glowed red-hot. Sir James dropped it and stared at his burned palm. Just for a moment the pain belonged to the man. A split second later the distant demon repossessed his soul.

'So it is true what they say,' the creature mused, using Sir James as his mouthpiece. 'You have the powers of fear and fire. You are the demon who can be all demons. How did you pick up my trail, I wonder? Still, it is of no importance. You are too late. You will never have the girl.'

For a moment Paul thought he meant Netty, then he realised it had to be a reference to the child in the carriage. Suddenly Sir James convulsed with agony. He shrieked and crumpled to the carpet. There he writhed and flailed, his feet drumming on the floorboards.

'What's happening to him?' Bullen cried, rushing to his friend's side. 'He was never subject to fits before.'

'This is Nathanael's doing,' Paul said. 'That was the voice you heard.'

'That is impossible.'

'Don't tell me what's impossible,' Paul said. 'Bullen, you are entering a dark dimension. You must be prepared for anything. Now, do as I say and restrain him.'

But Bullen had seen something that turned his heart to ice. Streams of blood were oozing from Sir James' eyes, ears and nostrils. 'James!'

Paul whispered into Sir James' ear. 'Where is your wife?' he demanded. 'Where has she taken Susanna?'

'Are you so unfeeling?' Bullen cried. 'Why do you torture a sick man with questions?'

'I'm sorry, Bullen,' Paul said, 'but it has to be done. We are too late to save your friend. We may yet rescue his wife and the child from their captors.' He turned towards the dying man. 'Listen to me, Sir James. You now know that I am telling the truth: Nathanael is in league with the demon master. Already, the monster's disciples will be on their way to find Susanna. Sir James, you must tell me where they are. Now that Nathanael is exposed for the evil creature he is, he has no further need of you or Lady Sarah. Do you understand? Whatever he does with Susanna, he will surely kill your wife.'

Sir James struggled on to one arm and clawed at Paul. 'Is this true, sirrah? Do not lie to me. I have suffered greatly of late and been sorely used. Will Nathanael's accomplices really kill her?'

'It's true,' Paul said. 'I swear it. Sir James, I'm her only hope.'

Blood was now spilling from Sir James' mouth. Only with the greatest effort did he manage to croak the address to Paul. Then he drowned in his own blood and died in Bullen's arms. Paul watched Bullen grieving for several moments, then he gripped his arm.

'There's nothing you can do for him now,' he said. 'If we are to save Lady Sarah and Susanna, there is no time to lose.'

'Have some mercy,' Bullen said. 'My friend has just died before my eyes. I can't leave him like this.'

'What will you do here?' Paul asked. 'Sir James is dead. You must fulfil his dying wish. For pity's sake, the demon brotherhood has already claimed one victim. Would you have two more on your conscience? Come with me and help save his wife.'

'Don't act as if you care what happens to Lady Sarah,' Bullen shouted as he tore himself away. 'You don't give a damn about her. All you want is this girl. That is the only reason you accompanied me here.'

'What you say is partly true,' Paul said. 'I do want to save Susanna, but don't you dare accuse me of not caring. I have sacrificed everything to fight Nathanael and his kind. The faces of the dead fill my nightmares.

Listen to me, Bullen, I don't want another innocent life destroyed because of Lud and his disciples.'

Bullen stared at Paul for a moment, then, closing his friend's eyes, he followed.

Bridget met them on the stairs. 'Where is Sir James? What were those awful cries I heard?'

'Don't go in there,' Bullen said as he followed Paul to the front door.

Bridget ignored him and entered. A moment later, her screams shattered the silence of the house.

'What will she think of me?' Bullen asked.

'Nothing you say will make any difference,' Paul told Bullen when he stopped and looked back. 'You must concentrate your mind on saving Lady Sarah.'

Bullen sighed. 'Very well.'

'Good,' Paul said. 'Now where are the stables?'

Bullen closed his eyes for a moment before leading the way to the back of the house. 'Come with me.'

As they rode out of the gates on to the Strand, they saw Bridget stagger to the door.

'Murderers!' she screamed.

Several passers-by stopped and stared.

'Stop those men,' Bridget shrieked. 'They killed my master. Murderers!'

The gathering crowd took up the cry. 'Murder! Foul murder!'

'We are outlaws now,' Bullen groaned. 'We will never persuade a court of law that we did not kill him.'

'None of that matters any more,' Paul said. 'The fate of the entire city is in our hands. We have to find this girl Susanna. The house is on Old Broad Street, near the church of St Peter le Poor. Do you know it?'

Bullen gave a last regretful look at the house and the distraught maidservant, then turned his horse north. 'Follow me.'

Fourteen

9 June 1645

Nathanael's behaviour in the tavern's upstairs room grew more erratic. Netty watched him aghast for a few moments before she began to understand. Somehow his mind had been transported elsewhere.

'Who is *that*?' he demanded, pointing into space.

Netty continued to watch her tormentor's movements. What would he do next? Within moments, he was clawing at the air, as if pushing some invisible figure aside. He was swatting shadows.

'Show him to me!' Seconds later, there was another shout. 'Reveal the intruder!'

Netty plucked up the courage to pass a hand in front of Nathanael's face. There was no reaction to her gesture. It was as if she had become invisible. He was too intent on the events that were unfolding before him in some other place. Nathanael mumbled incoherently for several moments, then a single word crackled across the room. 'Renegade!'

A buzz of anticipation swept through Netty. Renegade. That had to be Paul. 'Who are you talking to?' she asked excitedly.

She distinguished further fragments of Nathanael's conversation with his distant audience: 'How did you pick up my trail, I wonder?' and 'You will never have the girl.'

The girl, Netty thought, does he mean me? Is he talking to Paul? She ventured a question, hoping against hope that Nathanael might let the answer slip. 'Where's Paul?'

Nathanael didn't even register her voice. For all his earlier boasting, he seemed oblivious to Netty's presence. His mind continued to be preoccupied by distant events. Suddenly, the scene became more macabre still. A smile spread across Nathanael's lips. Simultaneously, he pressed his fingers into the sides of his own head. Netty watched as the veins throbbed in his face. A guttural snarl erupted from Nathanael's throat. That's when the blood came.

'What the Hell ...?'

Twin scarlet tears spilled from the corners of Nathanael's eyes, then from his nostrils. Finally, he spat as if bringing up phlegm, then a gout of thick, dark blood hit the floor. Still, he wasn't done. His eyes opened at last. They were washed with blood and bulged from their sockets.

'Riders!' he roared, his voice rebounding off the walls.

'What's happening?' Netty asked, her voice shaking.

Nathanel leapt to his feet, pushing her backwards against the wall, leaving her winded. He didn't even look at her. His eyes roved around, but he was gazing far beyond the walls of the room, completely preoccupied by events elsewhere. 'Riders,' he shouted again, striding to the door. He barked commands. Some of them were to follow him. Others were to guard the house. Sweeping past Netty, he gave one final order. 'Mistress Caulker, lock this door.'

With that, he was gone, boots pounding on the stairs. Mistress Caulker duly arrived, glancing over her shoulder at the commotion. When Mistress Caulker continued to be distracted by Nathanael's hasty departure, Netty saw her chance. The timing had to be just right. Mistress Caulker was staring after the riders as they leapt on to their mounts. Finally convinced that Nathanael had gone, Netty seized the bowl she had used to wash her face earlier and rushed her gaoler. Too late Mistress Caulker saw the danger and screamed, but by then the bowl had struck her on the temple and laid her out on the floor. Netty rolled the half-conscious Mistress Caulker on to her side and took her keys. Stepping over the landlady, Netty locked her in the room and allowed herself a smile. Gaoler had become captive.

Fifteen

9 June 1645

Lady Sarah crossed the sparsely furnished room on the first floor of Mistress Caulker's tavern and gazed out into Old Broad Street. She listened to the bells of St Peter le Poor chiming the hour. How much longer must they remain in these dismal lodgings? She was as much a prisoner as the child. Six long days and nights she had been confined in these four walls with only a nine-year-old girl for company and the early summer heat was suffocating. From time to time there was a knock on the door and food or freshly laundered clothing was delivered. It was a different person on every occasion. How she longed to flee.

She knew her imprisonment was at the behest of Nathanael Rector. Why had James admitted this wicked man into their home? Why, even now, as he languished in his darkened room, did her poor, deluded husband insist on Rector's every wish being carried out to the letter? Lady Sarah remembered the night James pleaded with her to go into hiding with the child. He had been completely under Rector's spell. Why did I not protest more? she wondered. She glanced at the strange, quiet child she had been told to guard. She looked at Susanna's bonds. Lady Sarah hated seeing the child's wrists tied behind her back like that, but Mistress Caulker insisted. Why? What harm could a tiny child possibly do? Mistress Caulker always gave the same answer. Master Nathanael's orders. Damn the fiend, she thought, but she didn't dare go against his wishes. Her husband's safety was at stake.

'Would you like some water?' she asked. 'I will hold the cup to your lips.'

Susanna shook her head.

'Why do you never speak to me?' Lady Sarah asked.

'I answer your questions,' Susanna replied.

'Yet you never speak of yourself,' Lady Sarah said. 'You have never even told me where you are from or what happened to your mother.'

'My mother will find me some day,' Susanna said. 'She promised. I have only to endure as my people have endured before me. You have seen my arm. When the riders came and tore us apart, we were each left with an identical mark. This wound symbolises the way they tore us apart. It will not heal until we are together again.'

'What an old head you have on your shoulders,' Lady Sarah said. 'There are times you do not sound like a child at all.'

'I speak according to my nature,' Susanna answered coldly.

'I have looked at this wound often,' Lady Sarah said, inspecting the deep, open gash. 'This is the first time you have explained its cause.'

'You know the reason for that,' Susanna said. 'You are not one of us. You would not understand.'

Not for the first time, the child had spoken of herself as part of a distinct tribe, or people. Lady Sarah let it pass without comment, though she couldn't help but wonder what the girl meant.

'I wish to understand,' she said softly. 'I would like to help you.'

'Help me?' Susanna said. 'You do not want to help me. You are little better than those monsters. You are my gaoler.'

'No, that is not true,' Lady Sarah objected. 'I believed that I was helping you.' Even as she said these words she thought how strange the request had been. 'My husband asked me to take care of an orphan child.'

'I am not an orphan!' Susanna cried. 'My mother will never abandon me. Even if I am removed to the far ends of the Earth, she will find me there some day. She gave her promise.'

Lady Sarah squeezed Susanna's shoulders. 'She must love you very much.'

'She does,' Susanna said. 'You must never call me an orphan again. You have no right.'

'Forgive me,' Lady Sarah said. 'It was ignorance. When I first took you into my care, I did not know the circumstances of your removal from her. My husband told me that you were alone in the world. I had no daughter of my own, so I was glad to look after you.'

'But you *are* my gaoler,' Susanna insisted. 'The riders stole me away from my mother. You continue to keep me from her. Even now, you allow Mistress Caulker to bind my wrists. I do not see any difference.'

There it was again, that prematurely wise voice coming from the mouth of a nine-year-old child.

'How can you compare me to the men who abducted you?' Lady Sarah protested hotly.

'You want me to believe that you're different?'

'Yes, oh yes.'

Susanna fixed Lady Sarah with a searching stare. 'Then let us put it to the test. If I tell you where my mother is, will you take me back to her? Will you release me from my bonds and let me go home?'

Lady Sarah looked away. 'You know that is not possible.'

'Why?'

'Nathanael Rector controls my husband's every thought and act,' Lady Sarah said. 'I fear that he would kill James if I disobeyed him.' She picked at her dress. 'Besides . . .'

'What?'

'Come and see for yourself,' Lady Sarah said. 'There is always at least one of your abductors watching us. Day or night, they are always there.'

Susanna slid off her seat and hurried to the window. Lady Sarah was right. She recognised the horseman standing by his mount some fifty yards down the street. He was one of the riders who tore her from her mother's protection.

'Susanna, there is something strange about our captors,' Lady Sarah said.

Susanna looked up at her, waiting for her to explain.

'They always cover their features,' Lady Sarah said. 'Have you ever seen their faces?'

Susanna shook her head slowly. 'It is as you say. They take care to mask their features. I have only seen their eyes.' She grimaced. 'I detect the shadows of Hell in them.'

Lady Sarah gazed at the watching figure. The rider wore a garb of brown and black. His lower face was swathed in dark bandages while his broad-brimmed hat shaded his eyes and brow.

'Their appearance is always the same,' Susanna said.

'Why are you so precious to them?' Lady Sarah asked. 'Why do they guard you so jealously?'

Susanna responded with her customary unsettling stare. Lady Sarah turned away and vented her despair.

'Oh, James dearest,' she groaned, 'what made you surrender yourself to Nathanael Rector? What happened to the man I married?'

She remembered Rector's growing control and her husband's decline into dependency on the monster. With each new visit, Rector had drained James of his willpower and independence. At that moment, she felt the child pressing against her.

'Look,' Susanna said.

Two more riders had joined their companion. The one on foot listened for a moment, then stared up at the window. Yet another rider clattered down the street at speed. There was something about their demeanour that caused Lady Sarah concern.

'Why are they gathering like that?' she asked.

'It is the first time I have seen them come together like this,' Susanna said. Her voice was trembling. 'See the way they stare at us.' She seized Lady Sarah's dress. 'They mean us harm. We must flee.'

'How?' Lady Sarah said, turning to speak to her. 'The door's locked.'

Her voice trailed off. Susanna's eyes were wide with terror. Alerted to the approaching danger, Lady Sarah returned her gaze to the street. Three of the riders were racing towards their lodgings, while the fourth held the horses' reins.

'They're coming to kill us!' Susanna cried. 'Look at them. Do you doubt their intentions?'

Lady Sarah started to tug at Susanna's bonds. 'That does it,' she said. 'I have gone along with this madness too long. We must flee.' She pounded on the door. 'Mistress Caulker, you have to let us out. For pity's sake!'

There were footsteps on the landing.

'Quickly!' Susanna cried.

Lady Sarah was still fumbling with Susanna's bonds when the door flew open. But it wasn't Mistress Caulker. Standing at the door was a young woman, the proprietor's keys in her hand. 'Follow me,' she yelled. 'They're coming.'

'Who are you?' Lady Sarah asked.

'Does that matter?' came the exasperated answer. When Lady Sarah continued to hang back, the newcomer huffed impatiently. 'Fine, I'm Netty. Now move!'

Together, Lady Sarah and Susannah followed Netty on to the first-floor landing. This part of the house was gloomy and illuminated by a row of lanterns set in recesses. Already, the first of the riders was pounding up the stairs. He ripped aside the bandages that covered the lower part of his face, revealing his hideous, ravaged cheeks and jaws.

'Stop!' he roared.

His face made a grotesque spectacle. Half the flesh had rotted away, exposing bare bone. Worse still, his teeth were curved and serrated. Lady Sarah and Susanna fled up the next flight of stairs.

'Give us the girl,' the rider hissed as he pursued them to the top of the house.

'You shall not have the child,' Lady Sarah said.

The second rider appeared at the shoulder of the first. 'Surrender her now! Your husband is dead. Give the child to us and we will spare you a similar fate.'

Tears spilled down Lady Sarah's cheeks. Her worst fears had been confirmed. 'James is dead?'

The riders were almost upon them. 'That is enough talk. Give us the child.'

'You could have taken her any time in the last three

months,' Lady Sarah yelled. 'What has changed? What made you kill my husband?'

The first rider made a grab for Susanna. Lady Sarah pulled her away from him.

'Save the child.' Netty hesitated.

'Run!' Lady Sarah cried.

Netty took Susanna's hand and they raced along the second-floor landing. Before them there were half a dozen steps. Netty climbed them and opened the door. 'Lady Sarah, the door leads on to the roof. We can get out.'

But it was too late for the woman Susanna had until that moment called her gaoler. The riders shrugged back their sleeves to reveal deformed, clawed hands.

'Save yourself, Susanna,' Lady Sarah screamed, 'you must go with Netty.' She snatched one of the lanterns that lit the stairwell and hurled it at the first of the demons. The monster batted it aside. Instantly, flames started to lick the wood-panelled walls. As Susanna was scrambling away Lady Sarah saw into the monster's mouth, where something evil lurked, something even more vile than its host. 'Oh, dear Lord, no.' The horror had just deepened. She resisted with all her might, but the struggle did not last long. Susanna heard the sound of cracking bones and turned away, mewling with fright.

Netty pulled the child to her. 'We've got to keep going.'

Susanna saw the flames that were licking up the walls and nodded.

'Get the child, Pitchcap!' snarled the first of the riders as he stepped over Lady Sarah's shattered form.

Netty and Susanna were already on the roof, scrambling across the tiles. Netty's heart was leaping as she fled. She had seen the riders' secret, their preferred way of killing their victims. The rider in the street howled the alert. 'There she is!'

Startled by his cry, Susanna lost her footing and slid towards the edge of the roof. She clawed at the tiles. Netty scrambled after her and seized Susanna's wrist.

'Look behind you,' the child cried.

Netty twisted round just as the riders emerged on to the roof after her. 'That way,' she hissed, pointing.

Agile as a monkey, Susanna scampered across the slanted roof. By now smoke was belching from the windows and billowing into the air.

'She's getting away,' the lead rider shrieked.

Netty tugged a heavy tile until it came loose and hurled it at him. He ducked and snarled.

It was at that moment Netty heard a voice from the street, one she recognised. 'Netty!'

It was Paul.

Paul stared up in disbelief at the slight, familiar figure on the roof. There was a strange cocktail of emotions; joy at seeing her again after all this time and horror at the danger she was in. 'How?' he cried.

Netty gazed down at him, eyes stinging. If she had ever doubted her feelings for him, all uncertainty was swept away in this moment. But she didn't answer his shouted question. The fire was consuming the building and the rider was closing on her. She turned to see Susanna sprinting towards the next house. The little girl would easily clear the space between the buildings. 'Jump!' Netty cried. As Susanna reached the gap, however, Netty's blood froze. A wall of flame was threatening their escape.

'Give yourself up,' the nearest rider said. 'You have nowhere to go.'

'Help us, Paul,' Netty shouted.

Paul didn't show a moment's hesitation. He plunged into the blazing building and started to fight his way up the stairs.

'What are you doing?' cried Bullen.

Paul vanished into the inferno without saying a word.

On the roof, the rider was moving closer to Netty and Susanna. 'Surrender,' he snarled. Susanna clung to Netty.

'Get away from us!' Netty cried. She was willing Paul to reach her. He was the only one who could confront this monster.

The rider grinned, but as he took a step closer, an agonised scream burst from his throat. Flames engulfed his clothes, transforming him into a living torch. Netty saw Paul appear behind him. This was his doing. For a few brief seconds the demon howled in pain and beat at his clothing. Then he fell heavily, rolling over and over down the slope of the roof before falling to the street three floors below like a fiery angel.

'That way,' Paul said, pointing.

'What about the fire?' Susanna asked.

Paul flung his arms wide. Instantly, the flames parted like theatre curtains. Seeing the way clear, Susanna took a run-up and leapt across the gap between the houses. The owners of the neighbouring house had appeared at a window and were waving the little girl off the roof.

'You're next,' Paul said.

Netty threw her arms round his neck and kissed him. 'I thought I was never going to see you again,' she cried.

Paul stroked her hair for a moment, then he pointed at the flames. 'Go,' he said. 'I'll follow.'

Netty's gaze held his, then she jumped the gap to the next roof. She took Susanna's hand and led her towards the open window. Paul was about to jump after them. Then there was a thunderous roar and the roof collapsed beneath him.

'Paul!' Netty screamed.

Sixteen

9 June 1645

The demon riders were now converging on Old Broad Street. Bullen was standing outside the building with the horses, wondering what to do. That's when he saw a young woman appear, leading a child by the hand.

'Are you Susanna?' he ventured.

'Who are you?' Susanna asked suspiciously. 'How do you know my name?'

'I'm Paul's companion,' Bullen explained. 'We came to rescue you. Paul's the one who saved you from that creature.' He gazed past the girl. 'Where is he?'

'In there,' Netty said tearfully. 'The roof collapsed beneath him.'

'God's blood!' Bullen murmured.

The demon riders saw the trio and wheeled towards them.

'We must flee,' Bullen roared, his skin crawling as cold, inhuman eyes examined him.

Netty shook her head. 'I can't leave. What about Paul?'

'Nobody could survive that conflagration,' Bullen said. 'We've got to go.'

Netty drew back. 'You don't understand. If anyone can survive, it's Paul.'

'Have you taken leave of your senses?' Bullen cried. 'No living creature could survive a fall into such a firestorm.' He lifted Susanna into the saddle, before climbing up behind the child. 'We have to go. In the name of God, mount the horse.'

'No,' Netty said, 'not without Paul.'

'I am begging you,' Bullen pleaded. 'The riders are almost upon us.' The danger didn't just come from the demons. The Trained Bands were arriving, a score of armed men. Bridget was with them.

'That's one of them!' she cried.

The militiaman next to Bridget raised his musket and squinted down the barrel.

'You must come with me,' Bullen urged. 'Please.'

Still Netty hung back. Terrified as she was, she couldn't bear the thought of leaving Paul. He had to be alive. The musket barked and the ball tore a chunk out of the wall behind her. 'Take Susanna,' she said. 'Save yourselves. I'm going to find Paul.' She turned her back on Bullen and Susanna and raced towards the burning building.

'No!' Bullen roared.

There was a second musket shot and he finally gave up hope of persuading Netty. Shaking his head, he kicked his horse's flanks and rode off down the street. Susanna clung to the horse's bridle and flattened herself against its powerful neck.

'Hold tight, Susanna,' Bullen said. 'We must get out of London.'

Seventeen

Present Day

Lisa Hussein, now DI Hussein, is finding it difficult to enjoy her promotion. She is working late. Except for a cleaner, she is alone in the office. She taps fitfully at her PC, thinking about a case that refuses to go away, no matter how many times her superiors have advised her to drop it.

'Where are you, Paul?' she murmurs.

Presently, she makes a decision. She makes a phone call and asks a favour. Half an hour later she is reviewing a tape of CCTV footage taken at the time of the Son of Ripper case. There were six murders and every one of them revolved around schoolboy Paul Rector and a sinister figure who went by the name of Redman. Hussein fast-forwards to the moment a Brick-Lane camera captured his face. She looks at the soulless eyes and shudders. Days after this footage was taken she encountered him in person. It very nearly cost her her life. Hussein picks up Paul Rector's photograph and compares it to Redman. There is no concealing the family resemblance.

A voice floats through the subterranean vault that is the evidence room. 'Are you going to be long?'

'No,' Hussein calls, 'I'm done here, Sarge.'

She collects the original foolscap file and signs it out. The sergeant at the desk logs it and glances up at her. 'This case has really got its claws into you, hasn't it?'

Hussein tries to make light of her interest. 'A serial killer, missing schoolchildren, echoes of Jack the Ripper, what more could a copper want?'

The sergeant grins. 'Closure?'

Hussein makes her way outside. Closure? She has a feeling it's going to be a long time coming.

Eighteen

9 June 1645

The afternoon sun was sinking over the wheat fields as three troopers approached the town where Grace was incarcerated. They were the Roundhead soldiers who had been in the inn the day she quarrelled with Beldam.

'The men no longer fear Prince Rupert's cavalry,' Cornet Leech said, swatting at the flies that were buzzing around him. 'Perhaps at last the campaign is beginning to turn our way.'

He was in a hearty mood in spite of the insects. The squadron had emerged victorious from its skirmish with a Royalist band. Now he and his companions, Cate and Ruddock, were riding homeward on the orders of General Ireton himself. They were to return with a string of sturdy horses in readiness for the imminent push into Northamptonshire.

'What's needed now,' Ruddock said, 'is a decisive engagement. This war has dragged on too long. The men want to be back in their fields, ready to bring in the harvest.'

'What do you think, Robert?' Cate asked.

Leech turned in the saddle. 'What's that you say?'

'His mind is on yonder town,' Ruddock said, 'and the fair lady who is being held in the town gaol.'

'Is that true?' Cate said. 'Is that why we took this fork in the road? Have a care, Robert. It will do your career no good if you are seen to be taking the side of a condemned witch.'

'There is not a shred of proof that Mistress Fletcher is a witch,' Leech said.

'You had your own doubts to begin with,' Cate reminded him.

'You are right, I did,' Leech admitted. 'But I have had time to consider the matter. She deserves a proper hearing at the very least. I pray that my father's intervention has helped quell the rumours. God willing, she may already have been released.'

Some way along the lane, they came across a carter repairing a wheel.

'Good evening,' Cate said, reining in his mount. 'My name is Edward Cate. May I know yours?'

'I am Bartholomew Fynche.'

'Do you live nearby, Master Fynche?'

Fynche pointed. 'Half a mile down that lane.'

'Then you know all the goings on, I warrant.'

Fynche squinted up at the trooper. 'Maybe I do.'

'What news from the town?'

'It's all bad,' Fynche replied. 'There's witchcraft in the locality. My neighbours report all kinds of strange happenings. They say milk is running sour from the cows' udders.'

'Have you tasted this turned milk for yourself?' Ruddock asked sceptically.

'Why no, sir, I have not.'

Ruddock glanced meaningfully at his companions. 'The witch hunt has taken hold of the people.'

'Does the town gaol still hold one Mistress Fletcher?' Leech asked, astonished that his father's intercession had produced no better result.

'Her and two more,' Fynche replied. 'There's Eliza Leverett and Cecily Mabb. Master Stearne took them in yesterday. It would be no surprise to me if there weren't more before the week is out.'

'Stearne?' Ruddock said. 'Who is this Stearne? I recognise the name from somewhere.'

'You should,' Fynche said. 'He and his partner are building up quite a reputation in the eastern counties. They can smell when a place has gone bad. We've got witch fever in the water now. There are new accusations by the day.' The carter looked at the troopers with some curiosity. 'What's your business here?'

'We have come to purchase horses,' Ruddock said.

'Horses, is it?' Fynche said. 'There is precious little horseflesh around here since Nol Cromwell mustered his army. The likes of you take all the good stock.'

Leech was indignant that he had changed the subject. 'Has there been no decision to try the witches in a court of law?'

'Not as far as I know.'

'I don't understand,' Leech said. 'Did my father not attend? He's a magistrate.'

'I know of no magistrate,' the carter told him. 'It is a man by the name of Hopkins who is running the show.'

'Hopkins!' Leech looked thunderstruck. 'Are you talking about Matthew Hopkins?'

'That's him.'

Leech gazed down the road towards the first of the

thatched and beamed cottages. 'When did that rogue come calling?'

'The town elders are paying him good money to look into our witchery,' Fynche said. 'They say the sum is twenty-three pounds.'

'Blood money,' Leech observed.

'I wouldn't let the townsfolk hear you talking like that,' Fynche said. 'They are most impatient to witness a hanging.'

'Before there can be a hanging,' Cate said, 'surely there must be a trial.'

'I don't know about that,' Fynche sniffed. 'The rumour is abroad that they mean to swim these witches.'

'Swim them!' Leech cried 'When is this to take place?'

The reply told him little. 'I don't know, sir. My wife is more excited by it than I am. I go about my own business and take care not to pry into the affairs of others. It is the best way to be.'

Tiring of the conversation, Leech jerked his reins and spurred his mount forward. The troopers entered the town at the gallop, attracting a small crowd. Leech made straight for the gaolhouse.

'Lampkin,' he barked the moment he saw the gaoler, 'what in God's name is happening here?'

Henry Lampkin looked startled. 'What do you mean, sir?'

'Don't answer a question with another one!' Leech cried. 'What has been happening since my departure? Who do you have in your gaolhouse?'

'There's Grace Fletcher, as you know,' Lampkin began, looking shamefaced. 'Then there's Elizabeth Leverett, Cecily Mabb and Catherine Martindale.'

'Do you mean that a fourth woman now languishes here?'

'Yes,' Lampkin said, 'there's four of them all right.'

'What of my father?' Leech demanded. 'I wrote him a letter urging him to come.'

Lampkin's face betrayed him.

'What do you know, gaoler?' Leech growled.

'It was none of my doing, sir,' Lampkin said. 'It was Jacob Beldam. He intercepted the letter. He boasted of it.'

'Did he, by God?' Leech said, turning his gaze towards the Swan. 'Then I'll be having words with this innkeeper.'

'Now, Robert,' Cate said, 'don't go losing your temper. We could be walking into the eye of a storm.'

It was too late. Leech clambered back into the saddle. Face stiff with rage, he rode to the inn. His companions followed. Dismounting, Leech strode through the front door and up to a nervous-looking Jacob Beldam. 'Did you presume to interfere with the letter I sent to my father?'

'Who's been accusing me?' Beldam stammered.

'I've a mind to run you through with my blade,' Leech said, cuffing the landlord across the head.

Beldam crumpled to the floor, where he knelt shielding his head with his arms. 'Don't beat me, sir.'

Disgusted by the man who knelt whimpering before him, Leech put a toe to his chest and shoved him on to his back. 'You are a craven cur, Master Beldam. You destroy a woman's reputation without a moment's thought, but when a man confronts you, you turn into a sobbing child.' He dragged Beldam to his feet. 'I should have you horsewhipped for this.'

It was at that moment his rage at the snivelling innkeeper was interrupted by a tread on the stairs. Leech turned to see a scarecrow of a man making his way down.

'You believe a woman's reputation has been destroyed,' the newcomer said. 'Would the lady in question be Mistress Grace Fletcher?'

'Yes,' Leech said. 'She is the persecuted woman. Who are you?'

'My name is Matthew Hopkins.'

Leech became aware of a second man at Hopkins' shoulder. 'You must be Stearne.'

'You have the advantage, sir,' Stearne said. 'Please identify yourself.'

'I am Robert Leech. I am an officer in the New Model Army. So you're the devils who have been stirring up so much trouble here.'

'Have a care who you're calling a devil,' Stearne growled.

Hopkins waved to silence his lieutenant. 'It appears,' he drawled, 'that you are the one causing the trouble.' He indicated Beldam with a lazy flick of the hand. 'Is it the job of Parliament's army to assault a man in his own home?'

'I am doing what I must to aid Grace Fletcher and the other innocent women you have ordered incarcerated in the gaolhouse,' Leech replied.

'How do you know they are innocent?' Hopkins asked.

His voice was quite passionless.

'I have met Mistress Fletcher,' Leech said. 'Damn me for a rogue that I was not made of sterner stuff when these allegations first saw light of day.'

'Have you met Mistress Fletcher's accomplices?' Hopkins inquired.

'You know that I have not.'

'Perhaps you should,' Stearne said. 'It is wise to appraise yourself of the facts before you go throwing your weight around.'

Leech could feel the ground slipping away beneath his feet.

'Did you know that all three women have confessed?' Hopkins enjoyed the look of astonishment on Leech's face. 'Yes, Elizabeth Leverett and Cecily Mabb named Mistress Fletcher as the high priestess of a secret coven late last night. Catherine Martindale made her confession this morning.'

'What did you do to extract it, damn you?' Leech bawled.

Cate saw that Leech was inviting trouble and tugged at his sleeve. 'Come away, Robert.'

'I will not back down in the face of tyranny,' Leech said.

'Tread carefully,' Cate whispered. 'We are three against almost the entire population of this town. Did you not see the way people looked at us as we rode here? Men were standing, pitchfork in hand, watching our every move. Robert, we would be outnumbered a hundred to one at least.'

For the first time, Leech looked less sure of himself.

'You would do well to take your friend's advice,' Stearne said. 'If you move against the gaolhouse, you will find the town united against you.'

'That is correct, Cornet Leech,' Hopkins said. 'I know all about your involvement in this case. There are twenty sturdy fellows, former members of the Trained Bands, who are armed and ready to defend the gaol. You would be foolish to make any attempt to free the accused.'

'I defy you, Hopkins,' Leech said. 'I do not believe the confessions.'

'That is an interesting comment,' Hopkins said. 'You believe that Mistress Fletcher is innocent though her child is missing. You reject the sworn statements of

118

three women though you have not even read their contents. Did you know that four witnesses have also come forward? Maybe you too are in league with Lucifer.'

The barely veiled accusation rocked Leech back on his heels. He was aware of Cate and Ruddock trying to guide him away. He delivered one last rebuke to the Witchfinder. 'Damn you. Damn you to Hell! I will read the statements. I will listen to your witnesses. I will find a way to rebut them all.'

'Please come away, Robert,' Cate whispered. 'You may be exposing yourself to great peril.'

Leech glimpsed movement out of the corner of his eye. During the exchange, twenty or so townspeople, mainly men, had made their way inside the inn. Several bore axes and shovels. One man sported a dagger. Yet another had a flintlock pistol tucked in his belt. The trooper could hear still more townsmen outside. They were angry.

'You will not have your way in this matter,' Leech yelled as he made for the door. 'This is not over!'

With that, he marched out of the inn, flanked by his companions. He barged his way through the sullen crowd to his horse. His neck was burning with humiliation.

Nineteen

9 June 1645

Nathanael Rector stood in a clearing, surrounded by the eight surviving demon riders. In the aftermath of losing the child, Nathanael's trademark arrogance had melted away. He looked anxious. Soon, the reason for his unease became apparent. A hot wind roared through the darkening woods. Debris stung the company's eyes and swarmed among the threshing branches like locusts. The earth began to ripple and become fluid, spinning faster and faster until a vortex formed. Deep within, a white chapel glowed. From its heart a silhouetted form rose.

'You summoned me, Nathanael,' Lud said, the malevolence in his voice so intense all those assembled before him shifted their feet with apprehension. 'Your reaction tells me that there is bad news.'

'The storm child is gone,' Nathanael admitted.

The white chapel pulsed with a searing light that

framed Lud and made his form darker and more menacing than before. 'Explain yourself.'

'It was the renegade's work,' Nathanael explained hastily.

'You had nine demon riders under your command.' Lud noticed that the dark squadron was short of one of its members. 'One of your brothers is missing. Where is Spitkettle?'

'Slain,' Nathanael said. 'But we believe the renegade died with him.'

'Did you see the body?' Lud demanded instantly. When there was no answer he grew impatient. 'Answer my question!'

'He fell into a burning building,' Nathanael replied.

'A burning building?' Lud scoffed. 'Do you know nothing? Fire is the renegade's element. He thrives on it. Of course he is not dead.' His translucent features glowed darkly. 'And the child? How did she slip out of your grasp?'

'The renegade had an accomplice,' Nathanael admitted. 'He spirited her away.'

'An accomplice?' Lud said. 'One man?'

'Yes.'

'So, in a city of four hundred thousand souls, Paul Rector managed to find this one precious child,' Lud snarled. 'How can that be?'

'I don't know, Lord,' Nathanael said. 'I swear on my life I left no clues. You know the carelessness was not mine. I was elsewhere doing your work.'

'I am not interested in your excuses,' Lud told him. 'When I advised patience and the adoption of a slower pace, do you think that I meant you to undertake a three-month sojourn in the London of the future?' His anger rumbled round the clearing. 'I grow impatient with my disciples' failures. I want solutions. The child

Susanna is vital to our interests. Now she has gone. Does the renegade understand her importance? Does he know why we need her?'

'I don't think so,' Nathanael replied. 'Even the child is too young to understand her gifts.'

'There is that at least,' Lud said, his bleak eyes glimmering like firelight on obsidian. 'It will take longer to break the seals, but I will see them destroyed.'

'Yes, Lord,' Nathanael said.

'It is possible to kill two birds with one stone,' Lud said. 'You will recover the girl and kill the renegade. There must be no more mistakes. I intend to be free.' His stare roved around the glade before alighting on Netty, who lay bound and gagged against a tree. 'At least you didn't lose this one.'

Nathanael omitted to mention that he had been lucky to discover Netty stumbling around the burning building, distraught and confused. 'No, Lord.'

'In this you have succeeded,' Lud said with satisfaction. 'We have something that is precious to him. Through her, we can break his sentimental heart and destroy his will to resist us. We may even transform a setback into victory. Pitchcap, Warboy, bring her closer.'

A pair of demon riders loosened Netty's bonds and dragged her before Lud.

'Yes, I remember this one,' Lud said. 'Redman wanted her. She was to be his work of art, his portrait of beauty and death.'

A tongue of black fire flickered out from the demon master and explored Netty's face. Each time it danced closer, she flinched. 'I can see why she pleases the boy.' Lud seemed to peer right into her soul. 'You bear some resentment towards the renegade. Now why can that be? Remove the gag, Nathanael. I will hear her voice.'

'Get away from me!' Netty cried.

'Do you hear that, disciples?' Lud said, amused. 'Why do none of you stand up to me like this? Why does an adolescent girl show more reckless courage than all the demon brothers put together? Where is the pure fire of rebellion in you?'

Netty felt the force of the demons' jealous stares. Their dark eyes made her flesh crawl. She knew her life was hanging by a thread.

'The bond between you and the renegade is strong,' Lud continued, 'yet there is some tension between you. What is its cause?'

'You won't get me to betray Paul!' Netty said bitterly.

Lud appeared amused. 'I rather think I shall,' he said. 'Consider this. You must know Nathanael's ability by now.'

Netty's breath caught in her throat.

'I see you do,' Lud said. 'Nathanael, penetrate her mind. Leave her conscious enough so that she can understand what is happening to her.'

Nathanael closed his eyes. Instantly, Netty gasped and convulsed in pain as his mind entered hers. His presence stole through every atom of her being, filling her with the clammy touch of evil.

'Let us conduct an experiment,' Lud said. 'We will explore your resistance to pain.'

Netty felt the pulse of Natahanael's mind as he invaded her will. She knew what he was preparing for her. 'Please don't hurt me.'

Netty had become a prisoner in her own body. She remained aware of the world around her. She could hear her own breathing. She could feel her heartbeat. Yet she had no control over her own actions, nor could she speak without Nathanael's permission.

'Walk to the fire,' Lud said.

The demon riders formed a circle and leant forward

expectantly. Netty sensed her limbs moving like an automaton. She took her place in the centre. Unable to speak, she screamed within.

'Hold your hand over the flame,' Lud said.

Nathanael directed Netty. She watched her own hand reaching out towards the campfire. Desperate as she was to withdraw it, she was helpless. She continued to extend it over the flames until her flesh started to roast. She could feel the blistering, the writhing of the blood in her veins. Soon she would smell her own skin burn.

'Do you wish to continue?' Lud asked. 'You know Nathanael can make you do anything he wishes.'

Netty found her voice. 'No more! I'll answer your questions.'

An instant later Nathanael relinquished his control over her and she screamed in agony, pulling her hand away. He splashed water onto her palm from a leather canteen. Netty stared at the blisters and the redness. She was gasping in pain.

'It will be uncomfortable for a day or two,' Lud said. 'There will be no permanent scarring. I wanted your knowledge, not your disfigurement. Even if you were returned to the renegade with a withered hand or arm, he would still welcome you. Oh, you can't imagine how much further I am prepared to go to attain my freedom.'

Netty sank to the ground and rocked back and forth, trying to ease the hurt. As she struggled with the throbbing pulses of pain, she realised the gravity of her situation. There was no point appealing to the creatures' humanity. They had none. Her captors wouldn't hesitate to inflict any torture.

'There is something I do not understand,' Lud said, breaking the brief interval of silence. 'Your anger is not directed solely at my disciples and I. You are angry with the renegade. You must tell me why.'

'It can't matter to you,' Netty said.

'All human behaviour is of interest to me,' Lud replied, contradicting her. 'To defeat your enemy, you must understand him.' When Netty continued to maintain her silence, he roared a command. 'Answer!'

Netty remembered the flames. There was no point trying to resist him.

'There was another girl,' she explained, 'in the War.'

'Ah yes, you mean Harry's London, don't you? I remember the girl Evelyn. She is dead, the victim of a stray bullet. It was Harry's doing. He always was careless.'

Netty stared into the fire. The image in the photograph leapt out of her memory. In her mind's eye she saw Paul and Evelyn walking arm in arm across Trafalgar Square, smiling through a haze of fluttering pigeons. For over three months she had harboured resentment against Paul and this other girl as if they were flaunting their happiness to spite her personally. She had never considered the possibility that this imagined rival might, like her, be the object of the monster's dark designs.

'Dead,' she whispered under her breath.

'Does the renegade still matter to you?' Lud demanded.

Netty twisted away from his eager stare.

'Don't be coy,' Lud warned her. 'Nathanael can get the answer for me.'

'Yes,' Netty admitted, wincing at the thought of further mistreatment. 'I still care about him.'

'More importantly,' Lud said, pressing her further, 'does he care for you?'

'Yes,' Netty replied. 'He was willing to risk his life to save me from the fire.'

'So how strong is the bond between you?'

Netty's earlier defiance leapt momentarily to life. 'It's none of your business!'

By way of persuasion, Nathanael stoked the fire with his sword. He allowed the blade to redden before advancing towards her. Netty tried to scramble away, but the riders blocked her escape. 'I could inflict great pain without spoiling your looks,' he told her matter-of-factly. 'Now, are you ready to answer the master's questions?' As the point smoked threateningly under her chin, she gasped out her surrender.

'Yes,' Netty said, tears spilling down her cheeks. 'I don't think I really knew until I saw him looking up at me today.'

'Do you *love* him, sweet Netty?'

She looked away.

'Answer!'

'Yes,' Netty cried. 'In time I think I could love him. Is that good enough for you?'

'That's what I wanted to hear,' Lud chuckled. 'You're in love. Oh, that's good. Yes, that's very good.' He turned his attention to his demon riders. 'Take her away and be sure to guard her well. She is important to our plans.'

As soon as Netty was out of earshot, Lud expressed his delight at his conversation with Netty. 'Did you hear her, Nathanael? The poor, deluded child thinks she might be in love. I like this emotion that mortal men value so much. It makes them irrational, impulsive.'

'It makes them vulnerable, Lord,' Nathanael said.

'Yes,' Lud smacked his lips. 'Vulnerable. What a delicious word. We must use this pathetic attachment. We will fashion it into an assassin's dagger.' He gave his orders. 'But be wary. Like Redman, Harry and Samuel before you, you have underestimated the renegade, Nathanael. You must learn your lesson if we are to triumph. His natural power is fire, but he has stolen other abilities. He can move small objects with his mind. He can feign death.'

'Each of those abilities was bought at the cost of a demon life, Lord,' Nathanael observed.

'Yes,' Lud replied, 'but it is advantageous to us in one respect. The circumstances of his birth have created a prince among half-breeds. He has the strengths and weaknesses of both man and demon. His weakness is that each time he steals a power, his mind becomes more susceptible to his demon instincts. '

'There are moments,' Nathanael said, 'when you sound as if you admire the boy, Lord.'

'Of course I admire him,' Lud said. 'In him, for the first time in twenty centuries, I see someone who has the potential to be my equal. That is why I must escape from my prison before his power can grow or mine wither. Time is of the essence, Nathanael. The game stands at stalemate. The enemy have the child Susanna. We have this girl. All is to play for.'

'Then I am keen to press our campaign to its conclusion,' Nathanael said. 'Instruct me, Lord.'

'At break of dawn you must ride east,' Lud said. 'The child is the key to a successful outcome. She can break the seals.'

'All of them?'

'Perhaps,' Lud replied. 'We will not know until we test the defences the fire priests have created. There are only two beings in this world who can channel her abilities. Naturally, I am one. Her mother is the other. You know what that means.'

'The mother must perish.'

'Yes,' Lud said. 'We thought it was enough to use a mother's love to paralyse her will. That may have been a misjudgement.'

127

Nathanael glanced across the clearing in the direction of Netty. 'What of this girl?'

'You may have to use her to neuter the threat of the renegade. Losing the child Susanna to Paul Rector has complicated our task, but we will still triumph.'

Nathanael bowed his head. 'I will not fail you, Lord.'

'I know you will not, Nathanael,' Lud said. 'You would not dare. Now, you must be silent while I discover the renegade's whereabouts. Before the night is out, our greatest enemy will have submitted to our will and the storm child will be back in our possession.'

Twenty

9 June 1645

There was a knock at the door. Bullen reached for his musket. 'Who's there?'

'It's me,' came a familiar voice. 'Let me in.'

'Paul!' Bullen pulled back the bolt to admit him. 'How did you survive the flames? How did you find us?'

'I struck my head as I fell,' Paul said. 'I lay dazed in the house for several minutes before I could recover consciousness.'

'But the flames,' Bullen said. 'You fell into the inferno.'

'Fire is my element,' Paul said. He noticed a candle and held his palm over the flame. 'As you can see, the flames do not blister my flesh.'

Bullen stared at Paul's hand. 'This is sorcery.'

Paul shrugged. 'Then I am a sorcerer. Now, enough questions. I am tired.'

Bullen wasn't finished yet. 'You must have had the Good Lord's help to escape the riders,' he said. 'What were those creatures? I've never seen the like.'

'They're Hell-fiends,' Paul said. 'They belong to the demon brotherhood.'

Bullen glanced at him, but made no comment.

'Do you still doubt that there are supernatural forces most men cannot fathom?' Paul asked, holding up the hand that the flames had not burned.

'I believe that what I saw tumbling from that roof in flames was no ordinary man,' Bullen admitted. 'I also know that you are possessed of powers that defy easy interpretation. How else could you have survived so intense a fire?'

'I am a half-breed,' Paul said, 'part-human, part-demon. I wander the centuries fighting creatures from Hell.'

'What are they?' Bullen asked.

'I am part-demon, as I said,' Paul answered. 'These monsters are what I would become if my human side were to wither and die. Each class of demon possesses a distinctive power.' He ran his hand along the back of a chair, leaving a line of flame. 'Mine is fire. I can snap my fingers and make it appear. I can use it as a weapon. There, are you satisfied now?'

Susanna appeared. She had an adjoining room. She saw the dying stream of fire.

'You can perform acts of magic!' she declared.

'Something like that,' Paul said.

'Show me again,' Susanna said eagerly. She scrambled to the table, where there was a jug of water, some cold beef, a loaf and a dish of butter. 'I will show you mine.'

Paul shook his head. 'Later,' he said. 'I want to talk to Netty. Is she in the next room? Go and get her for me.'

He saw the change in Susanna's expression. Paul turned from the girl to Bullen and saw the same troubled look. 'What's wrong?'

'It's Netty,' Bullen said, 'she wouldn't come with us. She went back to find you.'

'You let her go back!'

'I did everything I could to persuade her,' Bullen said. 'She insisted on looking for you.'

Paul seized him by the throat. 'If you'd done everything possible the way you say,' he snarled, 'she would be here now.'

'Please don't fight,' Susanna said, tugging at Paul's sleeve. 'Master Bullen is telling the truth. Netty wouldn't come. She ran back towards the building. She wouldn't leave without you. There is nothing Bullen could have done.'

Paul clawed at his face. 'Do you know what happened to her?'

Bullen and Susanna exchanged glances.

'What is it?' Paul demanded. 'Tell me.'

'I looked back as we rode away,' Susanna said. 'The demons took her.'

'I wanted to rescue her,' Bullen said, his voice flat. 'There were too many of them. Then there were the Trained Bands. I am no coward, Paul, but this was a battle I could not win.'

A resigned look came over Paul's face. 'You're right. I saw the crowd in the street. You would have had no chance against a company of demons ... or a body of militia. Forgive me.'

'There is nothing to forgive,' Bullen said. 'If I were in your shoes, I would be acting exactly the same.' He scratched his chin. 'We do have one thing in our favour.'

'What?'

Susanna smiled. 'He means me.'

Paul dropped into a chair. 'What do you mean exactly?'

'The brotherhood will want Susanna back,' Bullen said. 'They're not going to hurt Netty if they need her as a bargaining counter, are they?'

'You could be right,' Paul said. 'I pray you are.'

He cut a thick slice of bread and buttered it, before eating it with chunks of the cold beef. After a few moments he remembered something and turned towards Susanna.

'You said something about magic powers. What did you mean?'

'I'll show you,' Susanna said. 'You control fire, do you not?'

Paul nodded. Most people would have envied him his powers. They gave him little pleasure. They reminded him of the demon side of his nature.

'Show me what you can do,' she said. 'Heat the water.'

Paul shrugged and dipped a finger into the water. In less than thirty seconds it started to boil.

'Now me,' Susanna said. She placed both hands on the sides of the jug and started to take small, shallow breaths. In a similar timescale, the bubbling water grew still, and a sheen of ice started to spread over the surface.

'God's blood!' gasped Bullen.

In another thirty seconds the water was solid within the jug. Susanna turned it upside down to prove her point.

'What are you?' Paul asked, as amazed as Bullen.

'I must be the same as you,' Susanna said excitedly.

'That's impossible,' Paul replied. 'My powers come because I have the demon seed in my veins.'

Susanna pouted. 'Why does that matter?'

'For this reason,' Paul said. 'The demon brotherhood is exclusively male.'

'Why is it?'

'I don't know,' Paul said. 'It's just the way it is.'

'So explain the water turning to ice,' Bullen said.

Paul touched the frozen sides of the jug. 'That's just it. I can't.' He glanced at Susanna. He had an equal, somebody who, like him, could wield supernatural powers, yet remain human. He was overwhelmed. 'How long have you had this gift?'

'I don't know,' Susanna said. 'Always, I think. When I was very little, I made hail fall on Godfrey and Erasmus.'

'Who?'

'Godfrey and Erasmus,' Susanna repeated. 'They're two naughty boys who pulled my hair. The hail came so hard and fast it made them scream. Mother said we had to leave Brandeston after that.'

'So you went to live in Framlingham?' Paul said.

'That was later,' Susanna told him. 'We lived in Hoxne first.'

'Let me guess,' Paul said. 'Something happened there too?'

'How do you know?'

Paul pulled a face. 'Oh, it's just a feeling I get. So what happened in Hoxne?'

'It was two winters ago,' Susanna said. 'Wicked men tried to steal our chickens. They said they were soldiers, but I think that is too honourable a name for thieves.' She shuddered. 'They broke into the house. I think they wanted to hurt my mother too. One of them picked me up and tried to carry me outside. That's when the lightning struck.'

It was Bullen's turn to express surprise. 'You are able to bring lightning down upon your foes?'

'Yes,' Susanna said, 'a fork hit the house and set fire to it. The bad men ran from the farm and fled.'

'Did you make the lightning happen?' Paul asked excitedly.

'I think so,' Susanna said. Her face clouded. 'I don't know if I should tell you all this. Mother says it is dangerous to reveal my nature to strangers. Our kind has been persecuted for centuries.'

'Did I not save you from the demon riders?' Paul asked. 'Did you not see the water boil? I am your friend.'

Susanna's brown eyes were troubled. Her entire life had taught her to mistrust people.

'Can you control the things that happen?' Paul asked.

Susanna shook her head. 'Mother says that will come with time. At the moment the storms only occur when I am angry.'

'Do you know they are going to happen?'

'Never.' Susanna's bottom lip trembled. 'Mother has learnt to harness her powers over the years. She knows how to control the storm inside her, but it wells up within me in spite of myself. It is so frightening. It feels as if somebody else is making it happen, but I know it has to be me. I don't mean to hurt people.'

'But you have hurt them, haven't you?' Bullen asked.

'Yes.' Susanna's eyes filled with tears. 'I made Godfrey and Erasmus suffer for what they did to me. Their skin was sliced into strips. They looked as if somebody had taken a whip to them.'

Paul sensed that she hadn't told the whole story. 'There's something else, isn't there?' he asked.

Susanna nodded.

'Please tell us.'

Susanna pressed her forehead to her knees and mumbled into her lap. Paul and Bullen had to strain to hear. 'It was my fault we had to leave Framlingham.'

'What happened?'

'We had a neighbour,' Susanna began. 'His name was Marcellus Brindley. We paid rent to him for our cottage. A few months ago he wanted to increase it by six pence.

Mother said we didn't have the money to pay him.'

'So there was an argument?'

'Yes.'

'Tell me,' Paul said gently.

'I don't want to.'

'I need to understand,' Paul said.

Finally, Susanna relented. 'Mother was in the field. Master Brindley walked through the garden where I was playing. I could see that he was going to enter our cottage and take what we owed him, though it was all we had to pay for food.'

'So you tried to stop him?'

'I tried to plead with him, but he pushed me away and started to search for money,' Susanna sobbed. 'He began to ransack my home.'

'Did he find anything?'

Susanna looked up. Her face was awash with tears. 'He took everything we had. It was just a few pence, but it was all we possessed in the world. Then I made it happen.'

'What did you do, Susanna?'

'I screamed at him,' she replied, 'but it came out like thunder. Master Brindley fell to the floor and lay very still. Mother came and revived him, but the damage was done. From that day on he was stone deaf.' She held up a hand to prevent any interruption. 'The whole town was against us after that. They whispered about us when they saw us in the street. Somehow the rumours spread. The riders discovered our whereabouts. One night they came while we were sleeping.'

'And they took you away?'

Susanna told the tale, her voice raw with emotion. 'Yes, it was the night they took me from my mother, the night my heart broke in two. A sound woke me. Before I could cry out for help, I felt a hand being clapped to my mouth. I struggled and tried to scream, but the monster was too strong.' She turned tearful eyes towards Paul and Bullen. 'It was the riders. The one who seized me was called Ratshade. As he threw me onto the back of his horse, I heard the sounds of fighting in the house as Mother tried to reach me.'

'Why did you not use your powers?'

'I tried.' Susanna beat her little fists against her legs. 'You don't know how much I wanted to hurt them.' She thought for a moment. 'One of the riders pulled a bag over my head. He had something sharp against my throat. Do you think that's why the lightning didn't come?'

'It's possible,' Paul said. 'I remember once I was so exhausted I couldn't focus my powers either. I suppose we are the same as any living creature. If we are scared or tired, we don't function as well as we should.'

'But you do not know?'

'No,' Paul said. 'This is all new to me. I'm learning, just like you.'

'The creature took me,' Susanna continued. 'As we galloped away I heard my mother screaming.' There was a moment's hesitation, then she resumed her story. 'I heard her cry out.'

'What did she say?'

'I shall never forget her words. "Wherever they take you, my child, whether it is to the northern wastes or the southern oceans, I will find you again. Do not forget me, Susanna, no matter how long you are gone."'

'Is that everything?'

Susanna shook her head. 'I felt a terrible pain, as if somebody had driven a knife into my forearm and torn open the flesh. That's when I heard my mother's voice for the last time: "Your flesh is mine. Until we are reunited, this wound will never heal." Then she was gone. I don't know whether she's alive or dead.'

Paul and Bullen exchanged glances.

'Do you still have this wound?' Paul asked.

Susanna nodded.

'And it is still as livid as the day the riders took you?'

Susanna showed him the wound. 'Yes.'

'Then your mother lives,' Paul said.

'You think so!' Susanna cried. 'I think so too, but sometimes I despair.'

'Let me ask you one more question,' Paul said. 'It is about your mother. Are her powers the same as yours?'

Susanna stared at him for a long time before speaking. 'Yes, but she doesn't use them.'

'You mean they went away?'

'No,' Susanna said. 'It's not that. I think she could use them if she wished. She told me we must use our abilities sparingly. Many of our sisters have been persecuted because of them.' Her eyes welled with tears. 'Will I ever see her again?'

Paul tousled her hair. 'I will do everything in my power to make it happen.'

Within a few moments, Susanna had fallen fast asleep against his shoulder. Paul lifted her gently and tucked her up in bed. He was sitting at the table, wondering where the demons had taken Netty, when Bullen spoke.

'You shouldn't make promises,' he said. 'How is she going to see her mother again?'

'That's simple,' Paul said, 'we're going to return Susanna to her.'

'Why?' Bullen asked. 'How? I don't understand.'

'My destiny and Susanna's are linked to a prophecy,' Paul said. 'I am fighting a terrible foe, Bullen. His name is Lud. He is Nathanael Rector's master.'

'What is this prophecy?' Bullen asked.

'Lud is imprisoned beneath London's streets,' Paul

explained. 'He will be freed by fire, flood, storm or blood. Don't you see, Bullen? That is why Susanna is so important. She possesses the power to break his bonds. She is the storm child.'

Twenty-one

10 June 1645

Lud discovered his quarry at the Black Horse inn on the Stowmarket road. He relayed the news to his disciples and they rode eastwards across the sleeping countryside. It was approaching five o'clock in the morning by the time they spied the Black Horse nestling among ancient yew trees, and the first rays of dawn were illuminating the horizon. Dragonflies had started to dart back and forth across the rivers and ponds, predicting another hot day.

'Await my command,' Nathanael told the riders. He dismounted and approached the inn on foot. Pausing on the bank of a stagnant pond, he summoned the demon master. 'Which room are they occupying, Lord?'

Lud's image flickered dimly before him for a moment. 'The renegade is there, beyond yonder casement window. He shares a room with the storm child so that he can keep watch over her. His companion is asleep in the next room.'

Nathanael nodded as he digested the information, and his master vanished into the dawn mist. Nathanael closed his eyes and directed his thoughts to Nehemiah Bullen. In his room, Bullen started to toss and turn, his sleep disturbed by nightmarish visions of a phantom entering his mind and soul. The alien presence stole into his consciousness. Soon, Bullen was clawing at his throat and gasping for breath as the demon infection overwhelmed his brain. Though still asleep, Bullen's eyes flickered open at last, but it was Nathanael who saw the room around him. The demon directed Bullen as he swung his legs out of bed and dressed quickly. Nathanael made Bullen buckle his sword belt. Every movement was purposeful. His boots he left standing by the wall so that he could pad barefoot into the adjoining room. He eased open the door and stepped through. Paul was lying on his side in the bed on the far side of the chamber. Already the dawn chorus was flooding through the open window. That didn't prevent Nathanael using Bullen's ears to detect Susanna's soft breathing beyond a dividing curtain.

Bullen drew his sword and crossed the floor stealthily, taking light, cautious steps so as not to disturb either sleeper. He was soon just two yards from Paul. He gripped the hilt of the weapon. Lodged deep within Bullen's mind, Nathanael pictured the sword entering Paul's heart. How he longed to see the renegade's blood staining the bedsheets. Lud's disciple imagined his victim trembling on the point like a lark spiked on a thorn bush. *I will make you sing, renegade.* Drawing his arm back, Bullen lunged at his sleeping victim, but some primal sense of danger alerted Paul to the whisper of the sword through the air. He threw a hand up in self-defence and screamed as the steel sliced through skin and flesh. With his right hand impaled, he seized the blade with his left, desperately trying to guide it away from his chest.

'Bullen!' he cried. 'What the hell are you doing?'

A word burst from Bullen's lips. 'Renegade!'

It was a word from the vocabulary of the demon brotherhood. Realisation dawned.

'It's you, isn't it?' Paul gasped. 'Bullen is possessed by your spirit. You've come for me at last, Nathanael.'

'Don't resist,' Nathanael said, his words dripping from Bullen's lips. 'I will make sure it is over in a matter of seconds.'

Paul yelled his defiance. 'You won't have the child!'

Susanna had just appeared, her eyes startled and wide with fright.

'Hide!' Paul yelled.

Susanna scurried away to find a hiding place. In the same split second, Paul focused on the sword. It glowed first red, then white-hot. Molten steel dripped onto the bedclothes for a few moments, then Bullen let go of the weapon. Paul screamed as the liquid metal trickled on to his wounded flesh. He had no time to recover. Even as he clenched his teeth in an attempt to cope with the pain, the eight surviving riders surged through the door. They split into two groups, one making for Susanna, the other launching an attack on Paul. Pitchcap and Ratshade had almost succeeded in bundling the girl out of the room when there was an ear-splitting explosion. Susanna's scream had become a thunderclap, blowing out the windows. Part of the wall split asunder and crashed to the earth outside. She shrieked again, and lightning crackled across the ceiling, setting fire to the wooden timbers. Her resistance came to an abrupt halt as Claypin sprang upon her from behind. He jabbed his fingers into her throat and darkness took her. Pitchcap and

Ratshade accompanied Claypin as he carried Susanna from the room.

'Susanna!' Paul yelled, unleashing a fireball that enveloped the nearest rider, a snarling, screeching beast by the name of Lamedog.

Paul was about to torch a second attacker when he saw something that destroyed his ability to go on fighting. Nathanael had relinquished control of the now unconscious Bullen and appeared on the landing. It wasn't the sight of Nathanael that stopped Paul in his tracks, but that of his prisoner. Nathanael was dragging Netty, bound and gagged, into the room.

'Give yourself up,' Nathanael ordered.

Paul faced the riders, both hands glowing with liquid fire.

'Submit,' Nathanael continued, 'or the girl will suffer for your conduct.'

He enjoyed the look of resignation on Paul's face.

'You weren't expecting this, were you?' Nathanael chuckled. 'Hostages are a common feature of war, traitor.' He pulled Netty's head back by the hair. 'Suckvenom,' he said to the nearest rider. 'Show the renegade your claws.' Suckvenom traced a line down Netty's cheek with his razor-sharp fingernails. 'Believe me, my friend here could prolong her death throes for hours. He has the skill of a surgeon, but he doesn't use it to save life. Do you want to be the cause of such anguish?'

Flame rippled over Paul's hands and glowed through the veins that bulged in his arms. Netty fought against the gag, trying to make herself heard. Paul knew how brave she was. She was willing him to destroy them, no matter what they did to her.

Nathanael was keen to demonstrate his own powers. 'I don't even need Suckvenom's talents. There is a better way. Keep watching, renegade.' Entering Netty's mind, he made her take the dagger from his belt and press it to her own throat.

Paul watched in horror as the edge nicked Netty's skin and sent a stream of scarlet coursing into the hollow of her throat.

'Do you want her to press home the blade?' Nathanael asked. 'Do you want to hear her gasping for life as she opens her own windpipe?'

'You win,' Paul said. 'Whatever you want me to do, I'll do it.'

'Kneel,' Nathanael ordered.

Paul did as he was told. He loved Netty too much to put her life in any more danger. He put up no resistance when the riders bound his wrists and ankles and left him curled up helplessly on the floor.

Nathanael quit Netty's mind and made her kneel next to Paul. 'So this is the renegade everyone fears. This is the boy you care so much about.' Nathanael drew back his booted foot and drove it into Paul's ribs. 'Your power comes from your hands, I hear.' He stamped repeatedly on the boy's hands and wrists, and Paul howled in pain.

'Stop!' Netty cried. 'Please stop.'

Nathanael gave her a backhanded slap, making her yelp in agony.

'Don't tell me what to do, wench,' he snarled. He turned his attention to Paul. 'This is what is going to happen, Paul Rector. I will deliver your treasured Bernadette to the townsfolk. They are about to subject Grace Fletcher and her accomplices to the trial of water. I intend to enjoy the spectacle of the virtuous Christian folk swimming these witches.' He dragged Netty to her feet. 'There is nothing better than a witch-hunt on a summer's morn. Meanwhile the riders will convey the storm child to London. Unopposed, she will free my master. You have slain too many warriors of the demon brotherhood, renegade, but the time of your victories is at an end.' He leered down at Paul. 'You have lost. Say goodbye to your beloved Netty.'

'What are you going to do to him?' Netty cried as Nathanael dragged her to the door.

'Why, what do you think?' Nathanael said. He looked at the pair of murderous figures towering over Paul's prostrate form. 'Captain Toad, Halberd, you know what to do. End it quickly,' he added as he marched Netty downstairs, taking two of the creatures with him. 'Don't underestimate the renegade. Tear out his heart. Sever both his hands and his head. Burn the corpse.'

Paul gazed up at the dark riders. They shrugged back their sleeves to reveal deadly claws. Paul tried to summon the power of fire, but the demons had done their work well. Was it the way they had bound him that prevented him directing the flames? Or was it the searing pain in his damaged hand? Either way, he was unable to retaliate. The first demon dropped to one knee and drove his claws through Paul's shoulder. He screamed. Simultaneously, he saw the glint in the creature's eye.

'You're enjoying this!' Paul groaned, feeling the claws sinking into flesh and muscle.

The second demon crashed his boot into the side of Paul's head. 'Hold your tongue, renegade.'

Paul's senses were swimming. He clutched at a straw. In Samuel Rector's time, he had destroyed a pair of demons and absorbed their gifts. He remembered Jasper's ability to move objects with his mind. I am the demon who is all demons, Paul thought. He desperately tried to focus on the rope and felt it loosen. He shot out a hand and pulled Halberd's feet from under him. The demon fell heavily and awkwardly, cracking his head against a table on his way down, rendering himself unconscious. But before Paul could scramble to his feet, the second demon crashed a fist into his face, and Paul too lay motionless on the floor.

'Now you will perish, renegade!' hissed Captain Toad, beginning to press his claws against Paul's chest. He smacked his lips. The exhilaration of the kill lit his face. A moment later, the expression changed to disbelief. He swayed and his eyes rolled back in his head. A dagger had slashed his throat open. Gurgling his death rattle, the rider fell forward, his lifeblood pumping onto his unconscious companion and onto Paul. Bullen looked down at the crumpled form and wiped his blade.

'Paul,' he said, shaking the boy's shoulder. Nathanael had relaxed his hold on his mind, and he was his old self. 'Paul, can you hear me?'

But as Bullen bent forward, his heart missed a beat. He had heard somebody enter the room behind him. He spun round just in time to see Pitchcap coming at him.

'How?' he cried.

'We demons know when one of our brothers has lost his life.'

Bullen had no time to defend himself. Saving Paul was his last act on this Earth. He saw something unspeakable lurch from the depths of the demon's throat. 'Lord, help me!'

The creature held onto Bullen for several moments, fastening on his victim. For a few moments he gazed down at Bullen, gloating over the former soldier's death agony. Bullen was dead by the time he sank to the floor beside the others.

The newly arrived Pitchcap stared at the mayhem and started to inspect the bodies. Just as he had decided

145

everyone in the room was dead, there was movement amid the blood.

'My brother, you're alive.'

'You came back,' the bloodstained Halberd said.

'Nathanael ordered me to return.'

Halberd clapped Pitchcap on the shoulder. They dragged Captain Toad's corpse away from Paul.

'Dead,' Pitchcap said, checking the boy's pulse and heartbeat.

'We must be sure,' Halberd said. 'See if the renegade's heart still beats. Nathanael told us to tear it out.'

Pitchcap tore open Paul's shirt and pressed his claws against the boy's heart. He felt nothing.

'Rip off the head,' Halberd said. 'Sever it. We have to be sure.'

As Pitchcap crouched beside Paul's fallen body a voice barked a command. 'Get away from him!'

Pitchcap turned and snarled. Halberd fixed the newcomer with a hostile stare. The bewildered landlord had entered the room armed with a flintlock pistol. His wife followed. Their eyes roved over the carnage.

'I told you to get away,' the landlord ordered.

Without an instant's hesitation, Pitchcap flung himself at the newcomer. The pistol flashed and kicked, blowing away the side of the demon's head.

'Look out!' cried the landlord's wife.

Halberd hurtled across the room, slashing with his claws. The first swing severed the landlord's head. The second skewered his wife's heart. Halberd shook Pitchcap. When there was no response, he shook his head. Another fallen comrade. He gazed down at the landlord and his wife, then at Paul.

'All dead,' he grunted. With a shrug, he stamped out of the room.

Twenty-two

11 June 1645

Grace woke to the sound of the key turning in the lock. She scrambled to her feet and raked her fingers through her tangled black hair. Her captors had left her alone to break her will.

Lampkin entered. 'The other cell is too crowded, Mistress Fletcher. I've three of the miserable wretches in there now.' Grace smiled. With every day that passed Lampkin sounded more sympathetic to his prisoners. 'I thought you might like some company yourself.'

Grace's smile faded at the thought of some lonely old woman who had confessed in a desperate attempt to placate her interrogators. 'Must I tolerate some empty-headed ninny who confesses to crimes she has not done?'

'Oh, it's not one of the confessors,' Lampkin said. 'I wouldn't put those three in with you and subject them to your wrath, pitiable baggages that they are. No, this one is something of a wildcat. You will like her.'

'So who is she?' Grace asked suspiciously.

Lampkin went to get her. A young woman shuffled into the cell, shrugging away the gaoler's hand.

Grace watched her new cellmate stalk over to a corner and squat there, her eyes burning with resentment. 'Why is she here?'

'She is to suffer the same fate as the rest of you,' Lampkin said. 'She is condemned as a witch.'

Grace approached the newcomer and knelt beside her. 'What is your name?'

The girl averted her eyes.

'I do not recognise her, Lampkin,' Grace said. She stroked back her cellmate's hair, earning herself a warning glare. 'She is little more than a child!'

'She is not from these parts,' Lampkin said. 'I can only relate to you what I have been told. A gentleman delivered her to Hopkins this very morning, denouncing her as a sorceress and a Papist idolater. It was all I could do to keep the mob from carving open her pretty face there and then.' He rubbed his whiskery chin with his thumb and forefinger. 'These are bad times, Mistress Fletcher. I wish I were in a different trade, indeed I do.'

'I thank you for your kindness to me thus far, Lampkin,' Grace said. 'If it is possible, could you bring us some water?'

'I can do better than that,' Lampkin said. 'Hopkins has given me new instructions. From now on, you may eat and drink your fill.'

Grace looked troubled. 'Did he give you any reason for his change of mind?'

Lampkin hesitated.

'You must tell me,' Grace said. 'What has made Hopkins relent? I fear that it is not good news.'

'You're right there,' Lampkin replied. 'Hopkins knows he is never going to get you to confess. He is of the opinion that there is little point trying any more. You are to suffer ordeal by water.'

At Lampkin's words, Netty stared. Wasn't that how they exposed witches?

'So he aims to swim us, does he?' Grace said. 'When?'

'It will be tomorrow morning,' Lampkin said, 'an hour after dawn.'

Grace's breath caught in her throat. 'So soon?'

'If it means anything to you at all,' Lampkin said, 'not everyone hereabouts is behind Hopkins in this. Some of the townspeople refuse to be hoodwinked by talk of witchcraft. They think this whole affair is a miscarriage of justice. Sadly, we are too few to make much of a difference. The Witchfinder has the majority of the population behind him. Leech and his men continue to speak out, of course, but they are outnumbered. Several men armed with pikes arrived yesterday to reinforce the local Trained Bands.'

'There is little chance of rescue then?' Grace said.

'Mistress, there is none at all.'

Grace managed a smile. 'Still, it is good to know that not everyone is poisoned by this madness.'

Lampkin sighed and made his way to the door. 'I wish there was something we could do. I will bring some breakfast presently.' A moment later the key turned in the lock. Grace turned her attention to the girl.

'What is your name?' she asked.

'It's Netty.'

'I am Grace Fletcher.'

Netty was wary. It was hard to know who was friend and who was foe. 'I'd like to say I'm pleased to meet you.' Then she looked at the cell walls. 'Somehow that would sound stupid.'

Grace squatted next to Netty, wrapping her arms

round her legs. 'Lampkin said you were a Papist. You are not Irish though.'

Netty wondered where to start. 'My name's Irish, but I'm a Londoner.'

'You're from London,' Grace said thoughtfully. 'That is strange indeed. I thought maybe they had seized you from some Royalist baggage train. They say the King's men are nearby in Northamptonshire.'

'I don't know anything about your war,' Netty said, wondering how much to tell the other woman. 'I'm just trying to survive.'

'Yet here you are denounced for a witch.' Grace looked puzzled. 'How did this come about?'

Netty decided to say as little as possible. 'I was abducted.'

'So you were taken from your home in London and brought here?' Grace seemed perplexed and suspicious. 'But why would anyone take the risk in the middle of such a bloody conflict? And why would they remove you to a small, isolated place like this? There must be something more than you are telling me.'

Netty shook her head before dissolving into tears. Grace slipped an arm round the younger woman's heaving shoulders and allowed her to sob until she fell silent.

'I will press you no further,' Grace said. 'We all have our secrets and none have the right to demand that they are aired.'

Moments later, Lampkin entered with their breakfasts. They ate hungrily. Netty glanced at Grace as she chewed her bacon. Had she finally found somebody she could trust?

Twenty-three

11 June 1645

At the Swan, Jacob Beldam was also serving breakfast. There were three at table. Matthew Hopkins and John Stearne were there as usual, but there was a third guest, Master Nathanael Rector of London. Hopkins and Stearne were hanging on his every word. He had, after all, delivered a new and intriguing suspect.

'The girl is in league with the arch-fiend Prince Rupert, you say?' Stearne asked, eager to assign as many crimes as possible to their latest catch. Irish Papist, Royalist and witch, what could be more guaranteed to whip up the mob?

Nathanael smiled, revelling in the way the witchfinders were lapping up his lurid tale. 'When I came across the appalling scene, she was dancing around the corpses, singing the names of Charles Stuart, Prince Rupert and her liege lord, Lucifer himself.' He leaned forward. 'Her face was daubed with the victims' blood. She sang in French, then in some tongue I could not understand, Irish perhaps.'

'God's body!'

Nathanael was struggling not to laugh out loud. Hopkins was all but salivating with excitement. 'So distracted was the witch that I was able to creep up on her and club her unconscious,' Nathanael said. 'I heard that you had taken up residence here and resolved to bring the sorceress to you directly.'

'You did the right thing,' Hopkins said, nodding sagely. 'There are several dead, you say.'

'Ride out to the Black Horse,' Nathanael said, by way of an answer. 'You will see the corpses for yourself.'

'Stearne,' Hopkins said, 'gather up some sturdy fellows immediately.' The discovery of this girl was too good to be true. If the mob thought witchcraft was spreading, they would be his to command. He would have power beyond his wildest dreams. 'Ride out to this inn and witness the scene for yourself. Bring me back proof of what Master Rector has related. This is the strongest evidence yet that we have a most savage and powerful coven in our midst.'

Stearne nodded and almost ran from the room. He could imagine the twenty-three pounds he and Hopkins had been offered rising to thirty or forty before this episode was concluded.

With Stearne gone, Hopkins leaned forward to address Nathanael. 'Are you aware of the events that have shaken this small town to its foundations?'

'I heard that you had discovered witches,' Nathanael said.

'What we have here,' Hopkins said, 'is one of the most powerful and monstrous covens in all England.'

Nathanael made himself look suitably astounded. 'Is that so?'

'I have under lock and key four of Satan's spawn,' Hopkins explained.

'Five with the one I have just delivered,' Nathanael said, interrupting.

'Quite so,' Matthew said. 'Most of them are of little account. It is their leader and priestess I am most interested in. She is a fearsome harridan by the name of Grace Fletcher.'

'What will you do with her?' Nathanael asked.

'We swim all five of them on the morrow,' Matthew replied. 'Hanging will proceed immediately after the ordeal of water.'

'So long as the women are shown to be guilty, I assume,' Nathanael said, teasing Hopkins.

'Of course, of course,' Hopkins stuttered. 'We will follow due process of law.'

'It was my intention to return to London quite soon,' Nathanael drawled, 'but this is an opportunity to see the maids of Lucifer brought to account. I think I shall stay.'

'Your attendance will be most welcome, sir,' Hopkins said.

'So tell me,' Nathanael said. 'How does Mistress Grace Fletcher seem to you? I am asking you, you understand, as an experienced witchfinder.'

'She is sly, malicious and bold,' Hopkins replied hotly. 'I do believe that she sacrificed her own child on Satan's altar.'

'No!'

'That is my conviction,' Hopkins hissed.

Nathanael noticed that the Witchfinder's eyes were bulging and his knuckles white. He listened as Hopkins detailed every twist and turn in the interrogation of Grace Fletcher. Some forty minutes later, he called Jacob Beldam over.

'Do you have a room, landlord?' he asked.

'I do, sir,' Beldam said. 'There is a good-sized bed and the linen is freshly laundered.'

'I will take it,' Nathanael said.

'For how long will you want it?' Beldam asked.

'Two days will suffice,' Nathanael told him. 'Then I must return to London, where I have pressing business.' He was halfway up the stairs when he paused to address Hopkins. 'Would you send word when your man Stearne returns from the inn?'

Hopkins was quick with his answer. 'You will be the first to know.'

Nathanael was alerted to Stearne's arrival an hour later and made his way downstairs where there was great excitement.

'It was just as you described it,' Stearne said.

'You saw the bodies?' Nathanael asked.

'I did,' Stearne replied. 'They are being transported here as we speak.'

'What will happen to them?'

It was Hopkins' turn to answer. 'Four will be given a Christian burial.'

'How many are there?' Nathanael asked, frowning.

'Seven.' Stearne gave his interpretation of the scene. His description satisfied Nathanael that there had been at least one further struggle, triggered by the interventions of Bullen and the landlord, but that every one of the combatants was indeed dead, Paul included.

'May I inspect the bodies later?' Nathanael asked.

'You may,' Hopkins said. 'But why?'

'I have an interest in such things,' Nathanael replied. 'It is part of my Christian duty to confront the satanic.'

'I quite understand,' Hopkins said.

'You said there would be burials for four of the bodies,' Nathanael reminded him. 'What of the other three?'

'We are speaking of satanic creatures, abominations,' Hopkins said. 'They have been put on display in the town square to prove the justice of our cause to any doubters. Once the townsfolk have witnessed the nature of these monsters, the bodies will be burned. The parish minister has advised that the corpses must be reduced to ashes to prevent Lucifer, their master, raising them from the dead.'

'This is a wise move,' Nathanael said. 'But tell me, why is the same principle not being applied to Mistress Fletcher?'

Hopkins looked troubled. 'I do not understand, sir.'

'Hanging may be a suitable sanction for her four lesser sisters,' Nathanael said, 'but did you not tell me yourself that Mistress Fletcher was a high priestess?'

'Yes,' Hopkins said, 'that is my opinion.'

'So you consign a lesser demon to the flames,' Nathanael said, 'and permit the cause of your distress to get away with hanging. I am most confused.'

Stearne tugged eagerly at Hopkins' sleeve. 'I think Master Rector has something there. The townsfolk are happy with a hanging. Just imagine how they would howl for a burning. What say you, Matthew?'

Hopkins raised an eyebrow. 'Do you think it is the way to proceed?'

'I do,' Stearne said.

Nathanael adopted an expression of high moral gravitas. 'I too am in favour of a burning.'

'Then I am content,' Hopkins said. 'The four lesser witches will be hanged by the neck until dead while Mistress Fletcher will be burnt.'

'If they are found guilty, of course,' Nathanael reminded him.

Hopkins and Stearne laughed out loud. 'Of course, *if* they are found guilty.'

Twenty-four

12 June 1645

The following morning, at dawn, Lampkin roused his prisoners. First, Elizabeth Leverett, Cecily Mabb and Catherine Martindale shuffled from their cells and waited bleary-eyed in the corridor. Next, Lampkin unlocked the second cell.

'It is time,' he told Grace and Netty.

Grace took Netty's hand. 'Don't let them see you are afraid. Providence willing, we will endure all their insults.'

Netty forced a kind of smile and followed Grace outside. The three women who had confessed to witchcraft and implicated Grace kept their eyes averted. After a few moments, Catherine Martindale stammered an apology.

'Forgive me, Mistress Fletcher,' she said tearfully. 'I was mortally afraid and they promised to spare me the worst if I said what they wanted. Sweet Heavens, the nonsense they made me repeat.'

'I bear you no ill will, Catherine,' Grace said, 'nor either of you, my sisters. You are the victims of cruel tyrants, no more, no less. Try to show some courage. Maybe in that, you will find redemption.'

At those words, Elizabeth started to sob. 'I never thought to die like this.'

'Stop talking there!' Stearne barked as he arrived and made his way down the steps. 'Why are you not keeping better order here, gaoler?'

Lampkin scowled, but said nothing.

'Are you ready?' he asked.

'Lead the way,' Grace said, holding her head up.

Outside, a substantial crowd had gathered. It was made up mostly of men, but there were some women waiting to taunt Grace and the others. The noise swelled as the five women emerged from the gaolhouse, all blinking against the harsh sunlight. People ran forward, pointing and shouting. The accused women tried to shade their eyes.

'Do you see that?' Mistress Pettigrew shouted. 'They fear God's good sunlight.'

'It is a sure sign of witchcraft,' declared one of the churchwardens. The growing crowd took up the cry.

Grace noticed Leech, Cate and Ruddock at the edge of the crowd, looking on helplessly. She remembered Leech from the tavern. He was one of the few men to show her kindness in many a long day. Netty too saw a familiar face. It belonged to a man who made her heart freeze. It was Nathanael. There was no sign of Paul, and the demon's broad smile worried her. If he was here, then surely Paul was dead. Lampkin bound Elizabeth Leverett, Cecily Mabb and Catherine Martindale together, then fastened the loose end of the rope to John Stearne's saddle. In similar fashion Hopkins tethered Grace and Netty to his own horse. That done, the cavalcade set off through the town. Soon, gangs of boys were pelting the five women with stones and clods of earth. At one point, Cecily Mabb fell to her knees, before pitching forward onto the road, blood streaming from a gash to the head. John Stearne hauled her to her feet by tugging on the rope, making her tear the skin on both knees. Hopkins took little notice and led the way to the local river's deepest point, where a stone bridge crossed it.

'They're going to throw us in, aren't they?' Netty whispered.

'You must take a deep breath,' Grace hissed back. 'Kick for the surface with all your might.'

'But doesn't it mean we're guilty if we float?' Netty asked.

'You can try proving your innocence by sinking to the bottom and drowning if you wish,' Grace snorted. 'I intend to fight to stay alive as long as I can.'

Netty watched as the crowd surged forward to the riverbank in a frenzy of curiosity. Hopkins prepared to give instructions as to how the trial by water would be conducted.

'Swim the high priestess last,' Beldam urged him. 'Let her see what happens to her followers, then she will understand the fate that awaits her.'

Some of the townsfolk cheered his comment.

'Yes, Master Hopkins,' one cried, determined not to be outdone. 'Put the fear of God into the hag.'

'We will begin with Elizabeth Leverett,' Hopkins ordered.

Stearne pushed Mistress Leverett to her knees, then tied her left thumb to her right big toe, then her right thumb to the left.

'Behold,' Master Hopkins bellowed. 'In this way her arms will form the sign of the Holy Cross.'

The singing of hymns followed, then Stearne dragged the whimpering Elizabeth Leverett onto the bridge. There he lifted her onto the parapet with her legs dangling over the side. She gazed into the cold, cloudy river and started whining piteously.

'Mercy,' she cried, gesturing at Hopkins and Stearne. 'They made me say what I did. The witchfinders said I would be spared. I swear, all my life I have never hurt a living soul.'

'Tip the baggage in,' came a shout from the crowd.

Almost a hundred fists punched the air in agreement. Their owners shrieked in delight as Elizabeth Leverett tumbled face first into the river. Cecily Mabb and Catherine Martindale followed in quick succession, thudding into the grey-green depths. There were only twin rows of air bubbles to show where they were. In the minutes that followed only Mistress Martindale rose to the surface, coughing, retching, but alive.

'Witch, witch, witch!' chanted the almost hysterical crowd. They yelled and screamed. One or two of the women were so beside themselves that they fell to the ground in a faint.

Netty watched as some of the men in the front row went forward with long poles and fished in the river for the corpses of Cecily Mabb and Elizabeth Leverett. Eventually they dragged them onto the bank where they lay like sodden bundles.

'May God have mercy on their souls,' Hopkins cried. 'Be comforted that these good women will go to their Maker innocent of all crimes. They will enter the realm of Heaven.'

'Just listen to the filthy hypocrite,' Robert Leech said, a little too loudly, earning the glares of a large part of the crowd. Cate and Ruddock restrained him, fearing that they too might be swept up by the thirst for victims.

'But this woman,' Hopkins thundered, jabbing a bony finger at the gasping Catherine Martindale, 'this bride of Satan, she will be taken from this place to the gaolhouse. Tomorrow, she will dance the hangman's jig.'

The crowd met the announcement with noisy acclamation. After an interval, Hopkins raised his arms to call for quiet.

'It is time to test the last of the heretics,' he said, lowering his voice so that his audience had to strain to hear him. 'The first accused goes by the name of Bernadette Carney.'

The crowd booed. There were shouts of fury.

'Satanist,' shouted Mistress Pettigrew.

Nathanael looked around and added his own verdict. 'Papist traitor!'

The words earned him several enthusiastic pats on the back.

'Sorceress!' Hopkins screamed, not to be outdone. 'Confess your crimes, hussy. Describe the incantations and charms with which you have blighted this community.' He raked the crowd with a wild stare. 'John Stearne and I are convinced that this girl is second only to Grace Fletcher in wickedness. From the moment we placed the two together, there was much plotting and whispering.'

'Shame!' Nathanael shouted, getting into the spirit of things.

Netty bowed her head. Without a word she followed Stearne to the top of the bridge. He lifted her onto the parapet.

'Stay right where you are,' he chuckled. 'We'll duck you and Mistress Fletcher together.'

As he turned to collect Grace, he saw that Jacob Beldam had taken matters into his own hands.

'I've got her, Master Stearne,' he said.

'What are you doing?' Stearne hissed.

'I have a score to settle with this one,' Beldam whispered back. As he lifted Grace onto the parapet beside Netty, he murmured in her ear. 'I want you to take my laughter into eternity, Grace. No trollop slaps Jacob Beldam across the face and gets away with it.'

'I warrant, you'll be in Hell before me,' Grace retorted. She glanced at Netty. 'Trust me.'

Hopkins opened his mouth to speak, but Grace interrupted him. 'Keep your words for those that want to hear them, tyrant. None but I will decide my fate.'

She winked at Netty and tumbled forward. Hoping Grace knew what she was doing, Netty followed suit.

'Did you see?' Hopkins bawled. 'Did you see the eagerness with which she propelled herself into the water? Is this the conduct of a god-fearing woman?'

The impact of hitting the river took Netty's breath away. She could feel herself sinking through its slimy surface. But soon the cold made her so numb it was like being in the middle of a dream. As she sank into the depths terror invaded every fibre of her being. She was going to die.

Nearby, she made out a shadowy figure slowly gliding downwards. It was Grace. Disoriented by the cold and the shifting patterns of the underwater world, Netty saw her companion shrug away her bonds as if they weren't there. Simultaneously, the ropes that bound her own wrists and ankles fell away. When she turned to see why, there were four eels wriggling away into the murk. Grace pointed upwards at the sunlight dancing above them and they broke the surface together. Relief flooded through Netty as she gasped for air, but the torment wasn't over.

'There,' Hopkins cried, dancing about as if his feet were being roasted. 'They swim. They stand condemned as sorceresses, daughters of Hecate, witches.' He waved the men in the front row forward. 'Bring them to me.'

Grace and Netty struggled on to the bank, where they were brutally dragged across the flattened grass. All the while, the crowd chanted hysterically.

'Witch, witch, witch!'

None were louder than Nathanael, who spurred his neighbours on to ever more extreme demands for retribution. Soon, Grace, Netty and Catherine Martindale stood shivering before Hopkins.

'Do you have anything to say?' he asked them. 'You may yet save yourselves the worst agonies. Recite your profanities. Admit to your murders. Speak!'

'I will speak on behalf of my surviving sisters,' Grace said, her teeth chattering from the cold of the river depths. 'We are blameless of any crime. You want me to condemn myself out of my own mouth, don't you, Master Hopkins? We will not give you the pleasure. You are the demon here, yes, and you, Stearne.' She searched the crowd. 'I name Jacob Beldam among the guilty, and any man or woman who has cried out for our innocent blood.'

Beside her, Catherine Martindale started to weep. Netty comforted her while Grace concluded her speech.

'You have come to this place to damn me for a witch,' she cried. 'Well, say what you will. I don't care. I damn you, Witchfinder. I damn you to Hell!'

Hopkins' face was crimson. 'Take them away, Master Lampkin. Throw them back in their cell. Deny them food and water.'

Lampkin started to protest. 'But you said . . .'

'Yes,' Hopkins said. 'I showed them the milk of human kindness and allowed them the rights of any other criminal. How did they repay me? I have had to listen to a foul, sinful sermon delivered by one of the most

163

depraved creatures in this land. Give them no human comforts tonight, gaoler. Leave them to shiver and groan with hunger. It may make them ponder on their crimes.'

At the heart of the crowd, Nathanael was becoming bored.

'What will be their punishment?' he shouted, stirring the pot. 'Hanging is too good, say I.'

The crowd took up his demand for crueller sanctions.

Hopkins glanced at the speaker and remembered their conversation at the Swan.

'Bernadette Carney,' he said, 'you will be hanged by the neck until you are dead.' He turned to Grace. 'I will not go so easy on you, Grace Fletcher. You have been the instigator-in-chief of all the witchcraft committed in this place. Your punishment must be the more severe. You will be denied the abrupt mercy of the rope. You are going to get a first taste of the flames of Hell that will torture you for all time.'

In the crowd, Leech gasped in horror.

Hopkins raised his arms towards the heavens and concluded his peroration. 'You must suffer the ordeal of fire.'

Netty turned. For a moment Grace's lower lip trembled, then her resolve stiffened. She held her head high and started to walk back toward the town. 'Do your worst, Witchfinder. You'll not hear me grovel. Return me to my cell, Master Lampkin.'

Twenty-five

12 June 1645

That same morning the maidservant Bridget sat alone in Rokeby House wondering what to do. An officer of the Trained Bands had called the previous afternoon to tell her that Sir James' murderers were long gone and that little could be done. The country was torn by war. When every man was needed to fight the tyrant Charles Stuart, there was nobody to spare to pursue a pair of common criminals. The investigation was over. Bridget complained bitterly, but there was nothing she could do.

As a result she was left considering her options. There seemed to be only one. Should she return home to Southwark and ask her mother to put a roof over her head and food in her stomach? Bridget loathed the idea. The day she took the post at Rokeby House had been the happiest of her life. It had meant more than pay and lodgings. It had been the key to independence. She had left the little house in Southwark a girl. Earning her own keep had made her a woman. Was that all over? Bridget wondered what was to become of her. She had written to Sir James' family in Hampshire, but there had been no reply as yet. The war disrupted everything. She decided to delay the decision another couple of days, in the hope that the Rokeby family might find her employment. But how likely was that, when her negligence had allowed assassins into the house?

She thought of the dreadful scene she had discovered in Sir James' chambers. Her master was dead, the mistress too. Bridget drew a little comfort from the stories of Lady Sarah's courage in saving the child from her mysterious gaolers. Nonetheless she was burdened by the ever-present atmosphere of desolation. This had once been a house warmed by love and companionship. Now it was more like a mausoleum. It was as if ghosts lurked behind every door.

In spite of everything, Bridget still found it hard to blame Bullen. No, everything had changed the day he introduced that boy Paul into the house. His name was Rector, like that devil Nathanael. Had it all been some foul conspiracy? Had Paul and Nathanael been in league all the time? Oh, the boy had played a convincing part, but what else could she conclude? She tried to make sense of what had happened but the mystery remained unresolved. She sighed. If she encountered either of them again she would pray for the courage to take a knife and cut out their monstrous hearts. But what chance was there of finding them?

Twenty-six

12 June 1645

Fifty miles away one of the objects of Bridget's hatred was waking. At first there was only darkness. Then there was pain. His first instinctive thought bubbled to the surface of his mind: where am I? Paul breathed in the resinous smell of freshly cut timber. There was a rush of panic, immediately followed by intense, throbbing pain. He located its source. It was his right hand. At last he shook off the darkness and remembered the chaotic struggle at the Black Horse. He relived the moment when Bullen, his mind poisoned by Nathanael's will, had lunged at him and driven the rapier blade through his hand. But I'm alive, Paul thought. Then he remembered his last, desperate thought.

Play dead.

There it was, another of the powers he had drained from a demon brother as he died. Out of death had come life, a demon's death, his life. Such was the way of things in the brutal world of the demon brotherhood, to kill without mercy or hesitation was to live. Sensing that his right hand was too badly damaged to use, Paul raised his left and started to explore his surroundings. Instantly, he cried out as sharp stabbing pains screamed through his chest and shoulder. He remembered the ferocious fight and somebody stamping down on him. Squeezing his eyes shut for a moment, he flexed his left hand. He did it slowly and gently, trying to rise above the jagged edge of pain that stretched from his wrist to the base of his skull. After a few moments, he was able to lift the arm without crying out, though it still made him wince.

'Where am I?'

He asked the question out loud, as if he needed to seek reassurance in the sound of his own voice. Maybe he had to hear that he was indeed alive. Tensing himself, he pressed his fingers against the wooden surface above his face. It shifted slightly. OK, he told himself, a wooden box, a coffin. It isn't screwed down. That's good. He pushed again and gradually moved the lid back. A voice hissed excitedly in his head. I'm nearly there. With another shove, he sent it crashing to the floor. He lay there for a moment, gulping down mouthfuls of air as waves of pain and nausea swept through him.

He found himself in a newly made coffin perched on a sturdy oak table. As his eyes grew accustomed to the dark, he saw that there were three more coffins standing on parallel oak tables. With great difficulty, Paul finally managed to struggle out of his coffin and lower himself painfully to the floor. He explored the cellar. In the far corner he discovered the body of one of the demons that had been put on display in the town square. The corpse had been dumped on a crumbling wooden ledge and covered with a woollen blanket. Tugging at another blanket, Paul found Lamedog's corpse. As he gazed down at the creatures, he was breathing heavily and his face was covered with a sheen of sweat. All the while, both his wounded hands were throbbing with agony.

'I'm so ... weak,' he panted.

He leaned against the oak table for a few moments. That's when he heard the crunch of boots on the gravel outside. His newly acute senses confirmed that it was Nathanael. Paul's mind raced. I'll stand no chance against him if he finds me in my present condition, he thought. His eyes lit on Pitchcap's corpse, the creature's ruined skull plastered with blood and brain matter. Paul hoisted Pitchcap on to his shoulders, staggering under the weight, and deposited him in the empty coffin where he himself had been lying moments before. The door to the cellar opened and the footsteps started to descend. Paul limped across the stone floor and buried himself beneath the woollen blanket where he had found the first demon's corpse.

Moments later, Nathanael entered the cellar. Paul twitched at the edge of the blanket with the forefinger of his left hand and peered out. He tensed. Nathanael was carrying an axe. For a brief instant, Paul contemplated attacking, then he remembered the state of his hands. He watched as Nathanael lifted one of the coffin lids and peered inside.

'Bullen,' his enemy grunted.

Paul would have loved to have avenged his companion, but this wasn't the time. His first goal was survival. He held his breath. Would his luck hold? Nathanael lifted the next two coffin lids and identified the landlord and landlady of the Black Horse.

'Here lies Paul Rector,' Nathanael murmured as he reached the end of the row of coffins. He patted the lid.

'Do you know why I am here, descendant? The Master is afraid of you. He fears that you will rise from the dead.' Mirthless laughter followed. 'You won't when I've finished with you.'

Without even giving the contents of the coffin a single glance, he shoved off the lid with the axe handle and proceeded to hack at the corpse inside. He continued to chop until he was convinced the body was utterly dismembered, then he shouldered the axe and sauntered away. 'Farewell, renegade. Rise from that if you can.'

Paul held his breath and lay very still. Through the weave of the blanket he could make out Nathanael's form. He had stopped on his way out of the room. What was he doing? A moment later Nathanael spoke and Paul understood.

'So this is what they've done with you, brothers,' Lud's disciple said. 'Farewell, Captain Toad.'

Paul could make out Nathanael through a gap between the surface on which he was lying and the blanket. Nathanael was patting the lifeless body of the demon. He turned and Paul flattened himself on the ledge. He felt Nathanael's hand on his head. There was only the thin blanket between Nathanael's hand and his own face. To Paul's relief, Nathanael didn't remove the blanket.

'Farewell to you too, Pitchcap.'

Soon Nathanael's footsteps died away. Paul waited for several moments before emerging from the blanket. He swung his legs down to the floor. He gasped as his body howled with the effort. He was beginning to realise that his hands weren't his only problem. The blows and stamps he had suffered had bruised almost every inch of his body. His shoulder was scored with deep gouges, and it was so stiff he could barely move it at all. He tried to exercise his ability to produce fire. His left hand glowed weakly, but his suffering was too intense. Even after a few steps he had to stop to recover.

'Too weak,' he groaned.

He made his way back to the wooden ledge where he had discovered Pitchcap's body, lay down and pulled the woollen blanket back over him. Within minutes he was fast asleep.

When he came to, he gradually became aware of somebody moving about. Once more, he peered out from under the blanket. This time, it wasn't Nathanael. In his place, an elderly man was gazing down at the coffin containing the mangled remains of the demon.

'This is Satan's work,' he said. He scratched his head. 'I had better secure the other coffins.'

He went about his work systematically, moving from one to the next until they were all secure. Paul saw that the undertaker was about to go. It was time to make his presence known.

'Undertaker,' he said.

The man stumbled back, eyes wide with fright. 'By all that is holy, do you want me dead with a seizure? Whatever were you thinking, jumping out at me like that?' He treated Paul to a suspicious glare. 'Did you damage this coffin?'

'No,' Paul said. 'There was a man. He had an axe.'

The undertaker examined the room. 'You couldn't have inflicted such damage with your bare hands,' he said, 'and there is nothing you could have used. Maybe you are telling the truth.'

'I am,' Paul said. 'What day is it?'

'Day?' the undertaker said. 'Where have you been, boy? It is the biggest day this town has seen. My friend, Thursday morning is just dawning. It is a good day for an execution.'

Paul swallowed hard. 'Whose execution is that?'

'Them three witches, that's who. Two drowned during the swimming yesterday, you know.'

Fear twisted in Paul's gut. Not Netty. Please, not Netty.

'Who were the survivors?' Paul asked. 'Do you know their names?'

For a moment his throat was dry with apprehension.

'There's Catherine Martindale and Grace Fletcher,' he was told, 'aye, and some Papist trollop by the name of Bernadette Carney.'

Paul breathed a sigh of relief. She was alive. The undertaker paid no attention. He spat on his palms and rubbed them together gleefully. 'Before the day is out there will be three more corpses needing caskets. That will mean more work for old Osmyn.'

'Is that your name, Osmyn?'

'Aye, Osmyn Drone at your service. I don't recognise you, young sir. Will you come out of the shadows? My eyes aren't what they were.' Drone gazed up at Paul, then his eyes widened in terror. 'It can't be. You were a corpse the last time I saw you.'

'I wasn't dead,' Paul said, desperate to silence Drone. 'A blow rendered me unconscious during the struggle. The people who discovered me took me for dead.'

It was evident from Drone's expression that he didn't believe a word of it.

'There's something wrong here,' Drone said, 'something very wrong indeed. After all these years I know what death looks like, and you had passed over to the other side right enough. I swear, sirrah, there is no natural explanation for this.'

'You must be quiet,' Paul said, fearful that Nathanael might still be close.

'Why must I?' Drone demanded. 'I am not the one

172

who has been lying dead in this here coffin . . .' His voice trailed off.

'What's the matter?' Paul asked.

Drone thought for a moment, then glanced across at the ledge where Paul had been sleeping. 'Where's the monster I left lying there?'

'I don't know what you mean,' Paul replied.

'How did you dispose of it?' Drone demanded. 'Unless . . .' His eyes travelled along the row of coffins. 'What's going on here?' All manner of crazy thoughts were flying round his brain. 'You crawled out from under the very same blanket I used to cover that denizen of the underworld.' Drone ran his right hand over his bald head. 'I saw you with my very own eyes.'

'Don't work yourself up over nothing,' Paul said, his sense of apprehension growing.

'Nothing, is it?' Drone mused. 'What if you're one of the witch's familiars taken human form? Answer me that, you son of Lucifer?'

'You're letting your imagination run wild,' Paul told him. How could he shut Drone up? The man was going to put him in even more danger.

'Demon!' Drone cried. 'You're a demon come back from the dead. That's what I said to the churchwardens. We should have burnt the bodies, every one, then buried the ashes before sowing the earth with salt.' He started to make his way to the door. 'Get back from me, you Hell-fiend. Help! Help me, somebody. I am being pursued by a devil.'

'You've got to stop shouting,' Paul pleaded.

But Drone carried on kicking up such a fuss that the whole town was bound to come running. Paul made an agonising decision. Drone had to be silenced, and there was one sure way.

'Look at me, Drone.'

Drone turned and his eyes widened. My other powers have faded, Paul thought, but there is one that never goes away, the ability to cause death with a stare. He saw the terrified Drone reeling backwards, arms outstretched in a pathetic attempt to defend himself.

'What's this coming with its maw all sticky with blood?' the undertaker cried. 'What infernal beast have you raised from the depths?' He was descending into his own worst nightmares. 'Get it away. Get it away from me.'

For a moment, Paul wanted to break the spell and tell Drone there was nothing there. But if he was captured, what help would he be to Netty?

Drone was slapping ever more frantically at his clothing, batting away imaginary monsters. 'No!'

Paul ignored him and held the stare. Drone started to choke on his own terror. Soon, his eyes rolled back in his head and he fell to the stone floor, quite dead. When the deed was done, Paul too sank to the floor. He watched Drone's lifeless form for a moment, then buried his face in his hands. The next time he slept his nightmares would be worse than ever.

Twenty-seven

12 June 1645

Netty stirred. 'It must be light by now.'

'It is,' Grace said. 'I heard the birdsong when Lampkin brought our breakfast.'

'Didn't Hopkins order him not to?' Netty asked, stretching her arms and rolling her neck. 'I thought they meant us to fast as a punishment.'

'Master Lampkin ignores Hopkins' wishes when he can,' Grace said. 'He has helped me a great deal. I thank Providence for his efforts. He has taken risks on my behalf and been kindness itself.'

'Grace,' Netty said, 'what was that you did when we were in the river?' She was burning to know how they had escaped.

Grace pulled a lock of hair under her nose, sniffed at it and grimaced. 'I did nothing.'

'That's not true,' Netty said. 'I could never have broken free by myself. The cords were so tight, they were cutting into my skin.' She held up her scarred wrists to prove the point. 'I struggled for all I was worth, and I didn't loosen them one bit.'

Grace shrugged. 'What are you trying to say?'

Netty was growing impatient. 'For God's sake, Elizabeth and Cecily drowned.'

'Yes,' Grace said, 'and Catherine survived. Are you trying to say that I saved her and let them drown? I tell you, I did nothing.'

Netty gathered her thoughts before pressing on. 'Grace, I'm talking about the moment both of us hit the water together. We were bound hand and foot. Suddenly I felt something slimy against my arms and legs. The moment my bonds loosened I saw four eels swimming away. How do you explain that?'

'It was coincidence,' Grace said flatly.

'Don't lie to me,' Netty cried. 'Grace, we may have only an hour or two to live. Just tell me the truth. Maybe it was luck in Catherine's case, but how did *we* escape drowning?'

Grace relented and drew Netty to the far side of the room, as far from the door as she could find. 'You're right, I did do something to the ropes. I was too far from the other unfortunates or I would have done the same for them. We too would have perished in those slimy depths.'

Netty felt a surge of joy. 'You've got gifts.'

Like Paul. Until now he had been the only one who could stand up to the demon brotherhood. In Grace, had she found another saviour?

Grace was wary. 'You are imagining things.'

'Don't lie to me,' Netty said. 'I know somebody with powers.'

Grace seemed torn. 'What do you think I did?'

'You freed us by magic,' Netty insisted. 'That's right, isn't it? Well, if you can turn ropes into eels, why can't you get us out of here?'

176

Grace bowed her head. 'I dare not. Survival is one thing. If I were to escape this gaol, the consequences would be too terrible to contemplate.'

Netty frowned. 'But why won't you try to save your own life? It doesn't make any sense.'

Grace answered with a question of her own. 'How many people do you love, Netty Carney?'

'What's that got to do with anything?'

'Answer my question and I will answer yours.'

'I don't know how many,' Netty mumbled. 'There's my mum and dad, of course, my Nan, Paul. Why?'

'I love one person in this world, just one.' Grace said. 'That is my daughter Susanna.'

Netty seized Grace's arm. 'Say that name again!'

'Do you know something about my child?' Grace asked.

Netty nodded vigorously. 'There was a child called Susanna at the inn.'

Grace's eyes widened. 'You saw her?'

'I did,' Netty replied, 'though only briefly. Paul shouted her name.'

'Paul?' Grace asked. 'You have mentioned this name before.'

'He's my friend,' Netty said. 'He came looking for me. Grace, you have to believe me, he has powers like you. One thing I know for certain, he was trying to protect your daughter.'

'You say that Susanna is *here*,' Grace said, utterly bewildered. 'Are you sure you heard right? It was definitely my daughter's name he shouted?'

'I'm positive,' Netty confirmed. 'I can describe her if you like. She's about eight or nine years old. She has raven-black hair like yours.'

Grace was convinced beyond any reasonable doubt. 'But she has been missing these three months. How could she be so close by after all this time? Why would her abductors do that? Netty, where did you see her?'

'We were at the Black Horse inn.'

'The tavern on the Stowmarket Road?' Grace groaned. 'Are you really telling me that my child is that close?'

'I'm not sure about the name of the road,' Netty said, 'but it wasn't far. It was just a short ride, a half hour at most.'

'You must tell me everything you know,' Grace said urgently. 'I imagined my child many miles away.'

'A man kidnapped her,' Netty said. 'It was the same man who came for me. His name was Nathanael Rector. Does that mean anything to you?'

'No,' Grace answered. 'When the riders came, they took me by surprise. I heard no names and they were all masked. There was nothing I could do. What if they hurt her? Now you understand my shame, Netty. I failed to protect my own child.' She paused. 'Her abductor is a man called Rector, you say?'

'Yes,' Netty said, 'but I wouldn't call him a man in the ordinary sense of the word.' She trembled with rage and bitterness as she remembered her treatment at Nathanael's hands, then she stumbled through a hasty explanation. Grace listened without interrupting. 'Do you believe me?'

'I have no reason to disbelieve your talk of people with strange abilities,' Grace replied. 'Give me your hand.'

Netty did as she was told. Grace stroked her palm with a single finger, leaving a trail of sparkling frost. Netty stared in wonder.

'I knew it,' she said. 'I knew it the moment I saw those eels.'

Grace closed her eyes and ran both her hands over

her face, as if searching the depths of her mind. 'You said your friend had abilities like mine.'

'Yes,' Netty said. 'He does magic too. He can make things burn. He can scare people.'

Grace looked horrified. 'Repeat what you just said.'

'He can scare people,' Netty answered, realising instantly from the look on Grace's face that she had said the wrong thing.

'He scares them to death?' There was hostility in Grace's voice.

Netty regretted blurting it out, but there was nothing she could do about it now. 'Yes.'

'Then he must be part of the demon brotherhood,' Grace cried. 'Are you telling me that you are in league with the monster Lud?'

'How dare you!' Netty cried. Then she realised what Grace had just said. She had heard of the demon master. 'You know about King Lud?'

'Lud is the original cause of the persecution of my people,' Grace said. 'The creature has slain many of my sisters. If this friend of yours is in league with the demon master, then we have nothing further to discuss.'

'That's just it,' Netty said. 'Paul and Lud are sworn enemies. Don't look away, Grace. Paul is different.' She was searching for something, anything to persuade Grace. She relived the horror of her journey into Hell's Underground. 'Something happened when Paul was born. I don't really know the details, but Paul lived when he should have died.'

A look of astonishment crept across Grace's features.

'I know this legend,' she said. 'A boy will live who was doomed to die. A boy will harness the forces of evil to fight evil. Are you trying to persuade me that your friend Paul is the demon who can be all demons?'

'I've never heard it put in that way,' Netty said, 'but

yes, Paul is half-human, half-demon. You have no reason to trust me, Grace, but I swear I'm telling the truth. Paul's destiny is to find Lud and destroy him.'

They talked animatedly for the next twenty minutes. Netty set off on an explanation, telling Grace that she came from a time four centuries hence, and Grace immediately subjected her to a series of searching questions. Netty described Redman's attack and Grace submitted the account to the closest scrutiny. It was the same with every element of Netty's tale. She related the bare bones and Grace fired off a volley of questions. Eventually, Grace seemed satisfied and agreed to answer some of Netty's.

'You are a witch, aren't you?' Netty whispered.

'It is as good a word as any for what I am,' Grace said. 'It has nothing to do with the wild fantasies that possess the people of this town, of course. I serve no devil. I have no familiar but my daughter.' She displayed the wound that never closed. 'This is the mark of our separation. A sorceress and her child will never part until the daughter is ready to take a lover and have a family of her own. Until that time, there is no closer bond in the world. That is why the demon brotherhood acted as they did. My daughter is my most profound joy and my greatest weakness.'

'But what do they want her for?' Netty asked.

'My daughter may be young in years,' Grace said, 'but she has the power to unleash nature's most savage face. All she needs is a mentor who can help her channel it.'

'But that's you,' Netty said, 'isn't it?'

'There is one other,' Grace said, 'one so practised in the dark arts that he makes whole cities tremble, one who does not possess my scruples.'

Now Netty understood. 'Lud.'

'Yes, Lud. I know the creature only by reputation, but he is behind my torment.'

'But you must do something,' Netty cried. 'If you don't, we will die. Lud will break free from his crypt and plunge the world into chaos. You can't imagine the horror he can unleash.'

Grace sighed. 'Sadly, I can. I too have suffered at the hands of the creatures. When the riders took Susanna, they gave me a warning. If I tried to escape or thwart their aims, they would hurt her so badly I would not recognise her.'

'So you're putting your trust in *demons* to keep their word. You expect them to release her when they're done? Grace, are you mad?'

'What *can* I do?' Grace responded. 'If there is any chance at all that Susanna may one day be free, then I must submit to their wishes.'

'You will take this course even if it costs your life?'

'There is no suffering I will not endure so long as Susanna lives.'

'So what are you saying?' Netty demanded. 'Do you want us to go meekly to our fate? Grace, they are going to hang me, but just think what they've got planned for you. Can you imagine what it must be like to be burned alive?'

Grace lowered her head in resignation. 'There is nothing I can do. When you are a mother, you will understand. For the first time, you will love another human being so much you would lay down your life for them. I will do nothing to endanger Susanna's life.'

The mob didn't come for the three women until just after noon. The crowd had swelled to three hundred or more as people had poured in from the surrounding villages. Once more, Netty, Grace and Catherine were pelted with stones and clods of earth, though most of the projectiles sailed past them, striking other members of the multitude. Hymns rose into the cloudless sky. In almost every way, the day was flawless. There was only one blemish. Death was waiting like a carrion crow. The procession wound its way to a modest rise by the name of Bramble Hill some way outside the town. At a bend in the road, Catherine Martindale cried out. 'God help me!'

She had clapped eyes on the place of execution. Netty followed the direction of her stare and felt her blood turn to ice. A set of gallows had been constructed to the left and right of the occasion's centrepiece. This was a great mound of brushwood and logs piled around a solid timber that rose some ten feet into the air.

'Grace,' Netty whispered in a trembling voice, 'you have to do something. Please.'

Grace gazed at the place of death. 'I dare not.'

Netty hung her head. At that moment, all hope died.

Twenty-eight

12 June 1645

It was only with the greatest difficulty that Paul succeeded in hauling Drone's body on to the rotting ledge. Breathing heavily with the effort, he covered the corpse with the blanket and rested for a moment, bent double, his hands resting on his knees. He felt hollow with despair. Drone was a man who had been happy to go along with the witch-hunt, but he didn't deserve to die the way he did – *and I dealt the death blow.* Paul squeezed his eyes shut, trying to suppress his memories. It wasn't just Drone. So many had died. Hell's Underground was a slaughterhouse, a cave of bones. *And I am one of the butchers.* He swallowed hard. *I have taken decisions that have led people to their death. I have killed. It's true, I am a monster.* He struggled with his self-loathing for a few moments, then he remembered Netty's plight. Whatever crimes he had committed, he couldn't dwell on them. She needed him. Soon he was sufficiently recovered to test his powers. His right hand, still encrusted with dried blood from the sword wound, was as good as useless, so he had to concentrate all his efforts on his left. He finally succeeded in sending a single jet of flame some ten yards. It wasn't powerful enough to hurt anyone, but it might just sever a hangman's noose.

'That means I've got to get close,' Paul murmured.

He limped across the cellar and forced himself to climb the steps. It wasn't long before the wind carried the voices of the mob his way. Paul started his painful journey toward the sound. The whole town was deserted. Paul had to drive himself forward, gritting his teeth against the eddies of pain that racked his body. He turned a corner and saw three men in military uniform. One was sitting with his head in his hands. His comrades were standing to either side of him, their faces troubled.

'There is to be a hanging,' Paul panted as he approached them. 'Do you know where it is to take place?'

One of the troopers snarled his contempt, then stormed forward and grabbed Paul by the throat. 'Damn you for the carrion you are, boy. If you're so eager to see death, why don't you enrol in the army? There is slaughter enough on the battlefields of this land.'

'You misunderstand,' Paul gasped, sensing a possible ally. 'I don't ask because I want to see the accused dead. One of the condemned women is precious to me. I have to save her.'

The soldier released him and Paul rubbed ruefully at his neck. 'Are you telling us the truth?'

'Yes, I swear it.'

The seated trooper looked up. 'There's no saving them now, lad. The crowd at Bramble Hill must be three hundred strong. We came away because we could not bear to see the grisly spectacle to its conclusion.' A low groan escaped him. 'Dear God, I am partly to blame for this insanity.'

'How?' Paul demanded.

Leech explained.

'Then do something to redeem yourself,' Paul said, seizing on the admission. 'Please listen to me. If you can get me to the hanging there may be something I can do.'

'What's a lad your age going to do against a mob of three hundred souls?' the officer demanded. His comrades looked equally sceptical.

'Can't you at least give me a chance?' Paul cried, sensing the time slipping away. 'What can you lose by trusting me? I swear, I can make a difference.'

The three men exchanged glances.

'What do you think, Robert?' asked one.

The officer gave a shrug. 'Very well, boy, what harm can it do now? We will follow your lead. I am Cornet Robert Leech. This is Cate, and this Ruddock. What do you have, some fresh evidence? Will you try to make a final appeal to the Witchfinder's sense of justice? The mob has blood in its nostrils. Frankly, I don't give you much of a chance.'

'Just get me there,' Paul said. 'Please.'

Leech mounted and hauled Paul up beside him. It took them only a matter of minutes to reach the hill. At the approach of the mounted troopers, a row of pikemen stepped forward. Jacob Beldam pushed through the tightly packed crowd to confront the newcomers.

'Turn away, Master Leech,' he said. 'Get back to your regiment. They need you. We do not.'

'Stand aside,' Leech snapped. 'Don't give me orders, Jacob Beldam.'

'Nor can you command me,' Beldam retorted. 'You have no authority here, Leech.'

He shifted his attention to Paul. 'Who's this whelp you've brought with you?'

Paul heard the chanting and howling of the mob reaching fever pitch ahead of him. He made a grab for Beldam.

'I am Paul Rector.'

'Rector?' Beldam yelped. 'But there is one here called Rector already. What kind of mischief are you trying to stir up?'

'Look directly at me, Beldam,' Paul growled. Beldam saw a well of horror in the boy's eyes. He tried to twist away, but Paul had his attention. 'What do you fear?'

Even as the final word left Paul's lips, all manner of terrors started to flood Beldam's imagination. The sky filled with flying witches. Eyeless crones cackled and tore off lumps of his flesh like hungry dogs. Withered hags fell upon him, sinking their fangs into him and draining him of his blood. Beldam's mouth gaped open in a mixture of horror and disgust. Every superstition, every tale of witchcraft and sorcery took on solid form and danced before him.

'No!' he screamed.

The crowd shrank back, terrified by what Paul had done to Beldam. The three troopers swapped glances, but made no attempt to interfere. None but Beldam saw the terrors. None but Paul knew their origin.

'Now crawl back to your inn,' Paul told the terrified innkeeper, 'and never spread another false rumour about your fellow man or woman. I shall come after you if you do, and all the hounds of Hell will be with me. What you have witnessed thus far is as nothing compared to the nightmares I can dredge from your mind.'

Beldam pawed feebly at Paul's face. 'Let me be.'

'Leave this place now,' Paul said, 'or there will be worse to come. Go!'

Beldam stumbled away, sobbing like a child.

'What did you do to him?' Cate asked.

'I held up a mirror to his worthless soul,' Paul said. 'Now, do you want to stand here discussing it, or do you want to save those women from a terrible death?'

The troopers saw the impact of Beldam's humiliation on the crowd. With their spokesman gone, they lost their will to block the troopers' progress. Leech, Cate and Ruddock pushed forward, drawing their swords. Leaderless, the townsfolk offered a token protest before retreating. As the horsemen carved a path through the multitude, it was Stearne's turn to bar their way.

'You will not impede the law,' he yelled. 'Get back to buying horseflesh.'

'This is your law, scoundrel, not the Lord's,' Leech retorted. 'No merciful God would inflict such terror on innocent women.'

'The righteous people are against you, Leech,' Stearne protested, gesturing at the sullen onlookers around him.

'There is nothing righteous about murder,' Leech retorted. 'All I see gathered here are hundreds of poor, deluded fools that you have stirred up into a frenzy of hatred.'

'You shall not pass!' Stearne bawled. He appealed to the crowd. 'Close ranks against the heretics.'

Once more, Paul took charge, clamping the fingers of his left hand round Stearne's wrist. 'You demand ordeal by fire for Grace Fletcher,' he thundered. 'Maybe you would like to experience it yourself, then you might understand the anguish you intend to inflict.' His palm glowed and Stearne felt his skin beginning to blister. He shrieked in agony.

'Let me go!'

'Tell these people to back off,' Paul barked.

'Never!'

Paul squeezed Stearne's arm tighter and tighter until the Witchfinder felt his flesh begin to roast. The pain became too intense to bear. 'For the love of God, let them pass.'

With much murmuring and grumbling the throng parted a second time. Paul knew that, the moment they lost their terror of him, they would tear him limb from limb. He slid painfully from the horse and stumbled forward. He was still thirty yards from the brow of the hill.

'Stop!' he cried.

Hopkins waved his executioners forward with an urgency bordering on madness. 'Don't tarry, you fools. Delay and you will burn in Hell for all eternity. Carry out the sentence.'

While two of the executioners slipped nooses round the necks of Netty and Catherine Martindale, the third tossed a lighted firebrand into the brushwood at Grace's feet.

'No!' Paul cried.

Hopkins roared furiously at the crowd. 'This is the will of God. Justice will be done. You must resist His foes.'

The mood of the mob turned once more, this time from resignation to resistance. Encouraged by the leaping flames, they surged forward, surrounding Leech, Cate and Ruddock, who had to defend themselves at sword point. A fist struck Paul a sickening blow on the back of the head, and he fell forward.

Seeing his chance, Hopkins screeched a final command. 'Let the lesser witches dangle and let their priestess feel the fury of the flames!'

The executioners kicked away the benches on which

Netty and Catherine Martindale were standing. The two women started to twitch and jerk on the rope. Sprawled on the grass, Paul was surrounded by men, women and children screaming for his blood. Some spat, others punched and kicked. Through the chaos, he seized on Netty's familiar figure struggling on the rope. She was gasping and choking.

'No!'

Dazed as he was by the blows that had fallen on him, Paul mustered his last reserves of strength. His flesh glowed. Instantly, flame blazed from his wounded left hand, scorching through the rope. Netty fell to the ground, struggling for breath. She finally tore the noose from her throat and rolled on to her back, chest heaving. Astounded by the turn of events, the mob started to panic, surging this way and that in a desperate bid to escape the fire-throwing monster in their midst. Paul stumbled towards Netty before sinking once more to the ground.

'Thank God,' he panted, embracing her, 'you're alive.' He clung to her, tears glistening in his eyes. 'Are you going to be all right?'

'Yes,' Netty croaked, rubbing at her neck. 'Stop worrying about me. Help them!'

Paul threw out his left hand again. A jet of flame sliced through Catherine Martindale's noose and she too fell to the ground. Netty pulled off Catherine's noose and tended her. Finally, Paul turned his attention towards Grace Fletcher.

Hopkins shrank back amid the general panic. 'What manner of devil are you? Get away. Get away from me.' Then something occurred to him. 'You will not save the witch, Beelzebub.' Fear turned to triumph. 'What good is the gift of fire to her?' His hacking laughter mingled with the choking smoke.

Paul saw the truth of the Witchfinder's words. How exactly was he meant to fight fire with fire? Even as he watched, puffs of smoke leapt from the brushwood. Stearne had ordered gunpowder to be laid among the pile to hasten the conflagration. With a loud barking noise, the flames surged like sulphurous waves.

'Do something!' Netty screamed, her voice cracking. 'She is willing to die because the riders have her daughter.'

'Is that it, Grace?' Paul cried. 'You trust the brotherhood to release your child when they have done with her? Do you think they will be merciful? Do you believe that they will let her go when she has set Lud free? I know the demon brotherhood better than most. They will destroy her without a moment's thought.'

The flames were licking upward towards Grace's dress. The billowing smoke was starting to thin and she gazed down at him.

'You want Susanna to be safe,' Paul continued, knowing he had her attention. 'You are willing it with every fibre of your being. I understand the feeling. But don't fool yourself into believing it will happen just because you wish it. Your child has one chance of survival and it isn't to trust the demon brotherhood. They have no human feelings, Grace. Please listen, you are not alone any more. I know where the riders are taking Susanna. Together, you and I can thwart Lud's plans.' Grace turned her face from the heat of the flames. Any moment she would be engulfed by its fearsome heat. 'Listen to me. I spoke to your daughter. Do you know what has sustained her through these last three months? It was the thought of you. She always believed you would come for her.'

Grace was writhing desperately this way and that, trying to twist away from the hellish snap of the flames.

Paul searched for the words Susanna had reported to him. 'Do you remember what you told her, Grace? "Wherever they take you, my child, whether it is to the northern wastes or the southern oceans, I will find you again." Were they just empty words? Are you going to break your promise to your own child?'

The flames had almost obscured Grace. Paul redoubled his efforts, fighting his exhaustion. 'There was one more thing, wasn't there? How did it go? "Your flesh is mine. Until we are reunited, this wound will never heal." Was that a lie, Grace?' He saw Grace staring down at the wound of separation. 'Will you leave your daughter all alone to face who knows what horrors? Don't give in to the flames. Fight back!'

He could say no more. He slumped forward, hands planted on the sodden ground. It was up to Grace now. His words were followed immediately by an ear-splitting thunderclap. Livid forks of lightning danced above them and torrential rain poured from a hitherto cloudless sky. The lashing rain quelled the flames. Already, the mob was swarming away.

'Come back!' Hopkins cried. 'Pikemen, destroy the witch.'

But the pikemen had witnessed the fury of the storm. They were throwing their weapons aside and fleeing the scene.

'This is for your eyes only, Witchfinder,' Grace hissed, her voice mingling with the rushing columns of rain. 'How many months, years, have you been condemning women for witches? At last you have found one. Look at me, Hopkins. I am the sorceress you have sought so long.'

'No,' Hopkins wailed, 'for the love of God, do me no harm.'

Her bonds fell away and she rose, like a floating cloud,

191

into the air. She wasn't flying. There was no sensation of speed or effort. Quite simply, she had made herself weightless and free like the wind.

'Where are your insults now, Hopkins?' Grace demanded. 'Where is your proud boast that you will cleanse England of witchcraft?'

Hopkins fell to his knees to plead for his life.

'Do not presume to beg for your worthless life,' Grace told him before a single word had left his gibbering lips. 'I want no revenge. Take your minion and go. I have greater enemies than you to face.'

Hopkins looked around for Stearne. For a moment they hesitated, huddling together like chastised boys.

'Be gone!' Grace roared, her voice mingling with the bellowing wind.

By the time the storm abated, the pair had vanished.

Paul was still breathing heavily, exhausted by his efforts. He was aware of Lampkin helping Catherine Martindale to her feet. 'You probably think very little of me, Cornet Leech, but I must beg a favour from you. Catherine must get away from the town. The people have suffered a humiliating defeat. They will need a scapegoat. I fear for this poor woman. Can you help?'

Leech nodded. 'My father will know what to do. I will convey her to his household myself, then I must hasten to Northamptonshire. Rumour has it, the King's forces and ours will soon face one another again on the field of battle. What about you, Lampkin? Where will you go?'

'I will stay here,' Lampkin told him, 'in the town where I was born. Somebody has to try to bring these folk back to their senses.'

'Are you really willing to live among them after this?' Grace asked.

'I am,' Lampkin said. 'The way I see it, evil grows

when good men hold their tongues and do nothing. Most people are like sheep. The dog with the loudest bark turns them. That was Hopkins. I have learnt my lesson. The Lord will not find me wanting a second time.'

'Then I wish you good fortune,' Grace said. She looked around and frowned. 'Where is Netty?'

Paul lifted his head. 'What did you say?'

'I asked after Netty,' Grace said, her eyes full of concern. 'Where is she?'

The question provoked confusion among the handful of people still gathered on the hilltop. Lampkin held out his arms. Leech and the troopers shook their heads. Paul struggled to his feet and searched desperately for her, but Netty was nowhere to be seen.

Twenty-nine

Present Day

DI Lisa Hussein buzzes her boyfriend Mark into the flat. Leaving his suitcase by the door, he gives her a kiss. 'How did the interview go?'

'I got it,' Hussein replies absent-mindedly.

'You don't exactly sound over the moon,' Mark says.

'I know, something's bothering me,' Hussein tells him.

Mark switches his attention to the folders, printouts and newspaper cuttings that litter the floor.

'What's all this?' he asks.

'You may well ask,' Hussein says. 'It's a case.'

Mark sees one or two tell-tale headlines on the press clippings. 'Not the Redman case again?' he asks. He looks troubled. He remembers the effect the case had on her last time round.

'That's the one,' Hussein answers.

'Look, I thought you'd put that behind you,' Mark says. 'It really freaked you out. You took weeks to get over it.' He's been away on business and he has been

194

looking forward to relaxing in front of the TV. Now he knows that is out of the question. Lisa is on one of her missions. 'What's made you go back to it after all the grief it caused you?'

'Do you remember the boy who went missing?' Hussein asks.

'Yes, Paul something.'

'Paul Rector,' Hussein says. 'It's his girlfriend, Netty. She's gone too.'

Mark takes off his leather jacket and hangs it up. 'You're kidding.'

'I wish I was,' Hussein says.

'How long?'

'She vanished the day after you flew out to Hong Kong.'

Mark gave a low whistle. 'And nobody's seen her since?'

Hussein shakes her head. Mark runs his eyes over the documents. He picks up a photocopy of a press cutting. 'What's this got to do with the case?' He stares at the picture of a teenage boy and girl walking through Trafalgar Square. It is dated 1941.

Hussein takes a deep breath. 'The boy in the photograph,' she says. 'It's Paul Rector.'

Mark laughs, then seeing Hussein isn't joining in, he looks at the photo again. 'You mean he looks like Paul Rector.'

'No,' Hussein says. 'I mean it *is* Paul Rector.'

'But that's ...'

'Crazy? Yes, it is. That doesn't mean it isn't true.'

Mark drops on to the couch. He is utterly incredulous. 'OK, Lisa, what's going on here? I mean, are you trying to tell me this boy's some kind of Peter Pan? He never grows old?'

'No,' Hussein says, 'I'm saying that somehow this boy

has gone back in time, first to the Second World War, then God knows when.'

There is a long silence.

'You really are serious, aren't you?' Mark asks.

'Yes.'

Mark puts the photo down. 'Time travel?'

'Yes.' Hussein joins Mark on the couch. 'I know you think I must have gone completely insane, but this is the boy who disappeared. I tried not to believe it, but I can't ignore the evidence. I remember the night I encountered Redman. He didn't just scare me. He transported me into some alternative, terrifying world. Mark, after that I can believe anything's possible.'

Mark takes Hussein's hand and gives it a squeeze. He wonders what is happening to the usually calm, confident, sceptical woman he fell in love with. 'You sound scared.'

Hussein squeezes back. 'I am.'

Thirty

12 *June 1645*

'We need to rest,' Grace announced, reining in her horse. They'd been following Nathanael's trail for twenty miles and there was still no sign of the demon brotherhood or their captives.

'No,' Paul retorted. 'We have to go on. They've got Netty.' He was breathing heavily and his body was racked with torment. 'I let her fall back into their hands. I should have kept her close to me. It's all my fault.' He hugged his ribs protectively. 'Don't worry about me. I can make it.' In spite of the pain, every atom of his being demanded that they press on. He relived the moment when Leech and his men returned from their fruitless gallop down the Stowmarket Road to break the news that there was no sign of Netty. He had been inconsolable. He had torn at his face and fallen to his knees, crying out in helpless rage. Two hours later, he still had a ball of despair stuck in his throat. 'She resisted them, Grace. What if they hurt her?'

'You mustn't torture yourself,' Grace said.

'Why not?' Paul yelled. 'I should have protected her. Do you know what I am? I'm a pathetic loser. Hero? What a joke! Do you know what I do? I get people to put their trust in me, then I lead them to their death.'

Grace found the words strange, but she was careful not to add to his misery. 'You are exhausted,' she said. 'You must take some rest so I can tend your wounds.'

'No,' Paul said, 'we continue our pursuit.'

'Surely you know that we will not catch them now?' Grace said.

'We've got to,' Paul cried. 'We've just got to.' He tried to continue his protest, but he barely had the strength to stay in the saddle.

'Nathanael has taken her hostage as a bargaining counter against you,' Grace said as she reached out to steady him. 'Paul, it would have been better if it hadn't happened, but in a sense nothing has changed. She was a hostage before. She is a hostage now.'

'She is in the clutches of the demon brotherhood,' Paul retorted. 'She resisted them.' He shrugged away the helping hand. 'They can do what they want with her.'

'As they can do as they wish with Susanna,' Grace reminded him.

Her words brought him to his senses. He wasn't the only one who was concerned about the safety of somebody close to him.

'Consider this,' Grace said, her dark eyes flashing. 'If Nathanael orders them hurt, what good are they as hostages? He has no reason to do them any harm. He would be throwing away a bargaining counter. Just remember how long I have had to live with this fear hanging over me, Paul Rector. I learnt to endure. You must do the same.'

Paul rubbed the sweat from his eyes. 'You're right.'

He allowed her to ease him out of the saddle and support him as he stumbled over to a spot where a sluggish river wound between overhanging trees. Nobody but Grace could have persuaded him to rest.

'Lie down,' she instructed Paul. 'I will tend your wounds.'

Paul eased himself down and lay propped up on one elbow. He gazed along the road. Dusk was beginning to gather over the flat, open landscape. All he saw was a great emptiness. It spoke of Netty's absence.

'I hear what you say about the need to rest,' he said, 'but we can't stay here long. I'm not just talking about keeping Netty and Susanna safe. Even now, Nathanael may be preparing to break the seals that bind Lud.' He winced at the throbbing pain down his right side. 'I thought that you, more than any of us, would want to drive on towards London.'

Grace cupped her hands and let the cool water run over her face and through her hair. She repeated the procedure three times, then turned to look at him. 'There will be no attack tonight.'

Paul frowned. 'How can you possibly know that?'

'Look at the sky,' Grace said. 'It is almost cloudless from horizon to horizon. There will be no storm, therefore no attack.'

'I thought *Susanna* was the storm,' Paul said. 'Wasn't that the whole point of abducting her? Don't forget, I've seen what you can do.'

'What you saw was little more than a trick,' Grace told him. 'Nature is the power, not Susanna or I. We can conduct its healing powers and its wrath. That is our condition. We can even store the force of the elements in some measure and reproduce a small proportion of its awesome rage. That is all. Had Hopkins had the courage to defy me for another few moments, my power would have blown itself out and I would have been vulnerable once more.'

'So what are you saying?' Paul demanded.

'Just this,' Grace answered. 'The witch breed can imitate the storm for a few seconds, even minutes. After that, we will have exhausted our strength until the skies darken once more and we replenish it from our mother, the Earth.'

Paul laid his hand on her arm. 'Surely you're contradicting yourself. Are you now telling me Susanna is useless to Nathanael?'

'No,' Grace said, 'that isn't it at all.' She took a deep breath, a sign of her growing impatience with Paul. 'You told me the seals that prevent Lud's escape possess powerful magic.'

'That's right. They have resisted his attempts to rise for twenty long centuries.' He realised where he was and corrected himself. 'Well, sixteen centuries.'

Grace stared at him, trying to make sense of his curious stumble. 'Then Susanna could not break such powerful spells by herself,' Grace explained. 'She must harness the power of the storm and direct it against the seals. That is what Nathanael wants her for.'

Paul's eyes lit with the first rush of hope he had felt in several hours. 'So he can't do anything until a storm breaks naturally?'

Grace shook her head. 'We serve the spirits of the heavens. All depends on the storm. Soon it will break. Then and only then will my child be able to direct it.'

'When will that be?'

'I am a witch,' Grace said, shaking her head. 'The ability to harness some of Nature's force is my only power. I am no Cassandra. I am unable to predict the future.'

Paul allowed her to clean and dress his wounds. 'So

we are in the same position as the demon brotherhood? You're sure of that?' He was desperate for some kind of reassurance. 'Nothing can happen until a storm comes?'

Grace nodded. 'That is what I said. This is the reason for my confidence. The demons must keep Susanna safe until then, Netty too. We still have time.'

Paul raised his eyes to the darkening sky. 'Can't you even make a guess how long?'

'The sun has baked the land for many days,' Grace replied. 'There must come a release, and soon. It may be two days, three ... four at most.' She smiled. 'Now stop interrogating me and remove your shirt.'

Paul stared at her. 'What for?'

Grace was amused by his reaction. 'I will not be able to treat the rest of your wounds while you are still wearing it,' she reminded him.

'Oh, right,' Paul said and started tugging at it with his left hand. 'Sorry, I can't do much one-handed.'

He felt Grace's hands on him and allowed her to peel off the bloodstained shirt. Her gentle, healing touch made his sense of loss over Netty all the more acute.

'What did they do to you?' Grace gasped, looking at the tapestry of gaping cuts and bruising.

'They tried to kill me.'

Grace nodded. 'Relax and let my hands do their work.' She examined every cut and bruise closely, occasionally pressing his back or chest. Eventually she gave her verdict. 'There are no broken bones.'

'You're sure?'

She gave a nod of assent. 'By the time we reach London, you should have recovered much of your strength.' She gave him a sideways glance. 'Netty told me you have the power of fire.'

'Yes.'

'And fear?'

'That too.'

'Then you are the one who can break the brotherhood's power. Born to serve the demon master, you will become his nemesis.'

'How do you know about the prophecy?' Paul asked.

'My mother told me,' Grace replied. 'Her mother told her. It is part of the lore of our kind. One day a boy would come, forged in the fires of Hell, but destined to turn to the light.' As she dabbed away the encrusted blood, she put a question to him. 'You're in love with Netty, aren't you?'

This had new meaning for him. It was as if seeing her again had brought them both back from the dead. 'Yes,' he said. 'She's part of me.'

'I am going to say something you will not want to hear,' Grace said. 'You must be great-hearted enough to give her up.'

Her words stung him to the quick. 'What?'

'She must return home to her own time. She does not belong here.'

'She will return home,' Paul retorted, 'and I will be by her side. We're meant to be together.'

'It is not your choice,' Grace said, 'You must continue your journey until Lud is dead. Let Netty go or your affection for her will surely lead to her destruction.' She placed her palms on his cheeks. 'Please understand your fate, Paul. You may have occasional companions along the road. There will be people like me, but nobody will make the whole journey with you. You are destined to walk a lonely path.'

Paul sank into a resentful silence.

Grace said no more on the matter and inspected his shoulder. 'I will make a poultice to ease the pain.'

Paul watched the mist gliding over the river. Grace's touch started to ease his discomfort. In the late-evening heat he was feeling more and more drowsy. He listened to the hum of insects over the river and watched the leaves of a weeping willow brushing the surface of the water. On the far bank labourers were wending their way home. It all seemed so peaceful, but soon his pursuit of Netty would lead him back to London, where he would face a life-and-death struggle to thwart Lud. Grace went to the horses Cate and Ruddock had given them and handed Paul some bread and cheese. She sat next to him and they washed the food down with a little of the ale. They then watched the setting sun. Neither spoke a word. At last night fell. Paul gazed at the star-studded firmament. Grace watched him for a few moments, then she broke the silence.

'You give the impression you have never gazed upon the stars before,' she said, perplexed and amused.

Paul considered trying to explain about his world, where there was electricity and light pollution, but he thought better of it. Instead he gazed up at those countless points of light and he felt a sense of destiny catch fire inside him.

'I never saw stars quite like this,' he said.

Grace shook her head. 'You speak strangely, Paul. Now, turn around.'

'Why?'

'My body aches, just as yours does,' Grace said simply. 'I am going to swim in the river.' She chuckled. 'You are not going to watch me so you must turn around.'

'How can you laugh at a time like this?' Paul asked.

For a moment Grace's stare hardened. 'Don't you dare question my love for Susanna. For months I have thought of little else.' Paul tried to apologise, but she waved the attempt away. 'I had no idea where she was. Now, though she is in the hands of my oppressors, I at least know that she is still alive and that I have some chance of saving her. I have had a hollowness inside me. Now hope has taken its place. There is somebody I can fight. For the first time in months my life has a purpose.' The smile returned. 'Now turn your back,' she said again.

Paul shuffled round until he found himself looking down the road towards London. He heard the swish of Grace's clothes as they fell to the ground, then the soft lapping as she walked into the river. Presently, the sound of her scything through the water was interrupted by a familiar voice.

'You have found the witch, I see.'

For once, Paul was not surprised by Cormac's arrival. 'You don't usually visit me so often.'

'The brotherhood has your friend,' he said.

'Tell me something I don't know,' Paul grunted.

'You lacked vigilance,' Cormac said. 'That is unfortunate. The girl is your weakness.'

'She's got a name, you know,' Paul snapped.

Cormac's spectral figure glimmered in the warm darkness. 'Her recovery is a priority. While your ancestor holds her, your effectiveness is much reduced.'

Paul glowered at the fire priest. 'Don't you have any feelings?'

'I have feelings,' Cormac replied. 'I loved a woman once. Her death still haunts me. That is why I understand this girl's importance. You must get her back. When you do, you must return her to her own time.'

Paul scowled. 'Grace said I had to give her up.'

'Do as she says. If you care for Netty at all, you must relinquish her.'

Paul shook his head. 'Leave me alone.' He leant his forehead on his knees and tried to blot out the fire priest's presence. In his heart of hearts he knew that it was inevitable. He couldn't keep her here. But how could he ever let her go? When he raised his head, Cormac was no longer there. Paul's thoughts were soon interrupted by the sound of Grace gliding closer. She emerged from the water and padded over to her clothes. She had nothing to dry herself with so Paul waited for the warm air to do its work. Finally, he heard the sounds of her getting dressed. He turned and glanced at her. She was running her fingers through her still damp hair. Her skin seemed to glow in the moonlight.

'You should go for a swim,' Grace said. 'It will wash away some of the pain.' She winked. 'I won't look either.'

Thirty-one

13 June 1645

Bridget sat disconsolately in Rokeby House. She wore the silence like a heavy coat. 'It is my fault the master is dead,' she murmured. 'I was reckless with his safety. Why did I allow Bullen to invite that boy into this house?'

When she heard her words floating around the high ceiling of the scullery, she felt her flesh creep. Here she was still alone in a house where a man had been murdered. She had started to imagine all manner of terrors crawling from the walls, but not the one that was approaching at that very moment. Still uncertain what to do, Bridget picked at a leg of mutton before shoving it aside. She had had no appetite since Sir James' death. She was still turning over the unnatural events when she heard the sound of horsemen galloping into the grounds. She hastily licked her fingertips and pinched out the candle. What if it were Bullen and his accomplice Paul Rector returning to cut her throat? She started to pray. 'The Lord is my rock, and my fortress, and my deliverer – my God, my strength, in whom I trust.'

The horses whinnied outside and male voices boomed against the windows. Panicked by their approach, Bridget looked around for somewhere to hide. She chose the large pantry to her left and slipped inside, squeezing under a shelf and wrapping her arms round her knees. There she sat, heart pounding, until she heard the squeal of the hinges on the oaken door to the scullery.

'What made you choose this place, Nathanael?' growled an unfamiliar voice. 'I know you like the fleshpots, but this is a bit grand, even for your tastes.'

'Where would you have us lodge, Halberd?' came the reply.

Bridget recognised this voice. It was the blackguard, Nathanael Rector. Was his relative there too?

'We can't return to our former haunts,' Nathanael continued, striding across the scullery floor. 'This is as good a place as any.'

'I smell blood,' Halberd observed. He was sniffing the air like a dog.

'It belongs to Sir James,' Nathanael told him.

Bridget's heart turned over. What was this? Had she made a terrible mistake in thinking Bullen killed her master?

'I had to slaughter the deranged fool before the renegade got something out of him.'

Bridget covered her mouth with her hand. So it was true. *Nathanael* killed her master. Bullen was falsely accused. And who did he mean by the *renegade?* Was Paul also innocent? Oh Bridget, Bridget, she thought, why did you have to jump to conclusions? She had trusted Bullen once and he had vouched for the boy. Why hadn't she given him the benefit of the doubt a little while longer? But what was done was done. There was no putting it right now. All she could do was somehow bring the master's killer to justice.

'Take the girl upstairs,' Nathanael ordered.

'Which one?'

This wasn't Halberd, but another of Nathanael's cronies.

'The child,' Nathanael snapped. 'Netty stays here where I can see her.' He grew impatient. 'Get Susanna upstairs, Ratshade, and stay in the room with her.'

'I want something to eat,' Ratshade complained, 'and I'll not be satisfied with your leftovers.'

'We'll bring you something, you ugly rogue,' Nathanael said. 'Let me give you a word of advice. If you leave that room for any reason I will rip out your eyes and you can have them for your supper.'

'There's no need to threaten me,' Ratshade grumbled.

'Isn't there?' Nathanael barked. 'The child has given you the slip once, and it cost the lives of your comrades. I won't let it happen again. Now, no more of your belly-aching, you bag of maggots. Watch the girl well.'

'She's drugged,' Ratshade grumbled. 'What can happen?'

'Watch her!' Nathanael roared impatiently before lowering his voice and winking. 'Watch her, Ratshade. I'll let you have some tasty morsels to play with as a reward.'

'Puritans?' Ratshade asked. 'They're tastier than that beef.'

Nathanael grinned. 'Yes, I'll round up lots of Puritans for you.'

Placated, Ratshade left the room. Bridget heard his tread on the stone floor, then the slam of the door. It made the windows rattle. Would these intruders really devour human flesh? she wondered. Unable to contain her curiosity, she placed her fingers on the pantry door and eased it open a crack. She immediately wished she hadn't. What she saw made her senses reel. The figure nearest her was loosening the filthy kerchief that covered the lower part of his face. She witnessed a demon from Hell. The flesh was torn away from its jaw. Its tongue licked around the exposed, yellowish teeth. Fighting the temptation to cry out, she was about to close the pantry door when she glimpsed a young woman a year or two her junior. This must be Netty, she thought. Easing the door open a touch more, she viewed as much of the room as was possible. There was Nathanael and three more darkly garbed creatures. Bridget could also make out the shadow of a fourth. She was about to close the door when she heard the words that made her heart stop.

'See what there is to eat,' Nathanael commanded. 'A wealthy house has a good kitchen. Suckvenom, take a look in that pantry.'

Bridget flattened herself against the wall. Her whole body screamed with terror but she didn't allow a sound to escape her lips. Sweet Lord, my God, she prayed, protect me from this abomination. She heard the approaching footsteps and squeezed her eyes shut. She knew how Suckvenom got his name. His breath was as rancid as rotting meat. A sharp, yellowing fingernail, more like a claw, appeared through the crack in the pantry door. Any moment, he would discover her. That's when she heard Halberd's low growl.

'There's mutton over there in the corner,' he said, 'aye, and a pound of beef and some bread.' He ripped off a chunk and stuffed it into his mouth. 'The loaf is a bit stale but it will suffice.'

Suckvenom's claw twitched. Bridget bit her lip so hard she felt the salty tang of blood in her mouth.

'There is enough for us all,' Nathanael announced.

The claw vanished, and Bridget was able to breathe again.

Thirty-two

14 June 1645

Bridget slept fitfully in her hiding place, waking regularly and listening for every tiny sound that might herald the demons' approach. Finally she managed to doze off until a heavy tread woke her just after dawn. She knuckled the sleep from her eyes and turned painfully in the confined space of the pantry, easing herself round by tiny shifts of her body so as not to alert the creatures to her presence. She pressed her face to the slight gap between the doors and glimpsed a pair of leather boots. Her gaze travelled up the owner until she found herself gazing at Nathanael's brooding profile. His dark eyes made her shudder. This was the creature who had crushed her master's spirit and made him a slave. Soon she saw Nathanael smile, but what was he looking at? A moment later there was the crunch of boots on the gravel outside, then a knock at the door.

'You are punctual, sirrah,' Nathanael observed as he stepped back to admit his guest.

'I knew the house,' the newcomer said.

'Yes,' Nathanael replied. 'You are the one who directed the renegade here.'

The newcomer sounded surprised. 'You are well informed, Master Rector.'

Bridget strained to see the man, but he remained tantalisingly out of sight. If only Nathanael would address him by name.

'You use the word renegade,' the newcomer said.

'I mean the boy, Paul Rector.'

This seemed to confirm what she had suspected: both Bullen and Paul were innocent of the murder of Sir James.

'I understand that, but what do you want with him?'

Nathanael chuckled. 'You don't really expect me to divulge that, do you, Catchpole?'

Bridget's heart leapt. So that was his name, Catchpole.

'I suppose not,' Catchpole said. 'Why did you invite me here, Master Rector?'

'Paul trusts you, does he not?'

'I wouldn't go that far,' Catchpole said. 'We found that we had ... certain common interests. He told me precious little about himself.'

'I will get to the point,' Nathanael said. 'The renegade has been out of the city for some days. It would be to my advantage if I were told the moment he returned to London.'

'So you want me to post lookouts?' Catchpole asked.

'I do. I am told you have some expertise in the field.'

'I have a score of followers at my command,' said Catchpole. 'They are my eyes and ears in the city.'

'Your hands too, I hear,' Nathanael observed.

'If wealth is to be transferred from the rich man's pocket to mine,' Catchpole said, 'then I have need of hands.'

212

Nathanael nodded. 'Of course. So how will you find the renegade for me?'

'He could enter the city at several points,' said Catchpole. He named some of the likeliest. 'The more pairs of eyes I use, the more it will cost. It would be expensive.'

Nathanael produced a purse. 'Will this suffice?' He tossed it onto the table with a casual flick of the wrist.

Catchpole examined the contents, trying to disguise his eagerness. There was a note of satisfaction in his voice. 'That will buy you my time and that of my accomplices for a week.'

'Consider yourself hired,' Nathanael said. 'The moment Paul enters the city, I want to know immediately.'

'Oh, you will.' Catchpole made for the door.

'Master Catchpole,' Nathanael said, blocking his path.

'Yes?'

'Don't even think about crossing me,' Nathanael warned, his voice descending into a menacing growl. 'You are aware of Sir James' fate, I presume?'

'Yes, and Lady Sarah's too,' Catchpole answered.

Bridget thought she detected a slight shake in his voice. So I'm not the only one who fears this creature, she thought.

'Then we understand one another,' Nathanael said. 'You may take your leave.'

Bridget heard the door slam. She had still not seen Catchpole's face. She had even more pressing problems however. She was hungry, and desperate to stretch her legs, so long had she lain in the cramped conditions of the pantry. Five minutes passed while Nathanael ate a hearty breakfast, then Halberd entered. Bridget had heard enough to know that he was the captain of the demon riders.

'Are our brothers ready, Halberd?' Nathanael asked.

'They are.'

'Tell Ratshade and Warboy to watch the females,' Nathanael told him. 'We will make preparations.' He peered out at the sky. 'The storm is on its way. We must be ready.'

Bridget hugged her stomach, rocking back and forth to stifle the hunger pangs while the demon riders made their way out into the courtyard to mount their horses. Finally, they were gone. She listened. The house was quiet, but they were out there somewhere, the unspeakable creatures with their grotesque, malformed faces. The slightest noise, and they would come running. That would be the end of her. For an age she sat there, straining to pick up the slightest sound in the cavernous mansion. Finally, she made her decision. She must be bold and make her bid to escape or be imprisoned here until the monsters discovered her presence.

Taking a deep breath, she eased open the pantry door and stepped out. She straightened and winced at the stiffness in her joints and muscles. The sight of a platter of cold mutton made her pause, in spite of the danger. No sooner had she slipped out of her hiding place and hungrily stuffed some of the mutton in her mouth than she heard bare feet scampering down the passage towards her. She leapt back into the pantry, swallowing the meat and grabbing a crust of bread to take into her hiding place. Simultaneously, the door burst open. It was Lady Sarah's young charge, Susanna.

'Come here!' barked Ratshade as he followed her into the kitchen.

'Get away from me, demon!' Susanna shrieked, sprinting for the door.

But Ratshade reached her before she could make her escape. As Susanna kicked and struggled she saw Bridget staring at her from the pantry. The child's eyes widened and her lips parted as if to speak. Bridget shook her head in panic, warning her the little girl not to give her away. Susanna acknowledged the gesture with a slight twitch of her eyes and allowed Ratshade to take her back to her quarters. Bridget waited for a few moments, then she slipped outside into the grounds. Stealing along the boundary wall, she then hurried away down the Strand. No matter what it took, she would find Bullen and Paul Rector and warn them of the danger that was awaiting them.

Thirty-three

14 June 1645

Paul and Grace were being watched as they rode into the village. The observer stood under the overhang of a thatched and beamed inn. A shimmering heat haze hung over the village green as they reined in their mounts. Grace slid from the saddle and approached a passer-by. She wanted to know how many miles it was to London. Paul was about to join her when church bells began to toll through the sultry evening air.

'Why are they ringing the bells?' he asked.

'Have you not heard?' the man next to Grace responded. 'Parliament has won a resounding victory on Naseby Field. The King is routed.'

'Then it is a glad day,' said Grace.

The man nodded. 'It is, mistress.' He examined Grace for a moment before continuing about his business.

'I didn't know you were for either side in this war, Grace,' Paul said. 'After all, the people who tried to burn you supported Parliament.'

Grace smiled. 'Your innocence surprises me Paul. We are close to London, and London is also for Parliament. I told the good citizen what he wanted to hear. That is how to survive, by bending with the wind.'

'I can't imagine you bending to anything,' Paul remarked.

Grace folded her arms across her chest and pursed her lips. 'Are you saying I am a troublesome woman?'

'Would I dare?' Paul said with a grin. 'Let's eat. What's the name of this village anyway?'

'It is called Islington,' Grace said, 'and that is St Mary's Church, the bells of which are so eagerly proclaiming the Roundhead victory.'

Paul stared. He thought the past had lost its capacity for surprise, but it was hard to imagine that this modest village with its nodding elm trees would one day be transformed into the traffic-choked streets of north London. 'So Islington lies outside the city?'

'Yes,' Grace said, leading the way into the nearest inn, 'but not far. We should take our rest tonight and continue on into London tomorrow.'

They sat at a corner table and ordered bacon and a cup of hot broth. That's when Paul's expression changed.

'Is something wrong?' Grace asked.

Paul didn't answer. Instead he watched a familiar figure approach. It was Bridget, the maid from Rokeby House.

'I bear news,' she said.

'Sit down,' Paul told her. Wondering how she had got here, he leant forward and whispered to her. 'The last time I saw you, you were calling me a murderer.'

'I know that to be false,' Bridget answered.

Grace looked on, trying to make sense of the exchange.

'Maybe you would like to explain how you found me,' Paul said, 'and what brought you here.'

'Nathanael Rector dwells in my master's house,' Bridget began. 'He resides there with half a dozen devils. He boasts about killing my master. It was the monsters' loose talk that gave me an idea of your whereabouts.'

'Is anyone else there?' Paul asked.

'They have Susanna,' Bridget replied. 'There is also a young woman who goes by the name of Netty.'

Paul's pulse quickened.

'I was lucky,' Bridget explained. 'The devils said you would be entering the city soon. I guessed that you would most likely arrive by the Essex Road or by the Great North Road.' She smiled. 'By Providence, I picked correctly.'

The bacon and broth arrived, and Bridget looked at it longingly.

'Another serving,' Grace said. She watched the maidservant returning to the kitchen. 'It is but a few days since I earned my living like her. It seems like an age.'

'You are in danger, sir,' Bridget whispered, ignoring Grace's comment.

'You must call me Paul.'

'Nathanael has hired a man called Catchpole,' Bridget told him. 'He is a thief and ...'

'I know all about Tom Catchpole,' Paul said, cutting her off. The set of his face was grim.

'You sound angry.'

'It is nothing to do with you, Bridget,' Paul said. 'I am disappointed in Tom Catchpole. He's someone I thought I could trust.'

'Trust a thief?' Grace exclaimed. 'I said you were an innocent.'

Paul scowled and sipped some of the broth.

'Catchpole has his spies out at every entrance to the city,' Bridget said. 'The moment one of his lackeys sees you, he will warn Nathanael.'

The maidservant returned with Bridget's meal. She ate greedily.

'How long has it been since you last ate?' Grace enquired, watching Bridget spoon the broth into her mouth.

Bridget looked up from her bowl. 'I have had but a scrap of mutton in two days. I spent much of that time in a pantry, hiding from the monsters.'

'Did Nathanael see you?' Paul asked.

Bridget wiped her lips before replying. 'I am sure that he did not, sir.'

'Good,' Paul said. 'Now I need to make my way into London without being seen.'

Grace peered outside, observing the wisps of mist that hung over the elms. 'I think I can help you.'

In years to come people who lived in the villages to the north of London would remember the night a morning mist thickened so quickly that milkmaids got lost on their way home and travellers had to interrupt their journeys and sleep among the trees. They would tell their children and grandchildren how silvery clouds rolled across the landscape, blanketing every road, lane and meadow. None would know that it was the work of a witch who went by the name of Grace Fletcher. She led Paul and Bridget across the fields. Soon, in the distance, she pointed out a dark, hulking shape.

'That must be the city up ahead,' she said.

'I think I know where I am,' Bridget said. 'If I am not mistaken, that is the Charterhouse.'

'The name means nothing to me,' Grace told her. 'I have lived all my life in Suffolk.'

'It used to be a monastery,' Bridget explained. 'Part of the building is now used as a school.'

'So we're almost there?' Paul asked.

Bridget pointed out a few shuffling figures and a line of houses. 'Did you not notice? You are already within the city boundary.'

Paul examined what little of his surroundings he could make out in the fog. 'I think you can allow it to lift now, Grace,' he said. 'We have slipped past Catchpole's lookouts.'

As the mist began to thin they found an inn on the far side of Pardon Churchyard and paid for two rooms. Paul saw the two women installed in a large room with twin beds, then started to set off back down the landing.

'Are you not getting some sleep yourself?' Grace asked. 'If we are to free Susanna and Netty tomorrow you will need to recover your strength.'

'Later,' Paul said. 'First I have something to do.'

Tom Catchpole gazed out of his window at the mysterious fog that was blanketing London. It had held the city in its grip for several hours. Rarely had he seen such a thing.

'In summer too,' said Catchpole, his voice fading into the blankness of the night. 'Damn the elements, for they conspire against me.' He called to the accomplice who guarded his door every night. 'Mercer, send word to call off the watch. They'll see nothing on a night like this. If the boy arrives tonight he will slip by my men unnoticed.' Several moments passed. Catchpole frowned. 'Mercer, are you asleep, you idle rogue?'

He crossed the room and peered outside. Mercer should have been keeping watch, but the landing was deserted. 'Where are you, you craven dog?' He ventured a few steps further then he saw a leather boot. His heart starting to pound, Catchpole looked into the room from which the foot trailed. He made out a human form lying crumpled on the floor. He reached for a candle, but he already knew what he would find. Mercer was sprawled before him, eyes fixed. A stream of saliva trickled from the corner of his mouth.

'He's alive,' came a voice. 'He will recover presently.'

Catchpole felt a chill run down his spine. 'Show yourself.'

Paul stepped out of the shadows. 'Why did you do it, Tom?'

Catchpole saw a pair of eyes made in Hell.

'Why did you betray me to Nathanael?' Paul demanded.

Catchpole glanced down at Mercer. 'What happened to him?'

'I think you know,' Paul said. 'You've looked into Nathanael's eyes. I think you know what lurks there. The same darkness is within me.'

'What are you going to do?' Catchpole asked.

'I haven't made my mind up yet,' Paul told him.

Catchpole took a deep breath and turned to look straight at Paul. He saw the flutter of darkness in the boy's pupils.

'Why did you sell me to Nathanael?' Paul demanded.

Catchpole shrugged, a gesture of helplessness as much as anything. 'Money,' he said. 'What else?'

'How much did Nathanael pay you for my neck?' Paul asked.

Catchpole told him.

'That's what I'm worth, is it?' Paul said coldly. 'You betrayed me for a pittance.'

'It was business,' Catchpole said. 'You didn't think we were friends, did you?'

'Will you tell Nathanael I was here?' Paul asked. 'Will

you betray me again?' There was a long silence. 'Well?'

Catchpole swallowed hard. 'No.'

Paul examined his face. 'Close your eyes,' he said.

'Why?' Catchpole was trembling.

'Close them,' Paul commanded.

Catchpole squeezed his eyes shut. After a few moments he could stand it no longer and reopened them. Paul had gone.

Thirty-four

14 June 1645

Paul didn't return directly to the inn. He walked the streets. He had subdued his demons ... for now. 'Will fighting the monsters make me one myself?' he murmured, reliving the horror that had been with him for months. The fate of so many of his ancestors crouched in his memory like some foul, intruding vermin. Every member of the Rector line who had been born with the demon seed in his blood had gone on to serve Lud. They had all been prepared to kill on his command. 'Is that my fate?'

The fog with which Grace had wreathed London had relaxed its hold and the summer heat had returned. Paul leant against a wall and saw the swinging sign of the Saracen's Head inn. Even as he gazed at the image a familiar, swirling wind stung his eyes and it was the face of Lud that emerged from the cracked paintwork and stared out at him.

'You will never defeat me,' Lud gloated. 'The witch

permitted you to enter the city unseen. You could have left it at that, and we would never have found you. You couldn't do it, though, could you? It is not in your nature to use subterfuge. You had to seek out Catchpole. You had to have your revenge.'

Paul watched the features of his enemy, then he shook his head in a gesture of defiance.

'Are you ... smiling?' Lud demanded. 'You have nothing to be happy about. Your demon side is in the ascendant now, Paul. It can only grow stronger. You are torn, aren't you? You grow tired of the warring emotions that tear you apart. You are mine for the taking.'

'You think I killed Catchpole, don't you?' Paul retorted.

'You couldn't help yourself, could you?' Lud asked. 'You want to believe that we are opposites, but that's not true, is it? Forget the boy you were. He is dead. Surely you know that.' He seized on Paul's silence. 'You would like to portray yourself as the blameless hero, but are we really so different? I crush my foes. You crush yours. I use terror. So do you. Remember what you did to the undertaker. We are brothers, Paul, one flesh, one blood.' Paul tried to interrupt, to tell Lud they had nothing in common, but the demon master continued his speech. 'We are the lords of the dark. We are strong while others are weak. What was it like when you took Catchpole's life? Did you thrill to see him grovel before you? Did you draw strength from his strangled screams? Tell me how you felt as you broke him.'

Paul turned away.

'Look at me,' Lud said. 'Tell me you didn't relish your victim's fear. Let me hear it from your lips.'

Paul maintained his silence, preparing a surprise for his foe.

'It is time to make your peace with me,' Lud said.

'Why fight the inevitable? You can have Nathanael's place by my side. You can be prince of demons.'

Paul spun round, a look of triumph on his face. 'Catchpole's alive. I couldn't do it.'

In that instant Paul heard Lud's thoughts echoing through his mind. Suddenly Paul understood what the demon master wanted.

'This is a trick, isn't it?' Paul demanded. 'You appeared in an attempt to distract me. Even now you're searching for Grace. You've sent your disciples to kill her.'

Without another word he cast a fireball at the swinging inn sign and it burst into flames. Simultaneously, he heard horsemen thundering along Hosier Lane just a hundred yards away. *The riders!* Paul turned and ran across Smithfield in pursuit. He glimpsed the shadowy figures of the three horsemen galloping past the church of St Bartholomew the Great. They were extending their lead over him. Paul heard their hooves pounding over the ground towards the tavern where Grace and Bridget were sleeping. His flesh was burning with dread at the thought of what he might discover at the tavern.

Grace stirred. The night breeze carried a warning. 'Bridget,' she hissed to the young woman asleep in the next bed. 'Bridget, wake up!'

Bridget squeezed her eyes open. They were puffy with sleep. She had been exhausted by her uncomfortable vigil in the house on the Strand. 'What is it?'

'I thought I heard a voice. It came in my dreams.'

'What voice?'

Grace heard something, a deep, low rumble in the bowels of the night. She pressed a finger to her lips and strained to hear. There it was again, the thud of hooves. 'Follow me.'

Bridget obeyed, grabbing her boots as she followed Grace to the door. At the very moment Grace was stepping onto the landing in her bare feet, the front door of the tavern burst open.

'They're here,' Grace hissed.

Bridget stole a glance downstairs. 'Lord preserve us!'

Grace gestured to Bridget to follow, and the pair scampered along the landing. Lithe and agile as a cat, Grace sprang onto the windowsill. 'You too,' she commanded.

'But we can't jump from here,' Bridget said, looking down. 'We will injure ourselves.'

'I don't intend to jump,' Grace said, licking her finger and testing the breeze.

'What then?'

'No more questions,' Grace ordered. 'Put your arms round my shoulders and hold tight.'

'But ... .'

'Do it, you little ninny!'

Tears stung Bridget's eyes, but she obeyed nonetheless. Instantly, Grace launched herself out into the darkness. Bridget was about to cry out that Grace had promised not to jump when she felt a powerful force thump against her back. To her amazement they were not falling but rising. It wasn't flight exactly. They were gliding silently, following the trail of the night breeze. Somehow Grace was riding the wind. Behind them, they heard the snarl of the riders as they saw their prey drifting away into the gloom.

'How did you do that?' Bridget asked, gazing down at the streets below.

'I said no questions,' Grace snapped. They finally floated down at the corner of Long Lane and Aldersgate

Street. They were looking back at the tavern. 'Follow me. We're not safe yet.'

It was true. One of the riders had sprung down from the window. The other two were already emerging from the door they had kicked in. Candlelight was leaping at several of the windows. Grace seized Bridget by the hand and led the way down Aldersgate Street.

'They are coming,' Bridget panted. 'Let me go, Grace. You are so much faster than me. I will only hold you back.'

'I will not give you up to them,' Grace declared stubbornly. 'I have had to watch two poor souls die already. I will witness no more unnecessary deaths.'

Bridget wondered what she meant, but she didn't say another word as she struggled to keep up with the fleet-footed Grace. They turned towards the church of St Martin's le Grand. Grace was glancing back for some sign of their pursuers when Bridget screamed. One of the demon horsemen had just skidded into view ahead of them, blocking their escape. Grace chanced another backward glance and saw the remaining riders turn the corner behind them. Tugging her hand free of Bridget's terrified grip, Grace stretched out her arms. Hail lashed the streets, causing two of the horses to rear and whinny.

'Run!' Grace yelled.

Bridget followed Grace towards a narrow alley. Unable to pursue the two women on horseback, the riders dismounted and followed on foot. Grace stood still and unleashed a bolt of lightning that blasted the leading rider off the ground. His companions paused for a moment. When the fallen demon started to struggle back to his feet they continued the pursuit.

'They are gaining on us,' Bridget whimpered. 'Whatever it was you did, pray do it again.'

Grace looked despairingly at the clouds. 'Without renewal from the heavens, my powers are almost exhausted. Where is Paul? Why has he abandoned us?'

Grace's talk of powers made little sense to Bridget, but Grace's despairing tone filled her with dread. 'Are we to die?'

'Oh, you're going to die,' the first rider snarled as he approached. 'Isn't that right, Warboy?'

'Ratshade and I shall have the witch, Claypin,' said Warboy. 'You take the girl. We will bring their hearts to Nathanael as trophies. They will look pretty on a skewer.'

Claypin seized Bridget's hair and yanked her head back. He peeled back his scarf to expose his fleshless lower face. 'Give me a kiss, my pretty,' he hissed.

'Do something!' Bridget screamed.

Grace responded by laying her hands on Claypin's arm. Lightning snaked over his body, searing his flesh. For a moment, he screamed but already Grace's powers were fading. Ratshade gleefully clubbed her to the ground.

'Maybe you would like to swap,' he chuckled. 'The witch has turned your beautiful face to crackling, Claypin. You will think up a suitable punishment, I warrant.'

Claypin snarled as he slammed Grace against the wall. He stroked her cheek with his claws. 'I will cut your pretty face to ribbons for this,' he growled.

Grace recoiled from the menacing talons. 'Get it over with,' she cried defiantly.

Claypin shook his head. 'Oh, I am in no hurry. This is going to be very, very slow, witch. Now let's have that kiss. It is something you will never forget.'

Even as he drew the first blood from Grace's cheek and turned her mouth towards his, his eyes widened in agony as intense flame licked its way down his spine.

'The renegade!' Warboy roared. He raced forward to face Paul, but he too was engulfed in howling fire. As he staggered to and fro, beating at the tongues of flame, Ratshade cursed and fled.

'Where have you been?' Grace yelled at Paul.

Warboy and Claypin helped each other beat out the flames and staggered away.

'I shall have that kiss yet, mistress,' Claypin shouted.

Paul was about to go after him, but Grace seized his sleeve.

'Let the creatures go,' she scolded. 'I want an answer, Paul. Why did you not stay to protect us?'

Paul held up his hands in a gesture of apology. He hated himself for his lapse of judgement. He could hardly look at her. 'I let my emotions rule my head, Grace. Forgive me. I won't let you down again.'

Bridget was standing with her back against the wall, her face pale and contorted with fear. She looked as afraid of Grace and Paul as she had been of the demon riders.

'What are you?' she asked, her voice thin and afraid. 'This is the Devil's work. This is witchcraft.'

'Do not condemn us, Bridget,' Grace said. 'You surely understand that we are not like those creatures.'

'I know what I saw with my own eyes,' Bridget cried. 'You used flame and storm. This is most ungodly. I ask again, what are you?'

'We are the enemies of the creature that killed your master, Bridget,' Paul said. 'You have to listen to me—'

'I will not listen to another word you say!' Bridget retorted. 'You use the dark arts. This offends nature.'

Grace reached towards her, but Bridget pulled away.

'Don't touch me, Grace,' she said. 'I can remain in your company no longer.' Her voice softened a little.

'You saved my life and I am grateful for that, but what I have seen … ' She shook her head. 'This is Satan's work. I have to go. Do not stand in my way.'

'They may come after you,' Paul said.

'I will take that chance,' Bridget replied.

'Where will you go?'

'My mother still lives over the river in Southwark,' Bridget answered. 'I swore never to be a burden to her. I have no choice now but to take refuge under her roof.' She started plodding down the alley.

'Bridget,' Grace said, 'there is no need to fear us. You have to believe we are fighting a great evil.'

Bridget paused and glanced back. 'That may be true,' she said, 'but I am sore afraid, Grace. This night I have seen things that chill me to the depths of my soul. I am but a common servant. I do not have the strength for this. I must get away.'

'Let her leave, Grace,' Paul said.

They watched as Bridget reached the top of the alley. She turned and hesitated, gazing back at them. A moment later she was gone.

Thirty-five

14 June 1645

Warboy picked at his charred flesh. 'I will tear off the renegade's face for this.'

Nathanael shook his head. 'You may find it harder to do than you first thought. Our master says the boy has great power. Your mistake was to confront him in the open where he is strongest. You must get closer if you are to defeat him. It is the only way you can use that special trick of yours.' He rubbed his forehead. 'He has made his way into the city. There is no turning back time.'

'What do we do now?' Warboy asked.

'We don't have to do anything,' Nathanael said. 'The boy has been seen in the company of a maid who worked for Sir James. He will make his way here next. He and the witch will want to free the females we hold captive.'

'Then we should move them immediately,' Suckvenom said.

'You're right, of course,' Nathanael said. He paused. 'No, let me give this some thought.'

The five surviving riders stared at him.

'What are we waiting for?' Halberd grumbled. 'Our enemies could be on the way at this very moment.'

'Warboy, Claypin,' Nathanael said. 'Keep watch for them.'

The two riders left.

'We will move the witch child,' Nathanael said. 'She is vital to our plans. Without her, we will never breach the seals and free our master. As for Netty, we will use her as bait. This could yet turn to our advantage.' He explained what he had in mind. 'Now bring Susanna to me.'

Netty and Susanna were both sleeping when Halberd and Suckvenom burst in on them.

'What do you want?' Netty demanded, scrambling to her feet.

'Not you, crow-meat,' Suckvenom sneered.

Susanna gave a yelp of fright and pressed herself against Netty for protection, wrapping her arms round the older girl's waist. Halberd made a grab for her, and Susanna sent lightning crackling along his arm. He cursed, then seized Netty by her hair, dragging her towards him. 'Another trick like that, Susanna,' he warned, placing a claw against Netty's throat, 'and I will slit this scrawny wench's windpipe for her.'

'Don't hurt Netty,' pleaded Susanna.

'If you consent to follow us without further protest,' Suckvenom said, 'she will come to no harm.'

'You have my promise,' Susanna said. With a backward glance at Netty, Susanna followed Halberd meekly from the room.

'Where are you taking her?' Netty cried.

'That is none of your business,' Suckvenom told her. 'Now crawl into your corner and keep your mouth shut.' He shoved Netty roughly to the floor and watched her curl up against the wall. He noticed that she was trembling and enjoyed the power he had over her. 'That's right, just sit there and not another murmur out of you.' He slashed the air in front of her face with his clawed right hand. Fun over, he slammed the door behind him and locked it.

Halberd was still rubbing his arm when he pushed Susanna into the kitchen.

'What is the matter with you?' Nathanael demanded.

'It is this troublesome child,' Halberd complained. 'She is up to her tricks again. Her defiance knows no limits.'

'I will be good,' Susanna said hurriedly. 'Pray do not hurt Netty because of what I have done.'

Nathanael seemed amused by her pleading. 'Just be sure to obey my every command without protest,' he said. 'Do not forget, I can subject you to my will should you resist. Imagine how you would feel if I made you turn your powers on your new friend.'

'You wouldn't!'

'It might be fun watching you torture somebody you care about,' Nathanael mused. 'Did you know that you are aware of everything you are doing, even when I have control of your thoughts?'

Susanna hung her head in a gesture of surrender. 'I will do anything you ask,' she said.

Nathanael snapped his fingers. 'Halberd, Suckvenom, take the child to her new lodgings. She will give you no further problem.'

'Am I to go without Netty?' Susanna asked. 'I do not want to be alone.'

'You promised to obey me without protest,' Nathanael snapped. 'You are more use to me if you are obeying of your own free will, but if I have to assume control over your thoughts, I shall.'

Susanna bowed to the inevitable and fell silent. The riders bundled her outside to the horses. Once she was gone, Nathanael sent for Warboy and Claypin. 'The storm is about to break over the city,' he said. 'I must be at the child's side to control her actions. You will remain here with Ratshade.' He grinned. 'This will be your chance to gain revenge for the hurt done to you in your last encounter with the renegade.'

'Oh, we'll be ready for him,' Claypin said, running his tongue over his rotting teeth, 'and his friend the witch.' He leered. 'I owe her a kiss.'

By the time Paul and Grace arrived at the Strand stormclouds were gathering over the rooftops of the city.

'There will be a reckoning soon,' Grace said.

'Where will they strike first, I wonder,' Paul mused. 'Three gates remain. It could be any one of them.'

Grace dismounted and handed Paul the reins. 'Wait here.' She raced to the wall that surrounded the Rokeby residence. She climbed the obstacle with little difficulty and vanished into the grounds. Paul tethered the horses around the corner from the house and waited. After about five minutes he heard a stealthy pad behind him and spun round. Grace grinned at the look of surprise on his face, then the smile faded.

'Did you find out where they are?' Paul asked. 'Did you see Netty?'

Grace shook her head. 'Claypin was guarding the door. He is the only one I saw, but I overheard him talking to one of his comrades. Paul, I am certain that they have moved Susanna. Events are drawing to their conclusion.' A few drops of rain splashed the ground around them, hinting at the storm's arrival. 'We have no purpose here. We must stop the demons before they break the seals.'

'What about Netty?' Paul asked. 'Is she still in the house?'

'I think so,' Grace said. 'I fear this is a trap.'

Paul raised his gaze to the roof. 'We have to get inside.'

'Did you not hear what I said?' Grace protested. 'That is what they want you to do. Paul, surely you are not such a fool. You must not take the bait. The fate of London is in the balance.'

'I will not leave Netty alone with these monsters,' Paul told her.

'This is wrong,' Grace said. 'Helping Netty without defeating the demon master would be an empty gesture. If Lud rises, we are all lost.'

Paul shook his head stubbornly. 'You have to trust me, Grace. We can free Netty and still stop Nathanael breaking the seals. We've got to do this.'

Grace continued to object. 'You can't take the risk. There is more than one life at stake here. It is the future of an entire city for generations to come.'

'I won't go without Netty,' Paul insisted.

Grace stared at him for a few moments, then nodded. 'It is against my better judgement, but I will help you. What do you want me to do?'

'Can you get me up there?' He glanced at her. 'Bridget told me you can ride the wind.'

Grace looked up and down the road. 'We must be sure nobody sees us or we shall have more trouble.'

Once they were certain there was nobody watching, they glided onto the roof together and crouched, staring down at the earth below. The wind was picking up and snapping around them.

'The storm is breaking,' Grace whispered. 'Paul, please reconsider. There is no time left.'

Paul was conscious of the racing stormclouds overhead. 'Don't say another word on the matter, Grace.'

'How can you be so selfish?' Grace cried. 'They have my daughter. I understand your feelings but ...'

Paul interrupted her. 'My mind is made up. We must act now.'

He started peeling back the roof tiles. Grace watched him for a few moments, her face aghast, then followed suit. Soon the hole was large enough to let one of them squirm through.

'I will go first,' Grace hissed. 'I can land without making a sound.' She vanished into the murk of the attic, before reappearing a few moments later, her dark eyes gazing up at him. 'Lower yourself. I will guide you.'

He felt her support as he eased himself to the floor with just the slightest creak.

'There is a way into the house,' she told him, her voice low. 'It is over here.'

They crossed the attic floor, wincing at each creak of the floorboards. After a little while Grace held up her hand. Paul gave her a questioning glance. She looked troubled.

'Is something wrong?' he mouthed.

'I don't know,' she whispered. 'It is as if the house has been waiting for us.' He listened for some sign that the building's occupants were close, but Rokeby House was quiet except for the sigh of the wind in the eaves. The silence only increased Paul's anxiety. Maybe it was merely that Grace had transmitted her own unease to him or maybe they really were in danger. That's when he heard a key turn in a lock somewhere on the floor below. A demon voice said something about food. Then there was a female voice telling him to take it away.

'That's Netty,' Paul said, exhilarated to discover her location.

Grace nodded. They listened as the rider locked the door behind him and strode away along the landing.

Once they were satisfied that he had gone, they made their way forward to the room where Netty was held. Paul signalled to Grace to keep lookout then used his powers to unlock the door. He eased it open and saw Netty's eyes widen, first in horror, then in relief. He pressed a finger to his lips and crouched beside her. He used hand gestures to ask if she was all right. She nodded. Paul was about to lead Netty out onto the landing when he froze. What was that noise? There was no time to make sense of it. A split second later Grace fell backwards into the room, Claypin clawing at her. In quick procession, Ratshade came crashing through the window from outside. Running footsteps told Paul that a third demon was racing to join the struggle. While Paul put himself between Ratshade and Netty and started to grapple with the demon, Grace crashed to the floor with Claypin on top of her. She had the heel of her hand under his chin, desperately trying to keep his face away from hers.

'Paul,' she cried, 'beware the creature's mouth.'

That's when he saw the danger that lurked in the demons' ruined faces. Dozens of fat brown beetles were swarming over Ratshade's jaw and spilling from his tongue. It was these tiny creatures that had fed on his flesh and would feed on the monster's victims too. Worse still, instead of a tongue, a livid, scarlet reptile writhed inside Ratshade's mouth, snapping at Paul. For a moment Paul was almost paralysed by disgust, then he recovered and set his attacker alight. Even before Paul could push the blazing demon away, Netty screamed. Warboy had burst into the room and fallen on Paul's back. He felt the flesh-eating beetles spilling from Warboy's mouth and piercing his body. He cried out in agony as the insects started to tear off scraps of his skin. Then he saw the window and decided on his

237

course of action. With a roar, he seized both demons and leapt through it, taking Warboy and Ratshade with him.

The fall separated Paul from his attackers. He swept away the beetles that were still trying to devour his flesh. Warboy was the first to recover from the fall. As he rose to his feet, Paul torched him. A second jet of flame snaked down Ratshade's throat, ending the creature's resistance. In spite of his wounds, Warboy launched a final attack, but Paul was ready. Soon there was only ash to show that the monsters had ever existed. There was no time to dwell on his victory. Paul raced back into the house. He was halfway down the landing that led to the room where Netty had been held when there was a deafening explosion that threw Paul back against the wall. Thunder rolled through the house, booming again and again. Paul saw Claypin stumble from the room and feared the worst.

'No!' he cried.

Grace appeared a moment later, pursuing the rider. Claypin retreated, finding himself standing with his back to a casement window. Grace saw something behind the demon and threw out her right arm. Claypin spun round just in time to see a fork of lightning slash the sky. Instantly he understood his fate. With a cry, Grace pushed Claypin through the glass. As he pitched forward a second fork of lightning flashed from above and destroyed him.

'Grace,' Paul panted, 'where's Netty?'

'In there,' Grace answered. 'I just pray she survived the thunderbolt.'

Paul saw Netty crumpled on the floor and scooped her up in his arms. 'She's not breathing!'

'Give her to me,' Grace ordered. Propping Netty up with her left arm, she placed her right on her chest. For a few moments she looked concerned, then she smiled. 'Her heartbeat is strong. She will recover presently.'

Paul stroked back Netty's hair and sobbed with relief. He would draw little comfort from her recovery, however. Even as he and Grace supported Netty, there was a deep groan that seemed to rise from the bowels of the Earth.

'Oh no,' Paul cried. 'It can't be.'

'It is,' Grace said bleakly. 'Susanna has harnessed the storm. She has broken the second seal.' She tore at her hair. 'Do you see what you have done? You have handed Lud victory.'

Thirty-six

14 June 1645

Grace was standing at the edge of the smoking pit, staring into the abyss. In another time, Lud's disciples had broken the first seal by fire. Now the second of the magic chains that bound the demon master had been shattered by storm. Fire, storm, flood and blood – the prophecy was coming true. Grace turned and seized Paul's hand, dragging him away from the bemused onlookers. 'Do you see where your selfishness and pride have brought us?' She caught Netty's eye. 'I attach no blame to you. This was Paul's decision. He made the wrong choice.'

'You're right,' Paul murmured. 'You're right. All I could think about was ...'

Recovered from her ordeal, Netty took his hand and squeezed it. 'There are still two gates to fight for, Paul. It isn't over.'

The three of them stood in the drumming rain, the only ones among the throng who could make sense of the gaping hole a thunderbolt had torn in the middle of Aldgate. That's when Paul saw the shimmering form of Cormac waiting for him in an alley opposite. He pulled his hand from Netty's grasp and made his way over.

'I'm sorry,' Paul said, the rain streaming over his face.

'Words are pointless,' Cormac told him. 'What's done is done. You have to put it right or we are lost. Two gates are breached. Two remain to deny the creature his freedom. You must act now or Lud will triumph.'

Netty wandered over and listened to the conversation.

'You're right,' Paul said. 'I will find them.'

'First,' Cormac said, 'you must return the girl to her own time.'

'Netty's all I have,' Paul explained. 'I love her. Don't you understand? I left my own mother behind. I walked away from my home and my friends. Netty is here. I can see her, hold her. I love her.' He became aware of her presence. 'I can't give her up.'

'Did you say you loved her?' Cormac demanded.

'Yes.'

Cormac glanced at Netty, then snorted in derision. 'You do not understand what love means, either of you.'

Paul tried to protest, but Cormac raised a hand.

'When you have lived with another soul for twenty years,' he said, 'as I did with my beloved wife, when she has borne your children, then you may know the meaning of the word.' His eyes flashed. 'Because of Lud, I lost a woman who had been at my side for half a lifetime. Because of the Hell-beast, I lost my children, my home. For a time, I lost my very sanity. Do not talk to me of sacrifice, Paul Rector. You must do what is right or it may cost us all dear.'

Before Paul could say a word, Netty spoke. She had

come to a decision. 'He's right,' she said, joining in the discussion for the first time. 'I don't belong here.' Tears spilled down her cheeks. 'If I stay Lud will use me against you. Let me go home.'

Paul embraced her. 'I can't be without you again,' he sobbed, pressing his face against her cheek. 'Don't ask me to give you up.'

Netty peeled his hands from her back. 'Think it through, Paul. I'm not like you. I have no powers. You can't protect me every moment of every day. Sooner or later the demon brotherhood would destroy me, then what would you do? I don't belong here. I'm afraid and I can only do you harm. Let me go.'

Paul stood there, a wretched figure in the columns of rain. Finally, he nodded.

'Can you get her home safely, Cormac?'

Cormac nodded. 'There is one more thing to do, Paul.'

'What is it?'

'Nathanael travelled through Hell's Underground to abduct her. What's to stop Lud using the same tactic again?'

'What are you saying?'

'Listen to me carefully, Paul,' Cormac said. 'I demand one further sacrifice from you. The portal to the future must be closed.'

There was panic in Paul's eyes. 'Then how will I get home?'

'If you consent,' Cormac explained, 'the Courts of Destiny will seal Hell's Underground until your battle with Lud is concluded. None may go forward through time until there is a victor. Then you may return.'

Paul looked away. 'It's too much to ask.'

Grace approached. 'There is no other way. If the portal remains open, the demon brotherhood will use Hell's Underground again. Netty will never be safe.

They could seize your mother, your other friends. You must consent to this.'

Netty held him one more time. 'I believe in you, Paul. Say yes.' She pressed her lips to his cheek as she held him and whispered in his ear. 'I will be waiting for you when you return.'

Paul sighed. 'I suppose I knew it would come to this.' He fumbled in his jacket for something and handed Netty a letter.

'You already had it written?'

'I was afraid this moment would come,' Paul said. 'Read it when you get back.'

Netty smiled. 'I will.' Finally she drew away.

Paul wiped the rain and tears from his face. 'Do it, Cormac. Get it over with.'

Cormac turned his gaze to Netty. 'Walk to the end of the alley. You will see an oaken door. Step through it and you will be home.'

'As easy as that?' Netty asked.

'It is as easy as that.'

Netty strode to the end of the alley and opened the door. Paul watched her as she walked away. Then, as she stepped through the doorway, his resolve broke and he raced after her. But when he reached the end of the alley there was no door, just an uninterrupted board-and-plaster wall.

'She is gone,' Cormac said. 'You must accept it.'

'Lud was right,' Paul roared, torn by misery and despair, 'all you offer is pain and sacrifice.'

'I offer the only way Lud can be defeated,' Cormac answered. 'I offer London's only hope.'

'I will fight on,' Paul said. 'I will fight Lud to the finish, but I despise you for what you have done. Netty was the only person who might have made this journey bearable.'

'Hate me all you like,' Cormac said. 'What do personal feelings matter when measured against the fate of a city? I want only one thing from you, commitment to our cause.'

Paul scowled. 'You have it, now let me be.' He turned away. 'Come on, Grace, we have a battle to fight.'

Netty stood bewildered, staring up at Aldgate tube. All around her were the milling crowds of the capital. Occasionally, a passer-by would frown at her long Puritan dress and white bonnet, but few paid her any attention. Netty peeled off the bonnet and tossed it into the nearest litterbin. Examining her reflection in a shop window, she did her best to tidy her tangled hair and wipe the grime from her face. She fumbled in the folds of her dress, then laughed at her own stupidity. Of course there was no money for the Underground. Instead, she hailed a taxi. Mum would pay the fare when she arrived.

'Been to a fancy-dress, have you?' the cabbie asked, glancing at her in his rear-view mirror.

'Something like that,' Netty answered, settling back into the seat.

'It must have been a wild party.'

'It was.'

'Are you all right?' he asked. 'I don't mean to be personal, but you look a bit dishevelled.'

'I'm fine, honestly,' Netty told him.

The cabbie shrugged. He accepted that she didn't want to talk and got on with his driving. Netty watched the modern city rushing past and thought of the dark heart that beat beneath the streets. She pulled Paul's letter from her skirts and stared at it. Aware of the driver darting occasional glances at her, she decided to wait until she was in the privacy of her own room before reading it. She felt the rocking motion of the cab. Here she was, travelling down a tarmac road in twenty-first century London, but her thoughts were with a boy, fighting for his life, over three centuries before.

Thirty-seven

Present Day

An hour after Netty walks through her front door, DI Hussein receives a phone call. 'She's back? When?'

She races out of the police station and accelerates out of the car park. Within ten minutes she is sitting opposite Netty and her mother in their small, neat living room. Netty's father, divorced from Mrs Carney, is on his way from Essex.

'This is no thanks to you,' Mrs Carney snaps.

'Don't, Mum,' Netty says. 'There's nothing the police could have done. Where I've been nobody can follow.'

The colour drains from Mrs Carney's face. She has been lying to herself, forcing herself to cling to some rational explanation for Netty's disappearance. With her daughter's return, she is having to face the truth.

'Could I talk to Netty without interruption, Mrs Carney?' Hussein asks.

Mrs Carney tries to protest, but Netty cuts her off.

'I know you don't want to hear this, but she's got to know the truth.'

Mrs Carney gives a sigh of resignation and sags against the back of the couch.

'Did you see Paul?' Hussein asks.

'Yes,' Netty answers. 'I was with him just a few hours ago.' She stumbles through her story. 'You don't believe me, do you?'

'You're wrong,' Hussein says. 'I was there when Redman attacked you. I've seen the photograph of Paul walking through wartime Britain. I could try to dredge up some nonsense to explain it away, but I have witnessed this evil with my own eyes. I know you're telling the truth.'

'Thank God,' Netty says. 'For months I've been bottling it up. There were times I thought I was going insane.'

Hussein smiles. 'I've been feeling the same way. I lost a colleague and a good friend.'

'Detective Ditchburn,' Netty says. 'Of course, I didn't think.'

'What's happened to Paul?' Hussein asks. 'Is he ever coming home?'

Netty drops her gaze to the floor. 'I don't know,' she says.

'Where is he going?'

Netty buries her face in her hands. 'Deeper into Hell.'

Thirty-eight

14 June 1645

Paul and Grace made their way through the crowded streets. The rain was coming down harder, drenching to the skin anyone foolish enough to be outdoors. In the distance thunder rumbled, hinting that the storm's fury was still not spent. London was alive with talk of unnatural events. Some said the storm was the Devil's work. Secret Royalists whispered darkly that it was God's punishment against those who rebelled against the anointed King.

'What is Nathanael planning?' Grace wondered out loud. 'Fire and storm broke the first two gates,' she said, fighting to be heard over the howl of the wind. 'That leaves flood and blood.'

'I don't know about blood,' a voice said. 'You shall have your flood soon enough.'

The speaker was an elderly woman. She was swaddled in rags and was cowering in a doorway, sheltering from the downpour. Her face was scarred by disease and she was blind in one eye.

'Do you know something?' Paul asked. He was a little too eager and the woman stared at him suspiciously.

'Well?'

'Do not hurt me, sir,' she pleaded. 'I meant nothing by it. I should not have spoken.'

Her words served only to provoke Paul. He grabbed her wrist. 'Speak up, you said something about a flood. This is important.' Without intending to, he was tightening his grip. 'I don't have time to waste.'

'Get him away from me!' the woman croaked. 'I am only a poor beggar woman. The boy's possessed. I see it in his eyes.'

'Let me speak to her,' Grace said, gently removing Paul's hand from the woman's almost fleshless arm. 'Do not be afraid. My companion means you no harm.' She fished in her dress and handed her a coin. 'Pray use this gift to go to a tavern and nourish yourself. Dry those clothes before a roaring fire. What is your name?'

The woman was still cautious. 'I'm Annie.'

'Well, Annie,' Grace said gently, 'we are interested in what you just said about there being a flood. Where did you come by this information?'

'You won't take your money back when I tell you?'

'No.'

Annie was reassured. 'I was taking shelter by Cow Bridge when I heard the bargemen talking. There is a rumour the Fleet is threatening to burst its banks. That is the reason I made my way here. It is higher ground, you see, and more distant from the waters.'

'Where's this Fleet River?' Paul demanded. 'I've lived in London all my life, and I've never heard of it.'

'Do you know Cow Bridge?' Annie asked.

'Yes,' Grace said eagerly, 'we recently had lodgings near there.'

'Then you crossed the Fleet.'

'You can't call that a river,' Paul said, remembering the sluggish stream choked by garbage and offal.

'They cleaned it once,' Annie said, 'back in my grandmother's time but it became blocked again. The butchers throw the animals' entrails in. Then there is the sewage.' She glanced at Grace. 'You should see the waters now, mistress. A raging torrent is what you will find.'

'We are in your debt, Annie,' Grace said. She handed over a few more coins. 'Something tells me you are treated ill.'

Annie nodded. 'Since I was stricken with the pox nobody will offer me shelter.' She looked at Grace as if unable to believe her charity. 'I will not forget your kindness, mistress.'

Paul hovered close by, wishing he had Grace's way with people. Grace squeezed Annie's hands. 'God speed, Annie. I hope the money is enough for a bed for the night.'

Annie went on her way, glancing back from time to time.

'You heard her,' Paul said. 'Grace, we know where they are. It's got to be Aldersgate. They're going to use flood to breach the third seal.'

'Look,' Grace said. Great banks of purple cloud were rolling in from the east. 'This is not natural. Susanna is harnessing the storm.' Even as they gazed upwards, lightning slashed open the murk. 'She has begun the assault on the third seal. Paul, we must hurry.'

They mounted their horses and galloped westwards. Soon they saw the familiar hulk of St Bartholomew the Great. They were almost there.

'What do we do when we get there?' Grace cried.

'I don't know,' Paul answered. 'I suppose we fight.'

As they swept round the next corner Grace screamed. There was a rope pulled taut across the road. There was no time to rein in her mount. Her horse pitched forward, legs flailing, and spilled Grace onto the ground. Paul's horse hit the rope next. To avoid being crushed under the horse's weight, Paul threw himself clear. A jarring impact followed immediately and he lay half-conscious, groaning because of the pain that was racking his shoulder. The injury was the least of his problems. He was still rising groggily from the fall when he saw a pair of shadowy figures moving towards him. It was the final riders, Suckvenom and Halberd.

'Grace,' Paul shouted, 'are you all right?'

Suckvenom had already reached her. The demon scooped up the senseless woman like a rag doll and leered. 'Try and save her this time, renegade.'

Paul thrust out an arm in a vain attempt to summon flame, but Halberd was too quick, crashing a boot into the boy's chest. Paul went down and lay very still, barely aware of the world around him.

'Our master will be pleased,' Halberd said. 'There will be no mistakes this time.'

Suckvenom nodded. 'This is for our brother Claypin, you witch.'

Grace's eyes flickered open. Instantly she saw the hideous reptile that dwelt in Suckvenom's throat. Its jaws opened and closed, needle-like teeth snapping at her. Grace tried to struggle, but the demon had her in a grip of steel. She shrieked in terror, then hot blood sprayed her. For a moment she was unable to understand the turn of events. Then she smelt cordite on the air. As the gunpowder smoke cleared she recognised Bridget, who was holding a musket in her right hand. Grace pushed the dead Suckvenom from her.

'I thought you had left us for good,' she said.

'I did not even reach the Thames before I realised I could not just walk away from this fight,' Bridget replied.

'You will not save the renegade,' Halberd roared.

'She doesn't need to,' Paul said, both hands glowing scarlet. 'I can save myself.'

Paul unleashed the power of fire. Halberd burst into flame. As he rolled on the ground, shrieking in agony, Bridget aimed a second musket at his head and put him out of his misery.

'Where did you get the muskets?' Paul asked.

'They belonged to Sir James,' Bridget replied. 'When I decided to turn back I knew I must arm myself if I was to be of any use in this battle. I had seen him cleaning the barrels so I knew where to find them.'

Grace rested her hands on Bridget's thin shoulders. 'You did well,' she said. 'Now you must stay here out of sight.'

'Thank you,' Bridget said. 'I would not like to face Nathanael again.'

Paul and Grace continued towards Aldersgate. They shared Bridget's sense of apprehension.

Thirty-nine

14 June 1645

Nathanael was waiting for them. He had a surprise in store.

'God's blood!' Grace gasped as they stood in the middle of Aldersgate Street gazing up at the city walls.

'Surely you wondered what I was doing when you did not find me at Rokeby House,' Nathanael said, enjoying the look of horror on his opponents' faces. 'Did you imagine I would not be prepared?'

Paul's eyes travelled along the row of expressionless figures to either side of Nathanael and Susanna. A dozen men, women and children were kneeling, their heads bowed. They had nooses around their necks and were waiting for Nathanael's signal. To demonstrate his readiness to use his hostages, Nathanael projected his thoughts into the mind of a small boy at the end of the row. Without hesitation, he leapt from the city walls. Paul immediately cut the rope with a jet of flame and raced forward to break the child's fall.

'That is very impressive,' Nathanael said as the boy wriggled out of Paul's grasp and fled the scene, wailing with fright. 'But ask yourself the question, renegade: could you save the lives of all eleven of these good folk if they were to jump at once?' He stretched out his arms, and they rose to their feet as one. 'How many would survive? How many would snap their necks as they fell? How many would die an agonising death from strangulation?' He fixed Paul with a stare. 'How would you like to have that on your conscience?'

'I will destroy you, Nathanael,' Paul hissed.

'Fighting words,' Nathanael said. 'But here's the thing, my fiery young foe, how exactly do you propose to destroy me? Do you want me to tell you what you are thinking, Paul Rector? You are wondering how many minds I can control at once before I overreach myself. Unfortunately for you, I am not telling.'

'Let me take my daughter's place,' Grace said, interrupting them. 'You can master my thoughts, just as you have mastered hers. What difference would it make which one of us harnessed the storm to break the seals on Lud's crypt?'

'That is not worthy of you, Grace Fletcher,' Nathanael said. 'You want to be close to me, do you not? You want to be at my side so that you can use your abilities against me the moment I drop my guard.' He stroked Susanna's black hair. 'I prefer the arrangement I already have. With your daughter by my side, you are powerless.' He rolled his head slowly, loosening his neck muscles. 'It was always going to come down to this, you see. The lives of these mortals mean nothing to me.' He tugged on one noose and pulled the woman next to him to her feet. 'I could snap her neck like a twig.' He ran a finger along her throat. 'It is such a pretty neck too. I am single-minded, you see. I pursue my objectives and crush anything in my way. Whereas you two, the renegade and the witch, you want to be heroes. You want to come running to the world's rescue. The problem is, you are too soft-hearted. That is your weakness. It is for this reason I will break the seals here and at Ludgate and my master will finally be free.'

Grace glanced at Paul, willing him to come up with an answer to the demon's taunts. Nathanael noticed the gesture and laughed. The only sounds were the roar of the wind and the hiss of the rain on the road. Paul returned Nathanael's stare for a few moments, then bowed his head.

'What are you doing?' Grace cried. 'You are not going to give in to him!'

Paul tried to block out her words.

'What choice does he have, Mistress Fletcher?' Nathanael asked. 'A true demon would let these people fall to their deaths. He wouldn't give it a moment's thought.' He ran his fingers through his hair. 'You have shown flashes of that ruthlessness, Paul. You killed the undertaker but you acted out of desperation. That isn't enough. You must be able to watch the death of innocents without any feeling.'

'I'm not like you,' Paul mumbled weakly.

'That is why your long battle ends here,' Nathanael said. 'You have a simple choice. You can stay true to your human side and die or you can become all demon. Do it Paul, discard your human side. It is nothing but a burden. Embrace your demon self. Serve Lud. Be free.'

'Susanna,' Grace shouted desperately, 'you must resist him.'

But Susanna's eyes were dull. She too was under Nathanael's influence. There was no sign she had even heard her mother.

'Would you like to see how useless your appeals are?'

he asked. He whispered in Susanna's ear. She threw out her hands and lightning raked the earth at Grace's feet. 'It would only take a word from me, Grace,' he said, 'and your beloved daughter would destroy her own mother.'

Tears spilled down Grace's cheeks.

'Poor Grace,' Nathanael gloated. 'After all your trials, here you stand, defeated and broken in spirit. Tear the seal asunder, Susanna.' He ordered the hostages to take a step forward.

'Don't do it, Nathanael,' Paul said. 'I won't resist.'

Nathanael gave a satisfied nod and whispered in Susanna's ear. A wall of water swept down from Cow Bridge, swirling for a few moments through the Aldersgate. When it receded there was a great groan from the earth, just like the one Paul had heard from Rokeby House. The third seal was broken.

Nathanael started to descend from the walls, his hands on Susanna's shoulders. 'I will leave the hostages here. Go near them and I will know. They will hurl themselves to their death at my command. That should remind you not to follow me.'

Grace ran forward. 'If Paul won't stop you, I will,' she cried. Lightning crackled from her fingertips. 'You will not break the last seal.'

Nathanael patted Susanna's shoulders. The little girl turned the force of the storm on her mother and Grace was thrown off her feet.

'Don't make empty threats, witch,' he chuckled. 'You know you will never put your child in danger.' He started to walk towards Ludgate, where he would break the final seal and free his master. As he made his way across Long Lane a musket ball struck the wall behind him. He spun round, face twisted with rage. 'Who did that?' He saw Bridget and roared with laughter. 'Ah, Lady Sarah's maid. Do you think you are my equal?

This is not the same as polishing the furniture, you know. The renegade and the witch could not stop me. Do you really believe you can do any better?'

Bridget threw the empty pistol aside and aimed at his head with the second. 'For the sake of my murdered master and mistress, God willing, I will try.'

The words had only just left her lips when she felt the force of Nathanael's mind invading hers. In an instant she had no thoughts of her own. The dark hand of Nathanael's will now directed her every act. 'Put the barrel in your mouth,' Nathanael said. 'That's it, taste the gunmetal. Now blow out your brains.' He saw her starting to swallow the barrel and turned to go. A shot rang out. But when the smoke from the musket cleared it was Nathanael who lay sprawled on the ground, blood draining from his shattered skull.

'Annie!' Grace cried, seeing the reason for Nathanael's downfall.

The old woman had her arms round Bridget, her thin hands gripping the musket. She had wrestled the weapon away from the maidservant and turned it on Nathanael. On the city walls the eleven hostages stared down in bewilderment, barely understanding how they had got up there. The spell broken at last, Susanna squealed with joy at seeing Grace and raced into her mother's arms. Grace embraced her daughter and sobbed as she held her. After a few moments she looked up.

'You followed us, Annie.'

Annie nodded. 'You are the first soul to have shown me charity in many a long year. I knew something was afoot. I decided to repay your kindness.'

'I am in your debt,' Grace said, her face wet with tears as she swung the excited Susanna in a wide circle, 'and yours, Bridget. You showed great courage.'

'Mother,' Susanna squealed, 'my arm is healing.'

Sure enough, the open wound that had disfigured her arm for so long was mending. Grace smiled. 'Yes, and so is mine.'

Paul alone stood apart. He saw the tell-tale swirl of wind as Lud appeared some hundred feet away. He strode towards the demon master's apparition.

'This is no victory, renegade,' Lud said. 'Three seals are broken. Only one remains. You will not keep the Lud Gate sealed. Soon I will be free. When I walk the Earth again, I will crush you.'

'At least you did not win your freedom here,' Paul answered.

'Is that the only positive you can draw from this?' Lud asked. 'All you have done is delay the inevitable. You can claim no credit for this outcome. Just look at your companions. It was the witch and two mortals who delayed my liberation, not you.' His gaze was drawn to Nathanael's corpse. 'I regret his loss,' he said. 'He did well. He proved himself worthy of my trust. But for that crone, he would have succeeded where all the others failed. Know this, Paul Rector, I have your measure. When we meet again, you will die.'

With that, he was gone. Paul stood alone, lost in his thoughts. After a few moments, Grace approached him.

'Lud was here,' Paul said. 'He taunted me.'

'Why?' Grace asked. 'He has lost.'

'He has won,' Paul said, contradicting her. 'Three of the four seals that bind him are broken. He holds all the cards. No matter how many times I prevent his escape, he has to succeed only once.'

'But he didn't win,' Grace insisted. 'We are still standing and one seal remains to bar his escape.'

Paul stared at Annie. 'We owe it all to her. She succeeded where I failed, an emaciated, old woman.

Why?' He shook his head. 'It all came down to your act of kindness. When I was trying to drag you away, you took the time to help that old woman. That's what denied Lud total victory.'

'Maybe that is the lesson you must learn,' Grace said. 'Strength alone won't conquer Hell's legions. Without your human side, you are not complete.'

Paul didn't answer. Instead he asked Grace about her own path. 'Where will you go?'

'I will not return to Suffolk,' she said. 'There is nothing for me there. No, I will make a home for Susanna here, in this city. Maybe Bridget and Annie will play some part in our future. After what they have done here today, how could I see them reduced to penury? What does the future have in store for you?'

'I will continue my journey into Hell's Underground,' Paul replied. 'I will defend the last seal until the priests of Beltane believe I am ready to confront the demon master. Then we will fight to the death. It's my destiny.'

'When will you leave?'

'Now.'

'Do you have to go so soon?' Grace asked.

'You have a child,' Paul said. 'You have new friends. What about me? I have nothing but the clothes on my back. I don't belong here.' He grimaced. 'I don't belong anywhere.'

With that, he turned and walked away through the gloom.

'God speed, Paul Rector,' Grace said as he vanished into an unlit street.

Paul didn't look back. He didn't answer. His footsteps faded and he was gone.

Forty

14 June 1645

'You didn't waste any time showing up,' Paul grumbled when he noticed Cormac waiting for him in the shadows of Whitechapel. 'Are you satisfied now? Netty's gone. Nathanael's dead. One of the seals is still intact. I suppose we held the line against Lud. You've got what you wanted.'

'The result is ... satisfactory,' Cormac said grudgingly.

'Is that it?' Paul snapped. 'All that misery, all that horror and cruelty, and you call it ... satisfactory. Don't you have any human feelings at all?'

'Your business is finished here,' Cormac said, ignoring the accusation.

Paul sighed with resignation. 'I know. It's time to move on. I'm an outlaw. I don't belong anywhere any more.' He glanced back towards the heart of the city. 'OK, I'm ready. What's my next destination?'

'You will know soon enough,' Cormac said. 'Before

you depart, you have been summoned to attend the Courts of Destiny.'

'That again,' Paul said with a scowl. 'When are you going to let up?'

'Do not make light of a call to stand before the power in Hell's Underground.'

Paul stared. 'So these Courts of Destiny, they do exist?'

'Of course they exist,' Cormac replied.

'I often wondered,' Paul said. 'So all those questions I have been asking you, will the Courts of Destiny give me answers?'

'They have the authority. I do not.'

Paul sensed that Cormac was being evasive, but he let it go. 'Lead the way,' he said.

Cormac raised an arm. The slowing rain lifted and they stepped through a silvery portal into a shifting world where patches of light and dark slowly took form. Finally Paul was able to make sense of his surroundings. He was deep in an almost impenetrable forest, standing in an oak grove.

'Where are we?' Paul asked.

'This is the place where it all began,' Cormac said. 'Here Lud was created.'

'So is this the land London was built on?' Paul asked.

'No,' Cormac said. 'Lud was born far from the city he would later claim as his own. Should you succeed in your next trial, you will find your way here and face your nemesis in the final battle.'

'My next trial,' Paul said. 'Where will that be? Who is my quarry?'

Cormac looked away. 'Ask the Courts of Destiny.'

The rain stopped and the sun came out, spreading its light through the woods. A golden evening was born.

Paul saw that Cormac had almost faded from view. He was no more than a faint outline traced among the shadows. Paul's skin prickled as the air grew heavy with a growing presence.

'Is anybody there?' he asked.

The glades whispered with shifting, unseen forms.

Soon a voice floated by him. 'Is this the boy?'

'Who said that?' Paul demanded, spinning around.

'We ask the questions,' the voice said. 'You are Paul Rector?'

Paul turned again, as if expecting to see somebody materialise before him. Nobody did.

'I repeat,' the voice said, 'are you Paul Rector?'

'Yes.'

'What is your mission?'

'To prevent Lud's escape until I am strong enough to face him.' Paul glanced at the barely visible figure of Cormac. 'That's right, isn't it?'

'The priest of Beltane has no jurisdiction here,' said the disembodied voice. 'You alone may speak.'

A second voice chimed in. 'What is your nature?'

'I was born to serve Lud,' Paul said haltingly. 'I am part-demon ...'

'He is no demon,' a third voice screeched. It was inhuman, malevolent. 'He is a half-breed, a renegade. To have a dual nature is an offence against the universal order.' The voice took on a piercing intensity that screamed in his brain. 'Cast him out. He is an abomination!'

Paul turned towards the new presence. 'Who are you?'

More voices rustled through the leaves, fighting to be heard.

'He presumes to put questions to this assembly,' one said.

'That's because I want answers,' Paul said. 'I want to understand my destiny.'

The voices rose and fell like a tide.

'Do you hear how he addresses the gathering of the spirits? He lacks fear.'

'He lacks respect. Expel him from this place.'

Hundreds of voices broke from the shadows, raging around Paul like squabbling birds. They crashed in his skull until he thought his head was going to burst. 'Stop!' he cried. A hush ran through the grove. 'You're the ones who wanted me to undertake this journey. Why are you shouting at me?'

'We don't want you here,' came a hostile voice. 'We abhor you, renegade.'

'Order,' another, calmer voice interrupted. 'I am the speaker of this assembly. The conduct of the Courts of Destiny is in my hands. Step into the light, Paul.'

Paul took a few steps forward, finding himself in a pool of golden rays where the latticework of branches thinned to allow the sunlight through.

'You must understand the Courts of Destiny,' the speaker said. 'We are not of one voice. We are an assembly of all the spirits of the sky, the sea and the earth. The balance of forces changes constantly.'

'So this is a kind of parliament?'

'If you wish,' the speaker said. 'To your left sit the sons and daughters of man. You are their champion.'

Paul peered into the shadowy depths of the woods and saw nothing, but the sense of thousands of souls was heavy in the air.

'To your right sit the brotherhood of demons.' Darkness swelled towards him from this side. 'Long ago they chose Lud as their champion.' His words provoked chants of 'Lud, Lud, Lud.' This, in turn, provoked uproar as the other voices protested. For a few moments the

263

speaker struggled to restore order. Finally, he was able to make himself heard. 'Behind you sit the sisterhood of witches.' The wind strengthened, whipping around him. 'This is the meaning of destiny, Paul. It is a constant battle between warring forces. First one side, then the other holds sway. Long ago the demon brotherhood had the whiphand.' There was a roar of agreement. 'Then mankind grew in strength and wrested control from their enemy.'

There were cries of 'Shame!'

'And the sisterhood of witches?' Paul asked. 'Who is your champion?'

A female voice answered. 'We have always tried to prevent either the demon brotherhood or mankind having absolute control. Each of these tribes misuses the power destiny places in their hands.'

Another furious argument broke out. When order was resumed once more, the speaker continued his story.

'Lud was the last hope of the demon brotherhood,' he explained. 'They created him. His imprisonment was their greatest defeat.'

'There was no defeat,' the demon voices howled. 'London's dark prince was tricked. It was the work of the priests of Beltane.'

The speaker finally regained control and finished his tale. 'Now they await Lud's return. They see him as a kind of messiah.'

There was another chant of 'Lud, Lud, Lud.'

'But this is madness,' Paul protested. 'There are no rules.'

'What is it you want?' the speaker asked. 'You long for peace, don't you, an ordered universe where everyone obeys the same rules and holds the same beliefs?'

'What's wrong with that?' Paul asked. 'I thought that

was the meaning of the Courts of Destiny.'

'If you want some happy ending,' the speaker said, 'then you are in for disappointment. This is the way of things, Paul Rector. Time never stands still. The journey never ends. Good and evil are forever locked in a permanent struggle. The best any of us can do is to prevent things slipping into chaos, where all sides would be destroyed in mutual slaughter.'

'Is that my destiny?' Paul said. 'Is that the best I can expect? You want me to prevent Armageddon?'

'Let it come,' the demon brotherhood howled. 'In war and darkness the strong will triumph.'

'Are you trying to tell me there can be no final victory?' Paul asked. He stared at Cormac. 'Even if I win, it will still be like this?'

'There is no end to things,' the speaker said, by way of an answer. 'There is no such thing as final victory. The conquerors will never feel secure in their triumph. The vanquished will never accept their defeat. The conflict will last as long as time.'

'That's insane!'

'It is the way of things.'

Paul considered this bleak verdict, then he spoke again.

'I have one last question,' he asked. 'If I conquer Lud, will I get my life back?' He sensed hesitation. 'Will I at least be able to go home?'

'Defeat Lud and you can return to your own time,' the speaker said.

Paul turned his back on the assembly. 'Then I go on.'

There were boos and jeers, but there was also clapping and a few cheers. As Paul walked from the grove, insults were being thrown back and forth. He waited until they had left the clearing far behind before speaking. 'So that's your Courts of Destiny,' he said, 'hundreds of bickering ghosts. It's not what I expected.'

'It was ever thus,' Cormac said. 'Out of disorder, sometimes there comes a kind of order. It is imperfect, but such is our world.' He gave Paul a long look. 'Are you ready to continue your journey?'

'Not yet,' Paul said. 'Take me back to London. I have one thing to do before I leave 1645.'

Forty-one

14 June 1645

Paul returns to his lodgings and looks around. It is the last time he will sleep in that bed. It is the last time he will gaze up at that ceiling, trying to imagine Netty's face among the cracks. Why did she have to go? He is about to move on to confront who knows what dangers. He draws out the loose brick from the wall, behind which he has been hiding the lead-lined box. It contains his diary of 1645. He can imagine how people will receive Netty back in her own time. Will she even attempt to tell them the truth? If she does, this will give her all the ammunition she needs to back up her story.

Paul tucks the box under his arm and walks to the door. Within the hour he will have buried it in the foundations of a church. The building will rise and fall and rise again before the twenty-first century dawns. In Netty's time the latest church to be built on the site will finally be deconsecrated and turned into a luxury house. Before that happens it will stand empty. In that time

Netty will visit the derelict building and remove the box from its hiding place. Maybe it will help keep his face before her while she waits for him to return. He hopes so.